BY MARTHA GRIMES

The Man with a Load of Mischief
The Old Fox Deceiv'd
The Anodyne Necklace
Jerusalem Inn
The Dirty Duck

The
ANODYNE
NECKLACE

(Overleaf): In the City, in Temple Bar, that section of London where Royalty undergoes its annual ritual of begging entrance, there once was a pub called The Anodyne Necklace. Although I have taken the liberty of removing it to London's East End, the history of the origin of its name is true.

AN
ESSAY
ON THE

Ancient and Modern Use of Physical NECK-
LACES for Distempers in Children: as their
TEETH, Fits, Fevers, Convulsions, &c. With
a Particular Account of that Celebrated Anodyne

NECKLACE

Recommended by the late Dr. *Chamberlen* for the Easy Breed-
ing and Cutting of Children's TEETH, &c. More Children Dying of their *Teeth*, and Fits, Fevers, Convulsions,
and other Distempers caused thereby, then (generally speaking) of all other Ailments whatsoever.

Inest sua Gratia PARVIS. Virg.

By the Author of the PRACTICAL SCHEME.

THis Book (As also The Practical Scheme: The New System of The GOUT, and *Rheumatism*: And the Trea-
tise on Weaknesses, &c. in either Sex, as mentioned hereafter
in the Advertisement at the End of this Book) is Given Gratis
UP one pair of Stairs at the Sign of this NECKLACE
next the Rose Tavern without Temple-Bar.
  At Mr. Cooper's the Great Toy-shop the Corner of Charles-
Court near Hungerford Market in the Strand.
  And At Mrs. Garway's, the Sign of The PRACTICAL
SCHEME at the Royal Exchange (South) Gate, right over
against Exchange-Ally, on Cornhil Side.

The Ninth Edition.

Entered in the Hall-Book.

LONDON. Printed by H. Parker in Goswell-street. 1719.

THE
ANODYNE
NECKLACE

Martha Grimes

A DELL BOOK

Published by
Dell Publishing Co., Inc.
1 Dag Hammarskjold Plaza
New York, New York 10017

For Colleen and Jack

Map by M. Culpepper, S. Ford, and J. Kovacs

Dell ® TM 681510, Dell Publishing Co., Inc.

ISBN: 0-440-10280-4

Reprinted by arrangement with Little, Brown and Company, Inc.
Printed in the United States of America
One Previous Dell Edition
New Dell Edition
First printing—August 1985

Part One

LONDON
and
LITTLEBOURNE

ONE

∞∞∞∞∞∞∞∞

I

I T was a dead time in the London underground — after lunch and before rush hour — when the last plaintive notes of a Chopin nocturne floated from Katie O'Brien's violin down the tiled corridor.

Anything drifting in the air of the Wembley Knotts tube station besides wind you could taste the soot in was a rare occurrence. She plucked the strings and thought of what to play next. Ruefully, she glanced down to check the contents of the open violin case. Paganini hadn't earned her any 10p pieces. Neither had Beethoven. Indeed, there was only one addition to the coins she had put there herself, and that was five pence tossed in by a begrimed child of nine or ten who looked as if he should be spending it on milk. Yet he had given Katie his unqualified attention for the space of two minutes, his head nodding in rhythmic little jerks as if he had a small conductor trapped in there. Then, unsmilingly, he had deposited his coin and walked on, swallowed up in the warren of dun-tiled corridors. The boy had been her only audience for the last fifteen minutes. Charing Cross, King's Cross, Piccadilly: all of those would have brought more money, but also more risk. Police tended to be thick on the ground in those places, as if all they had to do was weed out the buskers — guitarists and accordion players — who kept sprouting up with their open cases and entertainment.

Five pence. At this rate she would never save enough, not even for a new lipstick, much less for a pink satin shirt she fancied. It had taken six months of stopping here playing just to collect the money for the jeans and blouse she was wearing.

She would have to go soon because she had to allow herself time to change back into her dress before catching the train at Highbury. The dress was neatly folded away in the big carryall that also contained the latest Heartwind Romance and a Cadbury bar. There was a *Telegraph* in there too, bought only to cover up the jeans and magenta shirt in case her mother looked into the bag. Katie O'Brien plucked the strings of her violin and sighed.

In the hollow tunnel, the notes echoed. A train rumbled in the distance and another pull of air, like an enormous indrawn breath, sucked hair round her face and blew soot in her eyes and bounced scraps of paper at her feet. Unmindful of her new blouse, she leaned against the wall and wondered what to play next, if it was worth playing anything at all. Across from her was an *Evita* poster. The corridor was lined with posters of films and museum exhibitions and adverts for travel. Evita wore a strapless gown, her arms shot straight up in the air in a sort of victory pose. Microphones bristled in front of her. A mustache had been penciled in over her pearly lips, prominent nipples had been drawn on the bodice, and between the upraised hands were a hammer and sickle.

Katie wondered when someone had found time and opportunity to muck up the poster and then decided it would be easy enough, at least now in the Wembley Knotts station. No one at all had come by except for the dirty little boy with the 5p.

She heard footsteps in the distance and tucked the violin under her chin. As the steps came nearer down the windy tunnel, she started in on "Don't Cry for Me, Argentina," hoping it would be more popular than the nocturne. She closed her eyes, simulating total absorption in the music. After a bit, she saw the feet halt in front of a grate below the poster, and added a few unscored flourishes to her song, waiting for the *ping* of coins in the violin case. But pretending indifference to money, she didn't look up.

That was why she didn't see it coming.

The brutal blow to the back of her head buckled her knees, and the dirty, ocher-colored floor of the tunnel came up to slap her in the face. She heard the sound of running feet. Darkness swept over her like sand, more and a little more. Before she was totally buried in it, she had time to wonder, almost whimsically, if Evita had stepped out of her poster, lowered the arms holding the hammer, and then hurried off, back to the Argentine.

Don't cry for me—

II

The small, woolly dog trotted across the Green with its teeth clamped round its latest treasure. It crossed the High and continued its walk, pausing at every portal, deciding none was a good enough hiding place for this particular treat, and trotted on.

The little dog belonged to no one in the village, but had been seen round and about. It had been noticed most often digging under the Craigie sisters' rosebushes, or chasing mice or elves in the Horndean wood. When the little dog saw a thin figure come out of the sweet shop, it paused, cocked its head as if debating the worth of this creature, and then rushed in a frolicsome way towards her. He recognized Miss Augusta Craigie, the one whose rosebushes he had lately left in tatters. Augusta Craigie tried to shoo it off. She quite loathed the dog.

The dog merely took the waves and flourishes as a friendly offer to romp. It barked and let the bone fall at Miss Craigie's feet. She started to kick it away, but the tip of her sensible shoe stopped just short of kicking. She looked closer at the bone and determined it was not a bone, but a finger.

The Hertfield police were there within ten minutes of the call from the village. But no matter what blandishments they used — bits of red meat, head-pattings, and so on — the little dog was not about to lead them to the rest of the body.

III

Superintendent Richard Jury was stuffing an extra pair of socks into a duffel bag, preparatory to his weekend in Northamptonshire, when the telephone rang.

He stared at the phone. No one in his right mind would be calling at seven-fifteen on a Saturday morning unless it was something he definitely did not want to hear. He listened to four more rings, telling himself not to pick it up, but then in the manner of all humans, who are convinced the one call gone unanswered must be The Call, the hot-line from the Universe, Jury weakened and plucked up the receiver. "Jury here."

"Su-per-in-ten-dent Jury." The voice made a double-treble of the word. Nor did the voice belong to God, although its owner at New Scotland Yard might have contested this. In plummy accents, Detective Chief Superintendent Racer began to set Jury up for the fall. "Well, well, not left yet, lad? I wondered why London was still so happy."

"I was just finishing packing," said Jury, refusing to rise to the bait.

The smooth voice became acerbic. "Well, you can just leave out the pink coat, Jury. You're not going to Northants."

Racer, who considered himself very county, assumed anyone with a title and a house the size of Ardry End must invariably ride to hounds.

"I don't quite take your meaning," said Jury, who took Racer's meaning perfectly. The phone was in the kitchen, and Jury was now leaning on the open fridge door inspecting the stark interior. One chicken leg and a half-pint of milk.

"My meaning, Jury, is that you're going to Hertford, not Northants, place called —"

While Racer turned from the phone to have a mumbled conversation on the other end of the wire, Jury took out the chicken leg, wondering if the role of the forlorn, possibly starving policeman fit his overall image, decided it didn't, and slammed the fridge door shut. He carried the plate and the receiver, cradled on his shoulder, into the sitting room and waited for Racer to get down to business.

"Littlebourne," came the irascible voice, and when Jury didn't immediately respond, said, "Jury!"

"Sir!"

A silence. "Are you being sarcastic, Jury?"

"Sir?"

"Don't 'sir' me, lad. You never did when you were inspector, so you damned well wouldn't be doing it now. I don't have time for your warped—and, I might add, *unprofessional*—sense of humor." Papers rattled. "Littlebourne. You got that? That's the one-eyed village you're going to. About three miles from Hertfield where the swells go to buy antiques. There's a down-train every half-hour from Islington—"

Jury cut him off. "I'm not on call. You do know there is a rota?"

The wire crackled in his ear as Racer said, "Rota. I'm well aware there's a rota. You trying to teach your grandmother to suck eggs, Jury? Perkins is in hospital and Jenkins is flat on his back with some kind of flu the Chinks are handing round. Hertfield police are shorthanded, and it looks like they've got an especially nasty murder. Trouble is, they can't find the body."

Can't find the body? Jury looked down at the chicken leg which lay congealed in a puddle of grease. "Then how do they know they've got a murder? Someone gone missing, or something?"

"Listen, and I'll tell you." More shuffling of papers. "Some woman named Craigie was out walking her dog. No, wait a tic. Not her dog . . ."

Jury closed his eyes. Racer would not simply hand over the facts; he would chronicle it. The Chief Superintendent considered himself a raconteur of bardic proportions.

". . . and then this woman comes out of a shop and tries to get the mutt out of her way and he drops the bone in his mouth. Only—"

There was a dramatic pause. Jury waited, inspecting the chicken leg with a sense of foreboding. *Only it wasn't a bone.* That had to be it.

". . . it wasn't a bone," said Racer with a good deal of relish. "It was a finger. Get cracking Jury. Take Wiggins with you."

"Sergeant Wiggins is in Manchester. He's visiting his people."

"He's giving all the Mancuneans the Black Death, that's what he's doing. I'll dig him out, never fear. With Wiggins that would be literal. Well, I'm sorry to delay your weekend in the country, Jury. No hunting, no shooting for you. A policeman's life is full of grief."

Click went the telephone at Scotland Yard.

7

Jury got out his address book and put through a trunk call to Ardry End. While he waited he sat with his head in his hand. A finger.

IV

Ardry End was a manor house of rose-hued stone, seat of the Earls of Caverness (when there were Earls of Caverness), hidden in its own wood of September gold and russet like a figure in an old tapestry.

The tapestry was even more faded, though, on this particular September morning, gray with mists and rain floating like gauze over the Northamptonshire fields. It was dark enough that the lamps glowed dully behind the mullioned panes of a downstairs room.

Thus a passer in the rain might have looked with longing through the windows of this room in the east wing—a room at once elegant and comfortable, a combination of Queen Anne couches and plumped-up pillows, of crystal chandeliers and cozy corners, of oriental carpets and warm hearths.

One might have taken its two occupants—a nearly handsome man in his early forties; a stout, dumpy woman in her late sixties—for mother and son, or old friend and young, or happy host and merry guest. Or, indeed, for any of those sentimental couplings we attribute to those sitting in the warmth of light and fire, while the poor, drenched passerby looks through the starry pane, envious of the comfort within.

One might have felt that there by the blazing fire, with the lumbering old dog at their feet, these two surely presented the most amiable picture in the world.

One might have supposed that *here* was friendship, *here* was intimacy, *here* was conversation at its best.

One would have been wrong.

"You're becoming an alcoholic, Melrose. That's your second shooting sherry," said Lady Agatha Ardry.

"If mere numbers count, you're becoming a fairy cake. That's

8

your third," said Melrose Plant, the last in the line of the Earls of Caverness. He returned to perusal of a road map.

She threw him a dark glance while she peeled the fluted paper from the little cake. "What are you doing?"

"Reading a road map."

"Why?"

"Because it's got roads on it." Melrose stoppered up the decanter and sipped from his morsel of Waterford crystal.

"You're being funny, Plant."

"I'm being literal, dear Aunt." Melrose had found Hertfield; but where was this Littlebourne village?

"You know perfectly well what I mean. You're not thinking of going anywhere, are you? If you're going up to London, I shouldn't. You ought to stay here and tend to your affairs. But if you *must* go to London, I should certainly like to go too. I've a lot of shopping to do and I want to stop in at Fortnum's and get some of their cakes."

Plant did not bother contradicting her, since she would have him up to London and back again faster than a flying carpet, and he could resume his map-study. He yawned. "Fortnum's don't do fairy cakes, Agatha."

"Certainly they do."

"Well, I expect we shall never know."

Lady Ardry regarded her nephew with suspicion, as if his remark held some nugget of meaning she must pry loose, like a gold filling from a tooth.

Gold was not the least of Agatha's concerns, either. She had just finished appraising Plant's latest acquisition, a small gold statue. She picked it up again, turned it every which way, and said, "This must have been dear, Melrose."

"I can show you the sales slip." He resettled his spectacles on his nose and looked at her over the rim of his sherry glass.

"Don't be vulgar. I've no interest in what you give for things."

He saw she now had her enormous purse open and was rooting through it, taking out and putting on the table all sorts of nondescript objects. Was she making room for the gold statue? Melrose occasionally visited her cottage in Plague Alley, partly as a gentlemanly gesture, partly to see some of his belongings. How she managed to get whole clumps of furniture out of Ardry End without his knowing was a mystery he had never solved. One day he would cycle up the drive to find a removal van in front of the door. Well, Ardry End was enormous, and he didn't really care, so long as she left the portraits in the gallery and the ducks in the pond. Then he spied something she had just transferred from purse to table.

"Isn't this mine?" he asked.

She colored slightly. "Yours? Yours? My dear Plant, whatever would *I* be doing with your calling-card case?"

"I don't know. That's why I asked."

"I'm not sure I care for what you're implying."

"I'm not implying anything. I'm saying you took my visiting-card case."

She thought for a moment. "You don't remember."

"Remember what?"

"Your dear mother, Lady Marjorie—"

"I remember my mother, yes. That was her visiting-card case." Melrose opened his own gold cigarette case and lit a cigarette. "Are you going to tell me Mother gave it to you?"

Rather than answer this directly, she began to reminisce. "Your dear mother, the Countess of Caverness—"

"You have a way of reminding me of particulars of my family history that suggests you believe I cannot sort them out. I remember that my mother was the Countess of Caverness. My father was the seventh Earl of Caverness. And your late husband, the Honorable Robert Ardry—"

"Stop trying to be funny again, my dear Plant."

"Allow me to continue. Robert Ardry was my uncle. And I, to everyone's consternation, am no longer the eighth Earl. There, now. All ship-shape and Bristol fashion."

"Kindly do not use such sordid, lower-class expressions. Your dear mother—"

"My mother was indeed dear and she swore like a scullery maid."

"No respect for the family. Never had."

"*You're* here, dear Aunt."

She played for time by rearranging the falls of bright-leaved chiffon, totally inappropriate for the day, and calling for Ruthven, Melrose's butler.

"Why are you dressed for an afternoon on the lawn, Agatha?" Melrose looked at her more closely. "And where'd you get that amethyst brooch? That looks like Mother's, too."

Ruthven entered and she requested some more cakes. She would stagger her 'elevenses' right into luncheon if he weren't careful, Melrose knew.

Ruthven shot her a glance like a poisoned arrow and swanned out of the room.

With that interruption she could now deftly turn the subject away from amethyst brooches. "I noticed Lady Jane Hay-Hurt paying special attention to you last Sunday."

Since Lady Jane was a fifty-eight-year-old maiden lady with prominent teeth and receding chin, Agatha no doubt thought it safe to imply a possible liaison between the lady and Melrose.

"I've no interest in Lady Jane. But I shall find someone one day, never fear. The Ardry-Plants have always married late."

That made her gasp, as he knew it would. "Marriage! Whoever said anything of *marriage?* You're a confirmed bachelor, Melrose. At forty-three—"

"Forty-two." He had found Littlebourne on the map and was ascertaining the best route.

"Anyway, you're rooted in your behavior and I really don't think it would be likely that any sort of woman would put up with your odd little ways. And there's no one round here for you to marry!" Triumphantly, she outreached her arms, making a sweep of the drawing room, as if once, indeed, marriageable females had crowded its couches and settees and wing chairs, but, alas, no more.

Certainly, certainly, he thought. She had convinced herself Melrose was just waiting to die so that he could turn over Ardry End, its grounds and gardens, its crystal and calling-card cases, its armoires and amethysts to her, his only living relative. And not even a blood relative. And not even English. Agatha was a transplanted American, not, however, of Jamesian sensibility.

Beneath his dressing gown, Melrose was wearing his traveling clothes. He had meant to get off around nine, but he had to spend a bit of time stalling her, putting her, indeed, off the scent. If she knew he was going to meet Superintendent Jury, she would be hiding out in the trunk of the Rolls. It had been sitting garaged for an age; Melrose had decided to take it as part of a cover he had not made up yet. You never knew when a Rolls would come in handy. He smiled.

"What's that smirk for?"

"Nothing." He folded his map. She thought she was such a dab hand at murder. Ever since Jury — Chief Inspector it had been then — had come to Long Piddleton, Agatha had been talking about their "next case." Keeping her out of his hair required a cunning befitting Crippen or Neil Cream. . . .

"Why are you looking at me that way, Plant?" As she took another fairy cake, he saw her ring wink in the firelight.

Where had she got that moonstone?

TWO

∞∞∞∞∞

I

LITTLE Burntenham was an ordinary village about forty miles from London, to which no one, until recently, had paid much attention. In the last year or so, Londoners had "discovered" Little Burntenham and its accessibility to the city — it was now a stop on the main line. This soon resulted in a burst of activity in the estate market and the plucking up of some of its falling-down properties that the villagers wouldn't have had on a bet. Great wads of money had exchanged hands, passing from those of the fools who would be parted from it to the estate agents always ready to grab it. The other change, which the older residents of the village greatly resented, was the respelling of the name so that tourists could find it more easily. It had been decided finally, that since Little Burntenham was actually pronounced *Littlebourne*, it might as well be spelled that way. It took a lot of the fun out of listening to strangers ask for directions.

Littlebourne, surrounded by pleasant, open country, with one side hemmed by the Horndean wood, was pleasant but undistinguished, no matter how the new inhabitants might spend money on rethatching roofs and exposing beams and painting exteriors in pastel washes. The village had its one street, called the High, which divided halfway along so that it flowed round an irregular patch of carefully tended grass called Littlebourne Green. The High had its sufficiency of shops, just enough so that the villagers weren't forced to go into the market town of Hertfield, four miles away, except when they wanted to browse through its many antique shops.

As some wags liked to put it, the High contained, among other things, Littlebourne's four P's: one pastor, one post office, one pub, and one police station. There was a fifth P with whom the villagers would happily have dispensed: Littlebourne's one peer.

The fifth P — Sir Miles Bodenheim — was presently giving one of the other P's the devil of a time. He was in the post office store making the postmistress's life hell. There had been only one other person waiting for service before Sir Miles Bodenheim had decided to rejuvenate the British postal system. Now there were twelve, snaking down past the bread tray.

"I should certainly think, Mrs. Pennystevens, that you could do the stamps a little quicker if you would keep the half-p's separate from the others. You would do better to have some sort of system. I have been standing here a good ten minutes simply trying to post this one letter."

Mrs. Pennystevens, who had been tending a gouty husband for fifteen years, was proof against practically anything. She even refrained from pointing out that the whole of the ten minutes had been taken up with Sir Miles's arguing the weight of the letter and claiming she was coming up too heavy. Finally, she had had to let him fool with the scales himself.

Back in the bread-shadows, a voice was heard to mumble, ". . . stupid old sod."

Sir Miles turned and smiled in a self-satisfied way, delighted to know that someone else was as quick at seeing Mrs. Pennystevens's deficiencies as he himself. He turned back to her: "I still believe that your scales are malfunctioning. But I daresay there's nothing to be done; the government has seen fit to place its faith in *your* judgment. Frankly, Mrs. Pennystevens, I would get a new pair of spectacles, were I you. Yesterday you shorted me two p on a half-loaf."

Shuffling, shuffling up and down the line and the woman behind Sir Miles whined that she was in the most dreadful hurry . . .

"Yes," said Sir Miles. "Kindly hurry it up, Mrs. Pennystevens. We've none of us all day, you know."

Mrs. Pennystevens looked at him with steel in her eyes and

counted out his change, which he slowly recounted, as he always did, naming each coin. One would have thought, given the puzzled expression, that he was unused to the coin of the realm or the decimal system. Finally, he pocketed the money, nodded curtly to the postmistress, nodded again up and down the line as if they had come not to buy bread and milk but to be received by Sir Miles Bodenheim, owner of Rookswood. He bade them all adieu.

Having accomplished the difficult task of posting his letter, Sir Miles proceeded farther along the High. He considered returning a handkerchief he had purchased in a tiny haberdashery next to the sweet shop, as he had noticed one loose stitch. Fifty pence, and the Empire couldn't even sew after all these years, he thought. There was only the one smudge, a tiny one in the corner when he had been eating a bit of chocolate, but that should make no odds. He was after bigger game, though, today. He was intent upon Mr. Bister's garage, down a few doors, where the owner had not given him the right change yesterday for gasoline.

Thus did Sir Miles make his daily rounds. The police station he was saving up for last, where he planned on spending the whole of the morning finding out from Peter Gere, the village constable, why the Hertfield police weren't moving more swiftly in the matter which had brought Littlebourne to much wider notice.

II

One would have thought that Sir Miles was the least popular of the villagers. This was not so. His wife, Sylvia, beat him out by a hair. It wasn't five minutes after her husband had left the village post office that she herself was on the telephone arguing with the benighted Pennystevens.

"I *simply* want to know how much it will cost to mail it, Mrs. Pennystevens. That seems a simple enough request. I want the parcel in this afternoon's post. . . . But I have given you the weight—you need merely look it up in the book." Sylvia Bodenheim's hand was clicking the garden shears which she had just used to cut the flowers, snapping each one as if it had been the head of a villager. "No, I most certainly will *not* send Ruth along with a pound note in case the postage is more. You know what servants are nowadays. I don't understand why you cannot undertake to give me the exact amount. . . . My scales are quite accurate, thank you very much. . . . Edinburgh, yes." The shears clicked now in time to the tapping of Sylvia's foot. "Fifty pence. You're quite *sure* that's the cheap rate?" Sylvia's mouth clamped in a grim line. "'As sure as you can be in the circumstances' is hardly a satisfactory reply. I hope it will not be necessary to send Ruth back again with more money if you've misjudged the weight." Abruptly, and with no farewell, she dropped the phone into the cradle and shouted for Ruth.

The other two contenders for the Littlebourne murders were the Bodenheim children, Derek and Julia. However, they fell far behind their mother and father merely because of proximity. Derek came down from Cambridge rarely; Julia (whose horse could have got into University before Julia could), was not seen all that much. She spent most of her time shopping in London or hunting with one or another of the local packs. Seldom did the villagers see her from any vantage point except up on her horse in her hacking jacket or black Melton, one hand on her hip.

When the four Bodenheims had to be together (at Christmas, for instance) they entertained themselves by noting the shortcomings of their neighbors, by reestablishing their own superior claims as feudal overlords, and, all in all, generally turning water into wine.

III

The Littlebourne Murders, as yet unfinished, had long provided practice in the gentle art of murder for Polly Praed. A moderately successful mystery-story writer, she often, when her plots came unglued, would divert herself by practicing various modes and styles of murder on the Bodenheims, singly or together. She favored the denouement which had the entire village coming together to murder the titled family. At the moment she was walking down the High considering a choice of weapons. A dagger passed from hand to hand was out — it had already been used. As she passed the garage considering poisons, she smiled absently at Mr. Bister, who raised his greasy cap. While she was thinking of that dreadful cliché of "arsenic-in-the-tea," she stopped.

About twenty or so feet away, parked outside of the tiny house which was Littlebourne's one-man police station, two men were getting out of a car. One was rather slight and ordinary-looking, though it was hard to tell, as he was apparently blowing his nose. But the other, the *other* made her understand the meaning of being rooted to the spot. He was tall, and if not *precisely* handsome ... but what else could one call him? When he reached to take something from the rear seat — was it a bag? was he *staying?* — a wind blew his hair. He scraped it across his forehead and turned with the other one and walked up the path to the station.

Polly stared at the air and felt mildly seasick.

It was nearly ten. She often went into the station to have a chat with Peter Gere; they were friends. Sometimes they even went across to the Bold Blue Boy for a bit of lunch or a drink. What was to prevent her from simply marching up the walk and feigning surprise — *Oh, do excuse me, Peter, I didn't know* —

Her hands shoved deep in the pockets of her coat-sweater, her mind busily worked over the scene that would unfold: there would be the stranger's open-mouthed astonishment that she was *that* Polly Praed (a name which had never seemed to get much of a rise even out of her publisher), an appreciation of her wit (which reviewers put on a par with her plots), a quiet appraisal of her beauty (seldom commented on by anyone). At this point she was so deep into sparkling repartee inside the police station that she forgot she was still on the pavement until she heard the raised voices.

She turned to look back toward the petrol station where Miles Bodenheim was waving his swagger stick in the air and Mr. Bister's face had turned the color of the little red Mini he had apparently been working on. Sir Miles made one last gesture with the stick, and started down the pavement, headed in her direction. Quickly, she crossed to the other side and shot into the Magic Muffin, fortunately open that day. It was a tearoom run by Miss Celia Pettigrew, a gentlewoman of slender means, who kept very capricious business hours. One never could be sure from one week to the next when the Muffin would be open: it was as if Miss Pettigrew were running by some other calendar than the Gregorian and some other time than Greenwich Mean.

Polly watched the progress of Sir Miles, who was marching down the other side of the street and was now just by the police station walk.

She could have died.

Coming down the walk and running bang-up against Miles Bodenheim were Peter Gere and the two strangers. The idea that this brief encounter should fall not to her but to Miles (who deserved prussic acid in his morning egg) made her want to scream. She watched as Peter Gere and the others maneuvered around Sir Miles and separated themselves from him — which must have been like picking a limpet off a rock. The three crossed the street and Littlebourne Green and out of her line of vision. Her face was nearly mashed against the glass.

"Whatever are you staring at, dear?" The reedy voice of Celia Pettigrew pulled Polly back from the window, the blood creeping up her neck as she took a seat at one of the dark, gate-legged tables. Its blue-and-white cloth matched the cottage curtains. "Might I have some tea, Miss Pettigrew?" said Polly in a strained voice. "And a muffin?"

"That's what we're here for," said Miss Pettigrew, moving briskly toward a curtained door at the rear of the room.

To resist further temptation, Polly had seated herself with her back to the windows, so that when the bell tinkled again, her heart leaped within her. Could his course have been deflected walking across the Green? Could — ?

No. It was only Sir Miles, come to hector Miss Pettigrew within an inch of her life. Although Miles Bodenheim vied only with his wife as the first one to dispatch in *The Littlebourne Murders*, she was almost glad to see him now.

It never occurred to Miles that anyone wouldn't be, so without preamble he dropped his stick and cap on the table and sat down.

"Saw you come in here. Thought I'd join." He twisted his large frame in the chair and bellowed: "You've got *customers* out here, Miss Pettigrew!"

Polly closed her eyes as the sharp rattle and shattering of dishes came from the curtained alcove.

"Butterfingers," murmured Miles. To Polly he said, "Well, Miss Praed, and are you working on your new thriller? Been a long time since you've had one out, but I expect the last reviews put you off your feed a bit, didn't they? Look at it this way, though. It's not what those idiots think, it's the sales, what? Though they weren't too brisk, were they? Sylvia tells me all the ones in the Hertfield shop are still there. Oh, well . . ." He ran his hands against his hair, smoothing it. There was a bit of dried egg on his lapel; since there usually was, Polly wondered if it were the same dried egg bit, or fresh from this morning. "We'll have to put your book down on the Christmas list for Ruth and Cook. Sylvia says they spend rather too much time reading trash — film magazines, that sort of thing. Where is that idiot woman?" He wheeled around in his chair again as Miss Pettigrew shuddered through the drapery, looking extremely pale.

"Yes, Sir Miles?" she said through lips nearly riveted together. "You needn't have shouted like that; you gave me the most awful fright —"

"You need something for your nerves. Bring another cup. There's enough in that pot for two. What are those things?" He poked at what were quite obviously muffins on the plate she deposited before Polly.

"Carrot muffins."

"Good God, woman! Bring me a scone."

"I don't do scones, Sir Miles."

He sighed loudly. "Bring me some of that anchovy toast."

"I only have that in the afternoon, as you know."

Elaborately, Sir Miles pulled a turnip watch from his watch-pocket, clicked open the case to let her know his time of day was more reliable than hers. True, it was only ten. So he settled for, "You really do not get enough custom to be always splitting hairs with your patrons, do you?"

When Polly observed poor Miss Pettigrew's narrow frame

visibly beginning to shake, she put in, "If it's not too much trouble, Miss Pettigrew, I'd really fancy some myself. You do make such *delicious* anchovy toast; I've heard people rave about it—"

As Miss Pettigrew, somewhat mollified, moved toward the rear, Sir Miles said, "Delicious? What's delicious about it? It's straight out of a tin. All the stupid woman has to do is spoon it up and slap it on some bread. But it's preferable to this muffin—" He poked the plate again. "How does she manage to make muffins the color of a mouse?" He hummed as they waited in silence for the toast.

Polly was about to break her rule of never asking Sir Miles a question when Miss Pettigrew appeared with a plate on a tray. "Too bad you had to be put to the trouble of making up two orders," he said breezily. "And Miss Praed has let the muffins go cold."

Stone-faced, Miss Pettigrew retreated behind her curtain.

His mouth full of toast, Sir Miles said, "Whole village has gone mad, far as I can see. First it's those beastly letters—" He smiled nastily—"didn't write 'em yourself, did you? Rather your line, isn't it?"

Polly reddened. "Poison-pen letters are *not* exactly the same thing as writing mysteries."

He shrugged. "Since you got one yourself, I expect it makes no odds. Though you could have done that to divert suspicion. Toast?" Handsomely, he shoved the plate in her face. "Not that I'm surprised Mainwaring and Riddley got one. Both of them carrying on with the Wey woman like that. No better'n she should be, that one. And now we'll be in all the papers, police putting themselves about looking for that body—"

It was the opportunity she wanted. Casually, she asked, "Who was that with Peter Gere you were talking to?"

Sir Miles studied the nibbled edges of his toast. "Policemen," was all he said.

That was the way with Miles. He'd talk the eyes off a peacock until you wanted him to say something and then he'd clam up completely.

"From where?"

He did not answer this, but said instead, "About time they sent someone to clear up this mess. If we had to depend on Peter Gere for protection we'd all be dead in our beds. I was about to tell him so —".

Polly was saved from stuffing the muffins down his throat by the fresh tinkling of the bell over the tearoom door.

The next person to enter the Magic Muffin was Emily Louise Perk, ten years old with no sign she had grown since she was eight. Her small-boned frame and triangular face, mournful brown eyes, strings of yellow hair hanging about her pointed chin, shabby little hacking jacket and jeans, all proclaimed her to be quite a pitiful child.

Emily Louise Perk was anything but pitiful.

Her unkempt appearance had nothing to do with a neglectful parent or a poor one. If her hair never looked combed and her costume never changed it was because Emily Louise was up long before her mother, up before the rest of the village, up before God, seeing to her interests, chief among them being her pony, Shandy. Shandy was stabled, oddly enough, at Rookswood, the Bodenheim manor. Emily was permitted to keep her own pony there in return for taking care of the Bodenheim horses. Since Emily Louise knew more about horses than anyone from Hertfield to Horndean, they let her alone. That she was not even plagued by Sylvia Bodenheim was in itself a remarkable feat, testimony to Emily's remarkable facility for either getting what she wanted out of grown-ups or ignoring them completely. She was permitted to slop about freely in the stableyard and even to enter the kitchen for tea and tidbits served up by the Bodenheim cook, who was fond of Emily Louise. Thus, unlike the other village children whom the Bodenheims gladly squashed like stray cats and dogs, Emily was permitted, metaphorically speaking, to live.

And live she did rather high on the hog because she knew everything that went on in Littlebourne. She was not a gossip, but she certainly knew the going rate of exchange. News flowed back and forth through her four-foot frame as if she were an electrical wire.

Polly happily called out to her and pulled a chair round for her to sit in. If anyone would know, she would.

As Emily sat down, Miles said, "Thought you were supposed to be up at the house currying Julia's horse." His iron-gray brows furrowed.

No frown, however, was any match for Emily Louise's. She always appeared to be in a brown study. "Today's Saturday. I don't do spit on Saturday." She looked at the muffin plate and sighed. "It's carrot again. I wish I had a hot cross bun." She clamped her hands atop her head and looked at Polly.

Polly called to Miss Pettigrew, who, seeing Emily, immediately procured a plate of buns and a fresh pot of tea. Miss Pettigrew was not immune to the charms of Miss Perk, either. They spent rather a lot of time over tea and talk.

"Thank you," said Emily, who did not place herself above manners. "There's a policeman in the village, a new one."

"I *know*," snapped Sir Miles. "Met the chap already." He dusted his trouser knees and drank his tea. "He's from Scotland Yard."

Scotland Yard. Polly's mouth dropped open. She cleared her throat. "What's he doing here? I mean, is he staying?"

Apparently unable to supply any more information, Sir Miles passed it off with a general comment about the inefficiency of police in general. "All running about cock-a-hoop, none of them seem to know what they're doing."

Emily ate her bun. "He's going to find that body, I expect. He's staying at the Bold Blue Boy. They dropped off their stuff there. He's a police superintendent."

"Did you, ah, happen to hear his name?" asked Polly.

Emily did not provide this essential bit of information. Instead, she drained her cup and shoved it toward Polly. "Tell my fortune, please."

Polly was loath to drop the subject, but perhaps the tea-leaf reading could be turned to that account. Sir Miles sighed hugely, as if they had chained him to his chair, forcing him to listen to this nonsense.

Polly tipped the cup and looked down at the meaningless pattern the small bits of black leaf left on its surface. All she saw was something that looked like a ragged bird. "I see a man, a stranger."

"What's he look like?" Emily's chin rested in her clenched fists. The eternal pucker between her brows deepened.

"Tall, good-looking, about forty—"

"*That* old?"

". . . chestnut hair, uh, brown eyes—"

"Gray."

"Gray?"

"Rubbish," contributed Miles.

"Go on!" said Emily.

Looking at the wingless bird, Polly said, "Some kind of danger, some sort of mystery." Polly shrugged her shoulders. Ordinarily her imagination was sprightlier, but today she couldn't seem to make it click.

"He's got a nice smile and a nice voice," said Emily, supplying the missing details. Then she stood up, her legs slightly bowed, her feet turned in. She had found a bit of string which she was winding thoughtfully about her finger. "Do policemen make much money?"

"Ho! Poor as churchmice," said Sir Miles, hoping it was bad news.

Apparently it was. "I can't marry anyone who hasn't got a lot of money. I'd need it for the horses. One day, I'm going to have a lot of horses." Then she turned and walked out the door.

Detective Superintendent Richard Jury had been in Littlebourne under an hour and had already turned two of its women to jellies.

Though Emily Louise Perk seemed made of starchier stuff than Polly Praed.

THREE

∽∽∽∽∽∽∽∽

I

IT was not the police who found the body to which the finger had lately belonged; it was Miss Ernestine Craigie, sister to Augusta. Ernestine had gone to the Horndean wood, as was her usual habit, in her Wellingtons and anorak, and with binoculars swinging round her neck. Ernestine was not only president, but was heart, soul and muscle of the Hertfield Royal Birdwatchers' Society.

The Horndean wood was a somber tract of oak, ash, and bracken which stretched its seemingly endless wetness (bog and marsh), an invitation to all sorts of birdlife, between Littlebourne and the much larger town of Horndean. The wood was unpleasant and unpretty; even in high summer it appeared to be sulking around the edge of winter, its shrubberies a dull brown, its leaves untouched by the usual autumnal glow. Except for the sort of mucking about Miss Craigie had been doing, it was a good-for-nothing, boggy place. Good for nothing, apparently, but bird-watching and murder.

Police hounds had snuffled through the last place the little dog had been seen rooting — the Craigie sisters' rosebushes. Fortunately for the sisters, the corpse had not been deposited beneath them. Otherwise the Craigies would have had a lot of explaining to do. They were having a bad enough time as it was. This particular corpse seemed fated to attach itself to them in one way or another. The body had been found not under Augusta's rosebushes, but by Ernestine: it was lying half-in, half-out of the muddy waters of a narrow stream which cut straight across the Horndean wood.

When Superintendent Jury and Constable Gere arrived on the scene they found a hard knot of police and dogs all seeming to jockey for position. One of the men peeled off from the group and walked toward them.

"'Lo, Peter." He put out his hand to Jury. "You're from Scotland Yard C.I.D.?" Jury nodded. "I'm Carstairs." Detective Inspector Carstairs had a beaked nose and somewhat predatory air. "Come on. We found her not half an hour ago. Or, to be more precise, one of the local ladies found her. I had one of our people take her back to her cottage; she held up awfully well, I must say. Still, it's a shock. She's there whenever you want to speak to her. Unless—"

"No. That's fine. Is that the M.E. over there?"

"Yes. Come along, then."

The medical examiner was a woman, and she was in the process of finishing up her preliminary examination, tossing her comments over her shoulder to an assistant who stood marking items on a chart of a human form.

". . . Hairs adherent to this hand; bag it. Nothing on this hand, but I'd bag it, too."

The reason, Jury thought, there might have been nothing on that hand was because it had no fingers.

The medical examiner dropped it, quite casually, back on the tree stump, with the direction, "Bag each finger separately."

Jury took a step forward but was stopped by her assistant's saying, "Don't step on that finger, please, sir."

He looked down and drew his foot back quickly. It was then he noticed the two separate, severed fingers. One had rolled off the stump. The victim, a youngish woman, in her late twenties or early thirties, lay in the shallow and muddy water of the stream. One side of her face was turned down in the water. The water itself was rusty with blood. Except for the one hand, the rest of the body appeared to have escaped mutilation; the cyanosed complexion told Jury she had been strangled.

The doctor rose and dusted her knees free of twigs and leaves.

She intoned her findings to Jury. "Dead, I'd say on a prelim, about thirty-six hours. I'd put it at roughly between eight and midnight, Thursday."

The police ambulance had made its way off the Horndean–Hertfield Road and was trying to maneuver inward along the public footpath. It had to stop some distance from the body. Two men carried over the stretcher and rubber sheet from that point.

"What about the hand, Doctor?"

She pursed her lips, looked at the plastic bag given over to her assistant. "Ax, apparently. It was done in a single blow. That one, there." She pointed to a small, double-bladed ax lying in the grass.

"Any ideas why the killer'd go to the trouble of cutting off the fingers?" asked Jury.

She shook her head, snapped her bag shut. A woman of few words. She wore a black suit relieved only by a pale shirtwaist, but even that was tied around the throat with a narrow black tie.

"Well, it couldn't be fingerprints," said Carstairs, "or he'd have done both hands. And taken away, ah, the fingers. The ax, Gere tells me, belongs to Miss Craigie. The one who found the body. She uses it to clear out underbrush and branches and so forth . . . to see the birds. Miss Craigie's big on birds." Inspector Carstairs pulled on his earlobe, as if embarrassed to drag this frivolity into it.

"Could it have been a woman?" asked Jury of the medical examiner.

Her every word was dipped in acid: "'Could it have been a woman?' Yes, Superintendent. You'll find that we can do all sorts of things—dress ourselves, ride two-wheelers, do murders."

Chalk one up for women's lib, he guessed. "Sorry." She left, and Jury and Carstairs looked down at the body. The black coat was scummy with algae and the hair was a net to trap twigs and leaves.

Sergeant Wiggins and Peter Gere tramped toward them, away from the clutch of Hertfield policemen looking the ground over.

Wiggins looked down at the mutilated hand as the woman was being wrapped in the rubber sheet. "Why d'ya suppose he cut off the fingers?"

Jury shook his head. "He wasn't just saying good-bye."

They were back in Peter Gere's one-room office on the High warming their hands around mugs of tea and coffee.

"No identification," said Carstairs. "Labels in her clothes were Swan and Edgar and Marks and Sparks. Anyway, you could tell from the quality she didn't do her shopping at Liberty's. Looks pretty much the shop girl type to me. Bit heavy on the jewelry, too. Only thing to tell us where she comes from was this." Carstairs drew a small envelope from his pocket and shook the contents out on the desk. "My sergeant handed me this just before we left the wood. A day return to London. Found it down in the coat lining, apparently slipped through a hole in the pocket."

Jury looked at the date, September fourth, two days before. "She wasn't a local, then."

"Guess not." Then Carstairs added, as if he didn't want to let the girl go entirely, "But we shouldn't completely discount that."

"Say she was," said Wiggins, holding his cup close to his nose and breathing in steam, "still, it's not likely she'd be having a walk along that footpath in the dark, would she? In that wood? And dressed the way she was?"

Carstairs looked at Wiggins as if he were a pile of unwashed socks, but had to agree, nonetheless. "This Miss Craigie, the one who found her. The Craigie woman said she must have passed by that spot when she was out that night having a tramp in the woods—"

"What time?" asked Peter Gere.

"She's uncertain about that. Nine or nine-thirty, possibly even ten. At any rate, after dark."

"What would she have been walking in the wood for at *that* hour?" asked Wiggins, handing his cup back to Gere for seconds.

Peter Gere answered: "Owls. Miss Craigie's the head of the local birdwatching society. Spends a good deal of time in Horndean wood. It's wonderful for birds, she claims—all nice and wet and boggy."

"Sounds a dim pastime," said Wiggins, pulling his jacket more tightly about him. The little police office's single night storage heater was no match for Wiggins. "So that puts *her* out there at the time of the murder, sir," he said to Jury.

Gere laughed. "Well, I must admit she's certainly got enough brute force for it—only, wait a moment: you surely don't think this was done by a *local*, do you?" With a worried frown, he was tamping tobacco down in his pipe.

"Maybe not, but you've had your share of troubles here, Peter. What about these?" Carstairs reached in his inside pocket and dropped a brown packet on the table. "Have a look, Superintendent." His smile was enigmatic, as if he could hardly wait for Scotland Yard to cast its eye on this little lot.

It was a plain, brown mailing envelope, postmarked in Hertfield and addressed to the Littlebourne sub-post office. Jury opened it and took out a packet of letters held together with a rubber band. He flipped through the envelopes and said, "*Crayon?*"

"Interesting, isn't it? Much more difficult for forensics than ink or typewriter impressions. They haven't come up with anything yet."

Jury opened and read the first, written in green crayon, to a Miss Polly Praed, Sunnybank Cottage. "It would appear Miss Praed has been getting up to all sorts of mischief without ever leaving her home. Gin. Dope." He set it aside and picked up the second, this one in orange, to a Ramona Wey. "Not very long, are they?"

"And not very naughty, either, except for the ones to Augusta Craigie and Dr. Riddley. Hard to write for very long in crayon."

Augusta Craigie's letter was done in purple. "Miss Craigie gets around, doesn't she? So far three different men have been cited here, in various states of dress and undress."

Peter Gere smiled. "If you knew Augusta—that's Ernestine's sister—you'd see it's very unlikely. She was rather proud of her letter, I'd say. We were wondering if perhaps she was the writer just so's she could send one to herself."

"It's not usual to do that," said Jury. "Seems a thin motive for writing all the others. Poison pen letter-writers usually get a sense of power from controlling other people's lives, like a voyeur or an obscene telephone caller." Jury opened the next one. "You got one, Peter, I see."

Blushing, Gere scratched his neck with the stem of his pipe. "Pretty dull. Done in gray, which is all my personal life deserves, I guess. 'Skulduggery'—there's an old-fashioned word for you—when I was working for LT."

Carstairs clucked his tongue at Peter in mock reproof. "The one to Riddley is a dandy. He's the local medic, young chap and attractive. Blue." Carstairs picked it out of the pile.

Jury read the detailed description of what Dr. Riddley was doing with Ramona Wey. "Is she that sexy?"

"Good-looking," said Peter, "but a bit of an iceberg. She runs an antiques business in Hertfield."

There were no addresses on the envelopes, only names. All of the letters had been stuffed in the one brown envelope and sent along to the local post office.

"So who got this lot?"

"Mrs. Pennystevens. Well, of course she thought it damned odd, but she just handed them over to the various locals when they came in for bread or stamps. She said she thought they must be party invitations, or something."

"Some party," said Wiggins, who was reddening up a bit as he scanned them.

"Ordinary Crayolas you could find in any W. H. Smith's or any home with kiddies in it."

"Or without kiddies." Peter Gere opened the side drawer of the desk and took out some stubs of crayons and a couple of coloring books which he tossed on the table. "Not mine, actually. They belong to a little girl here. Has a passion for coloring, Emily does. She leaves the damned things everywhere. I found these on the window ledge."

Jury shook his head as he reread the letter to Augusta Craigie. "These letters don't ring true."

Carstairs looked at him. "Meaning?"

"Meaning I don't believe them." He tossed the letter on the table. "They're like a game or something. They don't even *sound* serious."

"People round here are taking them seriously, believe me," said Peter.

Carstairs looked at his watch, set down his cold coffee cup. "Look, I've got to get back to Hertfield station. Anything I can do to help, let me know, Superintendent. We can have a mobile unit over here immediately, if you like. I only thought, that since Hertfield's so close—"

"That's fine. Just keep your men searching that wood."

Carstairs nodded, raised two fingers to his cap in a mock military salute and said, "Thanks for the coffee, Peter. You still make it out of steel shavings, I see." He smiled and was gone.

The packet of letters lay on the desk. Jury spread them out. "A veritable rainbow of poison-pennery. This girl that got murdered. Do you think there's any relationship between these and her?"

"I don't see how," said Peter Gere. "I hadn't thought of it, I expect. Are you talking about blackmail?"

"No. That wouldn't be a very lucrative way of operating, would it? To publish the sins and then try and collect."

Wiggins came out of the collar of his overcoat, where he must have been turning things over in his chilly way. "You know, it doesn't seem to me that ticket stub in her coat proves she was a Londoner. It could have been put there by someone else to make us *think* she was from London."

Gere touched the brown envelope. "These were mailed in Hertfield the Tuesday before last. But that doesn't prove a damned thing. What you say is possible, of course."

Wiggins went on to expound his theory. "Seems odd to me, the murderer having taken the rest of the identification and not going through the pockets."

"It was down in the lining, remember. Slipped through," said Jury.

Wiggins thought for a moment. "It's even possible, you know, it wasn't her coat."

"Why do you say that?"

"Well, there she was all tarted up in that green dress and eyeshadow you could take a shovel to"—Wiggins's tone was disapproving—"and all that costume jewelry. That black cloth coat doesn't fit the picture, does it?"

Both Wiggins and Gere continued to weave out of beautiful whole cloth their black-cloth-coat theory. Jury left them to it, assuming all the while that the ticket was just what it said: she'd come down from London and meant to go back that day.

Jury had a lot of respect for provincial police forces. Their incorruptibility was almost legendary. Some of their detractors in the M.P.D. liked to call them a "bunch of effing swedes," but that, to Jury, was sour grapes. He had still not gotten over the trials and imprisonments of some of his colleagues a decade ago. He was not naïve, of course; but he supposed he was a trifle romantic. He believed in the verities: Queen, country, and the football pools. He looked at Peter Gere, the village bobby, and felt a real respect. Still, it was difficult working over someone else's patch.

It was a pleasant patch, though, he thought as he tilted back his chair and looked out at Littlebourne Green. Not even the police descending on it seemed to have wakened the village from its golden September dream. The High seemed isolated from the violence that had invaded the wood beyond, like a stone heaved through a sunny window. Across the Green, an old man shuffled out of the single pub, the Bold Blue Boy. Farther along a woman with a basket over her arm went into a sweet shop. Only the cluster of three villagers who seemed to have collided in the middle of the Green was proof that something was going on, for there was much gesticulating and pointing toward the station.

No, not three, four villagers. A little girl emerged from the group and stood staring at the station or the C.I.D. car or both.

Jury was half-listening to Wiggins and Gere. The murdered woman was no local, he was sure. She fairly screamed London. He had seen dozens of her up and down Oxford and Regent Streets. Why not look for the simplest explanation?

While Jury watched the little girl with the straggly blond hair start a side-wise sort of dancing step, he said to the voices behind him, "Maybe so. But in that case, where's her coat?"

That the original coat would have to be accounted for seemed not to have occurred to them. Neither one answered.

Sunlight was painting lemon stripes across the floor through the venetian blind. Jury looked out again at the Green. The clutch of villagers had diminished by two, leaving the older man and the little girl. He had detached himself from the child and was walking purposefully across the High toward the station. The little girl followed, but at a distance. He was dressed in plus-fours; she was wearing a hacking jacket, too short in the sleeves.

"Do you think we could be going to the pub, sir?" asked Wiggins, rather plaintively. "That wood was awful wet."

"Sure. But who's this coming up the walk, Peter?"

A consortium of thrushes, busy up to that point with a discarded crust on the walk, thronged the air above the elderly man's head as if they meant to build their nest there. Jury watched him beat at them with his stick. His broad face and chest appeared gargoylelike in the pane of the door before he ushered himself in like a stiff September breeze.

"Peter! This *is* preposterous! I have been given to understand someone has been found dead in the Horndean wood!" The tone suggested that the local constabulary had better be quick off the mark in explaining this nonsense, or he would hold them strictly accountable.

Jury recognized in Sir Miles Bodenheim (introduced to Jury with noticeable lack of enthusiasm by Gere) the sort of village gentry which has nothing to do with its time other than to take itself very seriously. "Did you have some information you thought relevant, Sir Miles?"

"I know nothing, except I cannot understand why police find it necessary to cut across my south pasture. They're slogging about over my property as if they owned it."

"Is your property near the Horndean wood, then?" asked Jury.

"It certainly *is*. Borders it, as a matter of fact. Rookswood has quite extensive grounds."

"On the night before last, did you happen to see or hear anything unusual?"

Miles Bodenheim smirked. "Only Miss Wey in Dr. Riddley's office. Seems a bit late for an appointment, wouldn't you say?"

Wiggins had his notebook out. "What time was that, sir?"

Sir Miles's brow shot up. "Time? How should I know? I don't keep running records on my neighbors' affairs."

"Guess," said Wiggins, wiping his nose with his large handkerchief.

Sir Miles sputtered. "Oh, I don't know. Sixish, I suppose."

"I was speaking more of something happening in the wood, Sir Miles," said Jury.

"Nothing," he snapped. "I do not prowl the wood at night, keeping track of trysts, Superintendent. And why it's necessary to call in Scotland Yard is beyond me," he added for good measure, having forgotten his earlier opinion of the Hertfield constabulary. "But I might as well save my breath to cool my porridge," he added sententiously.

Jury imagined it would be the first time he saved it. "Is it usual for people to meet there?"

"I shouldn't think so. We only go there for the birdwatching. I'm secretary-treasurer of the Royal Birdwatchers' Society."

"I'll probably want to talk with you later, Sir Miles, if you can spare me a few moments."

As Jury predicted, Miles Bodenheim was partial to this beggarly attitude on the part of the police. "I could do, yes. I understand," continued Miles, *sotto voce*, "it was a particularly brutal crime. Severed arm is what I heard. I've just come from the Craigie sisters. Ernestine is still sedated. Shocking. I had tea with Augusta and got all the details. Terrible, the arm simply—" He made a clicking sound and took a swipe at his own arm with his stick. "Can't think why anyone would do a thing like that." Expectantly he looked at Jury, who remained silent. "But she was a stranger. Ah, well." The implication was that strangers had no one but themselves to blame if they lost their arms. "Well, I hope you Scotland Yard chaps can be a bit quicker than the local police. After all, that's what we pay you for, isn't it?" Continuing to converse with himself, Miles said, "Odd, isn't it? What would anyone have been doing out there in the Horndean wood? Except for us birdwatchers in the Society, I can't see there'd be any reason for anyone to be there. My wife, Sylvia, agrees." He was warming to his subject, which had taken an abrupt turn from grisly murder to trespassing. "After all, there's only the one public footpath, and that's all overgrown simply because no one uses it. Why should anyone want to go to Horndean *that* way? It's a very long walk and Sylvia says she nearly went down whilst she was out with the Society, and that it's best to stay away from the center of it altogether. Sylvia nearly sunk down a foot, she says—"

Jury took it from the expression on Gere's face that Sylvia would not have been missed if she had sunk up to her neck. He cut him off by asking, "You're saying that this wood has never been a place for picnics or lovers' meetings—?"

Sir Miles gaped. "Lovers? I should hope not!" The suggestion was that lovers, like rabies, were unknown in Littlebourne village. But now his attention was caught afresh by the letters lying on the desk, which Peter Gere had unsuccessfully tried to cover over with his arm. "This village has gone mad. Some pervert allowed to roam about freely amongst us innocent people. Well, *some* of us innocent people." He smirked. "Where there's smoke, you know. You'll be staying, I expect, Superintendent?"

"Yes. At the Blue Boy."

Sir Miles's gray mustache twitched. "Oh, not the Blue Boy, surely. It's not properly heated and although Mrs. O'Brien does prepare a fairly decent meal, well, I don't really *approve* of women publicans, do you? I know women are just chock-a-block all over the place these days, but Mary O'Brien . . . You heard, of course, what happened to her daughter? I'd almost forgot myself, what with everything else that's happened. And, I suppose, Peter, the police aren't any forrarder about that, either, are they? It's been two weeks, after all. Well, Superintendent, I should like to stop here and chat, but I must be going." Here he tapped his walking stick thrice on the floor as if in magical incantation. "We are at your service," he offered. "Do not hesitate to come to us at Rookswood for any help you might need." Then, having satisfied himself that he had set straight the nation's police forces, Miles Bodenheim threw open the door and sallied forth to mix hot air with cold.

"What happened to the girl?" asked Jury, putting the packet of letters in his raincoat pocket.

"Katie O'Brien. She's the daughter of the woman who runs the

Blue Boy. She's been going up to London twice a month for violin lessons and must have been getting some pocket money by playing her fiddle in the tube station."

"Stupid thing to do," said Sergeant Wiggins.

"Yes, well, someone landed a blow on her skull. They say it's a miracle she's not dead, though I can't say she's much better off the way she is. She's in the Fulham Road Hospital, in a coma. Been like that for nearly two weeks now and it doesn't look good."

As they stood up to leave, Jury asked, "Where'd it happen?"

"In the East End. Wembley Knotts tube station. The music teacher lives there somewhere."

Wiggins popped a cough drop in his mouth and offered the box round. "Not the healthiest part of town for a young girl to be mucking about in," he said.

FOUR

∞∞∞∞∞∞∞∞

I

No, she wouldn't. Yes, she would. No, she wouldn't.
Emily Louise Perk was standing on the Green, her feet as usual turned inward. Some part of Emily was always on horseback. She was watching the door of the police station through which Miles Bodenheim had just walked, turned, and started down the pavement. She was thinking about Scotland Yard.

According to Polly's books, there was something called a Murder Room. Emily Louise wondered what it looked like. Wax figures of murderers, probably. Manacles, axes. Blood. She had a strong aversion to blood of any kind and hadn't liked listening to the details of the person they'd found in the Horndean wood. Emily hated even the thought of blood. One of the reasons she was such an expert rider was because she knew if she weren't up to the mark, she might fall off and bloody herself. Her mother had tried to talk to her once about blood, and Emily had found the subject so revolting she had run out of the room. All of those passages in Polly's books about blood-bedizened bodies she had skipped over. In one there had been a severed head. And now it had happened right here. A severed hand. Miss Craigie had said the fingers . . . She wouldn't think about it.

It was one of the reasons she had not been to the hospital to see Katie. She was afraid of the smells there, of the blood which was not far off: operating tables. Doctors' knives. Dirty aprons and uniforms. And she didn't want to see her friend Katie lying flat out like a body on a stone slab.

Her frown deepened. Even for Emily, it was a huge frown. If

she could only find out what the police knew, then maybe she could figure out if what *she* knew was important.

The door to the station opened again and *he* came out. She would have to be careful; Scotland Yard could get information out of anyone. They could get secrets out of Shandy, if they had to. Out of the very trees, if they wanted.

And Emily had a secret. The trouble was, it wasn't really *her* secret. It was Katie O'Brien's.

II

No, she wouldn't. Yes, she would. No, she wouldn't.

Polly Praed slammed the carriage return so hard it nearly took the typewriter with it.

She was trying to muster her resolve.

Her cottage sat near the Celtic cross, just at the juncture of the Y formed where the High joined the Hertfield Road. The window of her tiny parlor, where she did her writing, commanded a good view of the High: she could see all the way across Littlebourne Green to the police station on her right and the Bold Blue Boy on her left.

Ordinarily, the comings and goings of Littlebourne street life registered dimly as she wrote. Her eyes took in movements, but her mind was busy with her story. At least it usually worked that way. Today, the process reversed itself.

She had just disposed of Julia Bodenheim by means of cyanide in a cup of party punch. Her fingers had a mind of their own when it came to disposing of any one of the Bodenheims. Consequently, her mind was really absorbing the details of the comings and goings round the police station. While her fingers poisoned Julia, her eye tracked the progress of the policeman from Scotland Yard and Peter Gere. They were walking across the Green.

What was Emily doing, Polly wondered, hanging about the Green? She blushed. Emily was doing the same thing Polly wished *she* were doing. Although it was after two o'clock, still, that wasn't too late for lunch. They must be going to have lunch. No reason why she couldn't, too. She would. No, she wouldn't.

Now her fingers rested above an arsenic-stuffed aubergine as she tried to come up with a conversational gambit: *"Scotland Yard? Oh! I wasn't aware the Hertfield police had called in ..."*

Pretty dim. What about, *"I suppose you can't stand to read mysteries about Scotland Yard, can you, Superintendent?"*

Inane. Could she seek his advice about Chapter Three? That would be transparent enough to lower her forever in his esteem. Was he supposed to stop his murder investigation to give her a short lecture on criminology?

Exasperated, she fell back in her chair and squashed Barney, her cat. The cat had appropriated the sunny part of the seat for his nap.

Severed fingers. Polly put her head in her hands and thought about it. She couldn't come up with a reason for cutting off the fingers. Polly leaned forward again, rested her chin on her folded arms, her arms on the typewriter, and stared out the window. She saw the gate of the Bold Blue Boy swinging. In, out, out, in ... Emily Louise, keeping an even closer watch than she was. When you were ten years old, you could bloody well be as obvious as you wanted.

This was ridiculous, she told herself, getting up, pulling down her twin set smartly. She would simply walk across the Green to the pub.

No, she wouldn't.

FIVE

I

"WHO's the little girl with the worried look?" asked Jury, looking through the open casement window of the Bold Blue Boy. She was swinging on the gate.

"Emily Louise Perk," said Peter Gere, eating a cheese-and-pickle sandwich. "She's always about. Her mum works in Hertfield, father's dead. Thanks, Mary."

The woman who set their pints on the table had, Jury thought, a vague and undefined look, like someone behind a rained-on windowpane. She was dark, middle-aged and had probably once been pretty, perhaps only two weeks ago, before her daughter's accident. She said nothing but that she hoped they'd be comfortable, and walked away.

Peter, who had been telling Jury about Katie O'Brien, continued: "What Mary couldn't understand was, when they found her in the tube station, knocked unconscious, she wasn't wearing the clothes she set out in. Mary always made her wear dresses. Katie'd changed somewhere and was wearing a bright pink shirt and jeans. There were cigarettes, too, in her shopping bag. And one of those books girls like to read nowadays. Heartwind Romance, I think it was. Well, her mother never let her smoke nor read books like that—"

"They're pretty innocent," said Sergeant Wiggins, looking a bit healthier now he had some food. "Not one of your bosom-rippers—" At Jury's questioning look, he said, "Well, you remember Rosalind van Renseleer. I read a few of hers. . . ." He turned his attention back to his sandwich.

"The mother's pretty strict, I take it?" Gere nodded. "What about the music teacher? You said he was supposed to meet her at the tube and walk her back."

Gere shrugged. "Don't know. 'H' Division handled it. You can get the report from Carstairs. Not the first time someone's been mugged in London, is it?" Gere gave Jury a bleak smile. "Hard on Mary, though, it is. Poor woman. But you know kids nowadays."

"What kind of jeans?" asked Jury.

Peter looked up, surprised. "What kind? Blue jeans. They're all alike."

"The hell they are. Most girls nowadays wouldn't be caught dead in anything but designer jeans. What kind?"

Peter frowned. "Well, I don't know, do I? Why's it important?"

"I'm just wondering how long she had to play for money in the London Underground to buy them."

"Jordache," said Mary O'Brien, twisting the corner of her apron as if it might have been the neck of her daughter's assailant. "And a pinky-purple shirt. I couldn't understand it. Her dress was in her shopping bag."

"Boyfriends? Did she have any?"

Mary O'Brien shook her head. "She's only sixteen. I told her there'd be plenty of time later for that."

Jury didn't comment. "The music teacher—what's his name?"

"Macenery." She watched Wiggins write it down. "Cyril Macenery. Lives on Drumm Street, not far from the tube station. I went there with Katie the first time. I wanted to make sure he was dependable. He *says* he walked with her to the tube stop and he didn't have any idea she was playing her violin for money."

"Don't you believe him?"

"I don't know what to believe. I'm surprised you're even interested. No one else is, now. After those letters, and now this murder in the Horndean wood. . . ." With the back of her hand, she shoved dark hair off her forehead.

"Of course I'm interested, Mrs. O'Brien. It's a terrible thing to have happen." That earned him a tiny, fleeting smile, like a leaf snagged on rock in a stream. It quickly disappeared. "Who's her doctor?"

"Dr. Riddley. The local doctor. There's nothing they can do, except to wait. I go to the hospital, talk to her. It's hard talking to someone who doesn't hear. I took in a tape recorder with some of her favorite music. Katie was a real musician," said Mary O'Brien, mustering some of the old pride she must have felt. "There was no one around here, no teacher good enough to teach her. She'd gone through them all. This Cyril Macenery was good enough, and cheap, too. I haven't got all that much, and she had to have the best. Katie helped out too. Her music meant a lot to her. She did odd jobs, mostly cleaning, for a lot of people — Miss Pettigrew, the Mainwarings, Peter, Dr. Riddley — quite a few others. She took care of the horses at Rookswood sometimes, too. Helped out in the Magic Muffin, waiting on tables in the summer when there was a lot of business. . . . If she hadn't had to have the best teacher we could afford, you don't think I'd have let her go roaming in that part of London, do you?"

Her defensiveness would turn into defeat if he didn't stop her. There was in her tone the rising note of hysteria. "The London police won't forget, Mrs. O'Brien."

"I'll just show you your rooms." As she led them up a dark staircase lined with old engravings of birds and bucolic country scenes, she said, "They say you never can tell what might trigger something for someone in a coma. I talk to her and play the music. You'd never guess what her favorite song was: 'Roses of Picardy.' Katie was so old-fashioned."

Jury wondered how she squared that with Jordache jeans and a bright pink shirt.

II

Jury's fascination with the little girl with the yellow hair was growing. She had got bored with swinging on the gate and had disappeared during his talk with Mary O'Brien.

Having dispatched Wiggins to question the postmistress and the Mainwarings, Jury was setting off for the Craigie cottage. His exit from the Bold Blue Boy and Emily Perk's from the sweet shop several doors up the High occurred almost miraculously, and certainly simultaneously.

Jury watched her for a moment while she looked off into space, ignoring him with near-spectacular indifference. He hadn't had anyone make such a display of not seeing him since he'd nicked Jimmy Pink, the dip who worked Camden Passage. She was bending her head over a screw of white paper, apparently debating which sweet to pop into her mouth. Still without seeing him, although he was the only person on the pavement, and a large one at that, she began hopping on one foot, then jumping forward and planting both feet, legs splayed across some invisible pavement pattern. Then she twisted herself in air and started the whole performance backwards, all the while holding tightly to the little white bag of sweets. Her formerly unkempt and straggling hair had been worried into two separate bunches on either side of her head, and when she hopped, the bunches bounced.

He crossed the High Street and got into his car, which he maneuvered round the bottom of the Green and back up the opposite side, past the Blue Boy. As he neared the Celtic cross, he looked in his rearview mirror. She was standing stock still, stuffing whatever sweets she'd got into her mouth and watching the C.I.D. car for all she was worth.

SIX

~~~~~~~~~~

I

AUGUSTA Craigie — or the woman in the unruly garden whom Jury presumed to be Augusta — seemed to be doing something to a bed of primulas when he unlatched the gate. Except for the one little patch in which the woman worked, the rest of the yard was a jungle. She was plying a trowel around tiny windmills and waterfalls, ducks leading ducklings off to war, frogs dressed in polka dots and sitting on plaster benches. There was even a tiny Ferris wheel. It was a carnivallike atmosphere.

"Miss Craigie?" She looked around at him, her mouth pursing in a small *o*. "I'm Superintendent Jury, Scotland Yard C.I.D." He showed her his warrant card.

Immediately, she pulled her collar up and her sleeves down, as if to cover any exposed skin. Hard to do, since Miss Craigie was already well covered, all in gray from her hair down to her lisle stockings. With her small eyes and sharp nose, she reminded Jury of a field mouse.

"You've come to see my sister. But I really don't think she's able . . . I mean, such a shock. You can imagine!"

"Yes, I can. But perhaps *we* could have a talk?" If he could get into the house he could deal with everyone's shock there.

"We? Oh. Yes, I suppose . . ." She looked uncertainly at her plaster ornaments, but finding no ecouragement from the ducks and frogs, she gave up and gathered her sweater even more tightly round her thin chest and led the way up the path to a small door. The roof was badly in need of rethatching. The heavy, wheat-dark collar round windows and door had long ago sprung from the netting meant to keep out nesting birds.

A long-haired cat with a down-drooping thug's face appeared from behind a bush and swayed along at her heels. Three others—Jury had the impression of gray and orange—were slipping like shadows round the corner of the house.

The look of the garden seemed to have reasserted itself inside. The Craigie sisters' talents leaned more toward ornamentation than housekeeping. Behind the front room, through a low-hanging beamed arch, was another room—a study or sitting room of some sort: before its one window sat a large library table overflowing with rolls of paper, writing implements, draftsman's tools. This was all overseen by a pair of lovebirds in a wicker cage.

Everywhere else there were birds, also. Only these were stuffed ones under glass, or porcelain ones on mantel and shelves. Augusta Craigie, who had seated herself in a bulky, cretonne-covered chair, said, "Ernestine is an ornithologist. That's why we've all the birds about. The lovebirds are mine. Sweet, aren't they? Ernestine has written a number of articles on birds. I just do the housekeeping." She moved her hands in an apologetic way, as if the hands were not quite equal to the task.

Jury did not know whether the three cats lined up and looking at him, paws neat and tails twitching, were the same cats come inside or other cats spawned in the darkness of the cottage. Even in midday a lamp was needed, and one was lit, a tall one beside Miss Craigie's chair. Its fringed shade cast a puddle of gloomy light. The thug-cat jumped up on her lap, dealing what should have been a death-blow, but Miss Craigie didn't seem to notice.

"Ernestine is the president of the Hertfield birdwatchers' group. She's usually up before five and out with her binoculars . . . so, you see, it's perfectly *natural* she might have come across the . . . poor woman."

Jury decided Augusta was an overexplainer and left her to it. She must have taken his silence as some assumption of guilt on her part and rushed ahead to embroider upon the circumstances. "She was out making one of her little maps, you see, for the birdwatchers. We all use them when we go out together, usually in teams, if there's something—like the Speckled Crackle—truly important . . ." A bitter note crept into her voice as she said, "You know, it was just as bad for *me*—quite as bad!" Even in the dull light Jury could see her face flush; she had blurted this out as if Ernestine had hogged the limelight long enough. "Seeing that dog come trotting up the street with that—*thing* in its mouth." Augusta sank back in her chair and then just as suddenly sat forward, sweeping the cat to the floor, who then set off to stalk the lovebirds. "I don't understand any of this *at all,* Inspector. We're being singled out. It's almost as if police—you— suspected *us.* First there was that other inspector from Hertfield coming here and asking all those questions . . . well, really, it's *most* unfair."

Jury let his demotion pass and said, "I hope you can understand how important it is to question anyone who had a part in discovering the body. We don't mean to harass you. If it hadn't been for you and your sister, she might still be lying out there in the wood." Jury smiled.

The sudden switch from victim to heroine brought Augusta's hand up to smooth her hair, then her skirt. Now she was able to let her naturally curious bent take over: "Who was she? Do you know?" Jury shook his head. "We'd never any of us seen her before, so maybe it is someone from Horndean or Hertfield. I was just saying to Miles Bodenheim—Sir Miles—and we both agreed, there must be some psychopathic killer, come down from London, maybe—" (On vacation? Jury wondered) "—and it puts us in mind of Jack the Ripper." Her small shudder seemed more one of pleasure than pain. "You remember the way he mutilated his bodies—"

"I don't think that's the case here."

But Augusta wasn't having that. She went after the gory details like a hound on scent, detailing the appearance of the corpse as described to her by her sister. That same sister seemed to be rousing, for there were thumpings and creakings and sounds of someone descending the stairs.

"That must be Ernestine. I can't think why she's up. I don't know why she didn't faint dead away—Ernestine! You really should *not* be up!"

If this were Ernestine blocking the archway, she didn't look as if she could be brought down by a gale wind. She was stout, square, determined. Any objections to her present course would obviously be beaten off with the blackthorn stick she carried. Even the cats scattered like buckshot. She was wearing a navy pea coat, buttoned tightly across her large frontage, and a knitted cap had been pulled down over her ears with such force, that nothing but a gray fringe of hair and the barest hint of eyebrow showed.

"*Out*, of course," was her snappish answer to her sister's timid question as to where she was going. "A nice lie-down, that's all I needed. Just got to get the Wellingtons on—"

"But you *can't* be going back to the Horndean wood. This is the police from Scotland Yard, and he wanted to ask—"

"Why shouldn't I go back? The Crackle won't wait forever. I expect police have tidied up by now. Right, Inspector?"

"We've taken the body away, ma'am. But you can't go into that part of the wood yet."

"Why not, I'd like to know? The Speckled Crackle is very nearly an extinct bird, sir. It's that part of the wood he'll return to, if any. They like the wet, you know." She was chugging toward a little window seat by the door where her Wellingtons waited, stiff as soldiers. Could only brute force stop her?

"This Speckled—what is it?"

She stopped. She turned. "Great Speckled Crackle. Don't tell me you've not heard of it?"

"No, I haven't. Is it rare?"

"Rare? *Rare?*" She walked back a few paces. "It's been sighted only five times in the last three years. Once in the Orkneys, once in the Hebrides, and once in Torquay. It's clearly off course, somehow."

"And you've seen it in the Horndean wood?"

"Think so, yes." Now she was unbuttoning her pea coat.

"I've a friend who saw a Spix's Macaw once." Jury offered her a cigarette which she absently accepted.

The eyebrows shot up, devoured further by the pull-down cap. "But that's impossible! The Spix's Macaw is only seen in Brazil. Somewhere in northwest Bahia. It's an extremely rare bird!" She sat herself down as if from shock in the twin of the cretonne chair.

Jury shook his head. "Maybe it simply got blown off course."

Regarding him with extreme suspicion, she said, "I can't believe this person saw one. I'm an ornithologist and keep abreast of such things. I've heard no report of Spix's Macaws." Her eyes narrowed as she puffed on the cigarette she held between thumb and index finger. "Describe one." She might have been interrogating a murder suspect.

"Well, it was blue, he said. Darker blue on the back and wings. And about, oh, two feet or so long."

There was a brief, amazed silence as Ernestine stared at her sister. At first, Jury thought she might be going to accuse Augusta of having something to do with this spurious Spix's Macaw report. But what she said was, "Augusta, don't be sitting about like a sparrow. We're peckish and it's nearly twelve. Let's have some sandwiches." To her sister's resigned and departing back, she yelled: "Minced chicken in the fridge!" Then she settled back for more bird-talk. "The Spix's Macaw is . . ."

Jury gave it exactly three minutes and then decided she was primed enough to get off birds and onto birdwatchers. "How often does your group meet?"

"Once a month, third Monday."

"Who belongs to it?"

"The Bodenheims—Miles and Sylvia. Mainwaring and his wife, when she's about." Ernestine smirked a bit.

"I take it she's not about very much?"

"Trouble there, if you ask me."

Augusta returned with a plate of sandwiches so neatly cut they looked hemmed. Jury refused the food, but accepted a cup of coffee.

"Tell me, Miss Craigie, you must have speculated on who this girl might be, or at least a reason for her to be walking in the wood."

Making no attempt to hide the fact her mouth was full of chicken, Ernestine said, "None whatever. Some shop girl, probably."

"Why do you say that?"

"Don't know. Just looked the type. Bit tartish, you know, all

47

those bangles and earrings. 'Bedizened, beringed, and bejeweled,' as our old mum used to say. But all from Woolworth's is my guess."

"You observed her rather closely if you saw all of that."

"Saw the body through these first." Again she lifted the binoculars. "Wasn't sure what it was, though, and I tramped over. I didn't spend too much time looking—you can imagine—but, being a trained observer, it wouldn't take much to see what I saw. I went off straightaway to the nearest phone and called the police."

With the answers flowing freely now, Jury hesitated to ask his next question. "The, ah, damage to the body was done with a small ax found near the stump. I understand it was yours, Miss Craigie. Why did you keep it there?"

But it would take more than bloody axes to put Miss Craigie off. "To chop through thick stuff, of course. Small branches, that sort of thing. Get a better view."

"Anybody else ever use it you know of?"

"I expect so. It was always lying about. Not necessarily *there*— the birdwatchers wielded it now and again, so it might have been found anywhere round about there."

Jury changed the subject. "Tell me, did you know Katie O'Brien?"

They didn't, for a moment, seem to comprehend. "Oh, that O'Brien girl. Forgot about her. Got coshed on the head, didn't she, about a fortnight ago? Well, if the mother will let her run about London, it doesn't surprise me."

Augusta said, more to disagree with her sister than to defend Katie, Jury inferred, "Katie always seemed such a nice girl. She did cleaning for people in Littlebourne to help out. And she was very thorough; I had her in to help me often. She worked, Katie did. A responsible child. Not like some of those others that go to the comprehensive."

Ernestine made a deprecating gesture. "Nice as ninepence, maybe, but I always say still waters, that sort of thing. Bet she'd be off with a boy soon as say knife."

"Perhaps," said Augusta, "it was the girl for Stonington."

"Stonington?" said Jury.

"Why yes, that's the Kennington place. I heard Lady Kennington was looking for someone to do typing for her. Stonington's just the other side of the wood, on the Horndean Road. I'm quite sure Mrs. Pennystevens told me that she — Lady Kennington, I mean — had a prospect she was expecting to interview a day or two ago. Maybe this person in the wood was one of them."

"Doesn't it seem unlikely that such a stranger would be walking through the Horndean wood, though?"

Augusta said brightly, "But, Inspector, perhaps she was *dragged* there. You know. Killed somewhere else. Or *executed*. Really, it does sound like some sort of *ritual* crime. Had you thought of that?"

Jury had to admit he hadn't.

"Oh, bosh, Augusta. You've been reading too many of Polly's thrillers. She's our local hack," she said to Jury. "Not a bad sort, actually. Tried to get her in the birdwatchers —"

Jury's mind was on the Kennington place. Why did the name seem familiar? He couldn't remember Carstairs or Peter Gere mentioning it. "Are you on the telephone?" he asked the Craigies.

"Of course," said Ernestine. "Got heaps of calls to make about the Society. Yes, of course you can use it," she said to Jury's next question. "Back in the study there. Mind you don't knock my maps about!" she called to Jury's departing back.

"Stonington?" said Inspector Carstairs with some surprise. "No, no one mentioned the woman's being for Stonington. The bus driver says he remembers a woman of that description getting off the Hertfield-Horndean bus in Littlebourne. It was the last bus for Horndean, and got to Littlebourne at 8:05. It was dusk."

"This Kennington. I seem to have heard the name somewhere before —"

"It was in the papers about a year ago. Lord Kennington had a collection of jewels, among them an emerald, very rare and very valuable. The secretary, a villain named Tree, walked off with them. Or it, I should say. Poetic justice, maybe, but Tree was run down by a car a few days later. The necklace is still going missing, as far as we know." Carstairs turned away from the telephone to make some comment to someone there, then he was back. "I'll

49

get onto this Stonington business straightaway. Lady Kennington lives there now. Husband's dead."

Jury thanked him and rang off.

When he returned, they were arguing about the letters. Augusta's favorite candidate, it seemed, was Miss Praed.

"Old Polly?" said Ernestine. "For pity's sakes, she's too sensible for that sort of thing. Keeps herself busy enough in her mind she doesn't have to go about wasting her imagination that way."

"It's because she's *got* the imagination," snapped Augusta.

Ernestine shoved the mean-looking cat, who had been rummaging among the sandwich rinds, from the table. "Got to admit, old sweat, that letter to you would *take* some imagination!" Ernestine guffawed and beat her blackthorn stick to the floor. "Augusta here wouldn't say boo to a goose."

Jury wouldn't bank on that, seeing the look on Augusta's face. Ernestine, though, apparently having got the lion's share of whatever went round all of their lives, didn't appear to notice the look of murderous rage. And as the cat, frustrated in its play for minced chicken, stalked the lovebirds again, Jury also wondered what odd little mental quirk had one sister keeping cats and caged birds where the other was an ornithologist.

"Who's your own candidate for that lot of letters?" he asked Ernestine.

Chin resting on crossed hands atop her stick, she gave it some thought. "Derek Bodenheim's my guess." She ignored her sister's shocked expression. "Peabrain, Derek's got. Sort of child who tore wings off insects. Or it could be old Sylvia, if it comes to that."

"You're accusing one of your own *birdwatchers?*" said Augusta.

"Rubbish. Just because you like birds doesn't mean you wouldn't take an ax to your mum, does it?"

"No, it doesn't," said Jury, shoving his notebook in his pocket. "Thanks very much for your time. I might be wanting to talk to you later. And no going into the Horndean wood, Miss Craigie." Of course, of course, was her reply. He knew she'd be off like a shot the moment he left.

At the door, as Jury was handing them one of his cards, Augusta said, "I *do* hope this awful business won't postpone our church fête, will it? It's to be tomorrow, and I've got my tent and costume all planned out."

Ernestine hooted. "All kitted out in fortune-teller's rig. Madame Zostra. Damned silly business. If the church needs money, why doesn't it go whistle for it?" She was studying over Jury's card. "Said you were Inspector, didn't you? This says Superintendent. What's the difference? You in charge of the whole boiling, or what?"

Jury smiled as he scanned the vault of the blue sky. "Not much difference. Just look at it this way: not all policemen are inspectors, and not all birds are Crackles."

II

As he drove the short distance back to Littlebourne High Street, Jury tried to remember what it was that one of them had said that nagged at him. The wood, the body, the birds . . . ?

The detail lay buried, sunk like a stone. Driving slowly along the quarter-mile of road toward the Celtic cross, he thought of the possibility of the woman's having been on her way to the Kennington estate. As Jury ran over the list of people he wanted to see — Peter Gere; the doctor, Riddley; the Praed woman; the Bodenheims — he was conscious of the hurried *clop clop* of hooves. When he looked in his rearview mirror, he saw a brown pony, topped off by the little girl with the yellow hair.

He was clearly being kept under surveillance by one of Littlebourne's most resourceful citizens.

III

"It was about a year ago," said Peter Gere, feet planted on the desk in the one-room police station. "It was Trevor Tree — Lord Kennington's secretary — called me sometime round about midnight saying the place had been burgled. Kennington kept his collection in a glass-topped case in a study that had a French door leading out to a courtyard and windows on the other side overlooking the gravel drive. The reason I mention that is, we didn't see what Tree could possibly have done with the stuff except to toss it outside to someone else waiting there. There wouldn't have been time to do anything else except maybe drop it in a vase of roses. We searched the people, the house, the grounds." Peter Gere shrugged. "And they were all watching one another from the time the alarm went off—"

"The case was wired?"

Gere nodded. "So was the house. Besides Lord and Lady Kennington, there was the old cook, and a housekeeper who's no longer with them, a gardener, and Tree. It wasn't the first time Kennington had missed stuff. Some odds and ends of antique jewelry—brooches, some Egyptian-like stuff, a ring shaped like a snake, a diamond in a gold setting, some lapis lazuli—he'd bought from Ramona Wey. She's got a shop in Hertfield. They weren't all that valuable; Kennington thought he'd misplaced them himself until this other thing happened.

"It was clever of Tree. He breaks the case, disposes of the emerald somehow, calls the police himself," Peter went on. "It couldn't have taken Lord Kennington more than two minutes to pull on a robe and get down to the study, and there was Tree on the phone. Kennington didn't really suspect him until later, next morning, when he was gone. He would have got a lot more of a headstart if it hadn't been for the cook, who couldn't sleep and saw him going down the drive at six in the morning. But even *then* she thought he had some reason. Tree was a smooth fellow. A charmer. Clever, sophisticated, very plausible. I met him once or twice over at the Blue Boy. You know the type. . . .

"Well, it was then that Kennington knew what had happened. We had police waiting in London, at Tree's digs. The necklace wasn't on him and it wasn't in the flat. They nicked him, but hadn't any proof. Police in London watched him for several days. Then comes the irony. Tree gets run down by some bleeding teenager in the Marylebone Road. And no one ever found that emerald. Worth a quarter million, it was."

"That's a lot of money to trust an accomplice with. If you think Tree handed it over to someone else, what makes you think the someone else didn't unload it?"

Gere scratched his neck. "I never thought he had a mate. Not him. And that's the main reason. He'd never have trusted anybody else. Kennington must've been a mug to trust him."

Jury smiled. "Hindsight's great."

"Yes, I expect so. I didn't like him, not by half. Cheeky sort, he was. Kennington apparently thought he knew enough about jewelry to have him buy it. He was showing the stuff he bought from Ramona Wey round in the pub, saying what a bargain he'd got. To tell the truth, I wondered if he didn't have something going with her. Two peas in a pod, those two."

"You don't care for her, I take it?"

"Oh, she's all right, I expect. Anyway, what's all this in aid of?"

"I don't know," said Jury. "Littlebourne just seems to come in for more than its share of grief."

IV

"Stupid old sod!" said Nathan Riddley, yanking down the knot in his tie like a hangman's noose. They had been discussing Augusta Craigie. "Polly ought to have her up for slander. Tell her to get stuffed."

Dr. Riddley sat smoldering in his swivel chair, turning it from side to side, his anger deepening, Jury thought, with every turn.

"Far as I'm concerned," Riddley went on, "you don't have to look any further for the author of those stupid letters. I know what you're going to say—that she got one herself." Riddley shrugged. "So she sent it to herself. I'm sure that sort of thing happens often enough. Diverting suspicion, and so on. *Hers* was almost flattering. 'I knew what I wanted to do when I saw you stark through the chink in the curtain.' Bit of a giggle, that's what most of us would have if we saw Augusta stark." The swivel chair creaked as he leaned forward to get another cigarette, then sat back again, rolling the chair from side to side. All the furniture in the surgery was old, wooden, pockmarked, except for the aluminum table used for his examinations.

"How'd you know what was in hers, Dr. Riddley?"

"She was *showing* it round, man. Doing, she said, her civic duty." There was a silence as Riddley smoked and turned his lighter in his fingers. The ashtray was already full to overflowing.

53

His fingers were stained with nicotine. He seemed a nerve-wracked young man. Youngish. Jury put his age in the mid-thirties. He wondered if having a surgery in even such a small village as Littlebourne were still a pressured existence. Looking at him, Jury thought it was no wonder women fell in love with doctors, and Riddley would be odds-on favorite for a romantic candidate: unattached, good-looking, probably chauvinistic enough to fascinate. With all that going for him, he might even live down his Irish ancestry — those blue eyes, that copper hair.

In the expanding silence, Riddley tapped ash from his cigarette and said, "Superintendent, I confess in the face of your relentless questioning."

Jury smiled. "To what?"

"Anything, anything. You've asked exactly two questions since you walked in the door. No, three, with that last one. You've simply let me yammer on and on. So what have I said that's going to see me in the dock? Of course, you've read the letter about me and Ramona Wey. All in blue. Writer didn't have much imagination, though, since he chose Ramona as the object of Mainwaring's affections, too. Sort of like throwing darts at a board and seeing which will hit the bull's eye and which fall wide."

"What *is* your relationship with Miss Wey?"

"Oh, there you go again. Questions, questions. My 'relation-ship' with her is doctor-patient. Period. But Mainwaring's—" Nathan Riddley's blue glance flicked away from Jury's eyes.

"Mainwaring?"

Riddley shrugged. "Let the Craigies and the Bodenheims do the gossip, please."

Jury changed the subject. "What about Katie O'Brien?"

That did make him stop rocking his chair. "Katie? My God, I'd almost forgotten. . . . You heard she'd been attacked in a London tube station." Jury nodded. "She's in a coma. Been that way for two weeks and the longer it lasts, the worse her chances. Whoever hit her wasn't kidding around. Landed a terrific blow to her skull. She suffered a tear of the brain stem, sort of thing you might get in an auto accident. Whiplash. And you know, of course, the longer the coma keeps on, the worse the chances of any sort of recovery. We don't see many miracle awakenings, except in books. It's really terrible."

"What hospital is she in?"

"Royal Marsden. It's in the Fulham Road." As Riddley made a jab at the ashtray, the pale red-gold hairs along his wrist glinted in the sunshine. "Mary's taking it awfully hard. I'm really worried about her."

The worry seemed to be more than clinical, Jury thought. He would not have thought of Riddley and Mary O'Brien. Perhaps he was older than he looked. More likely, Mary O'Brien was younger than, at this awful moment in her life, *she* looked.

SEVEN

❦❦❦❦❦❦❦

"I'LL simply have them kill one another off. That way I can get rid of them faster."

Polly Praed announced her plan to Barney, her cat, who lay like a paperweight atop her manuscript pages.

Polly was not much interested in the motive for these multiple killings — she was only interested in the method. *Tap, tap, tap* went the typewriter keys, painting a clear image of Julia Bodenheim threading an embroidery needle which she had recently dipped in curare:

> *"Oh, do be careful, Mummy," said her daughter, Angela, whilst flipping through a fashion magazine. "Remember, you've no thimble."*

Of *course* Mummy had no thimble. Polly smiled. Angela had taken pains to hide it.

> *Angela was only pretending to read. Actually she was watching closely the flying fingers of her mother as they deftly drew primrose thread round the edges of the hoop. "Oh, Mummy! There, you've gone and pricked your finger!"*

Polly shoved the glasses to the top of her head and sat back. Matricide? Would the public go for that? Or would it be rather too sickening? Sophocles, after all —

There was a knocking, like doom, on the door.

She jumped. Then, annoyed at the interruption, shoved her glasses down. Why was someone knocking now, just when Mummy Sylvia was about to die a very painful death? (Clutching her throat? Clawing at the air?) And thinking how she really ought to read up on poisons, Polly went to the window to peek out —

Oh, good God! Him!

Wildly, she turned, searching the room as if she might find a gown of beaten gold to take the place of the dreary twin-set. *Why* hadn't she put on her blue frock this morning . . . hair, awful . . . no lipstick . . . God! Another knock!

"Ju-ust a mo-ah-ment. . . ." She tried to flute it, but her voice cracked. She ran to the bathroom for a comb.

Humming tunelessly, Jury waited on Polly Praed's stoop and looked over the pleasant prospect of Littlebourne Green. He was wondering when Melrose Plant might get there, was rather surprised he hadn't turned up by now, as he had called him early this morning. Lady Ardry had probably shackled herself to him, and Plant was looking for an acetylene torch. . . . The other half of Jury's mind was looking up and down the street for the girl with the yellow hair. He was sure she was out there somewhere. Um-hm. In the doorway, suddenly, across the Green. That tearoom with "Muffin" in its name —

Sunnybank Cottage's door opened.

The woman looked, he thought, rather newly minted, in the sense of a makeup job that had the stamp of someone about to appear on a film set. Yet, despite the layers of thick mascara and a totally inappropriate green-gold glitter of eyeshadow, he could see the eyes beneath it all were wonderful. Perhaps it was the film-set notion that made him think of Elizabeth Taylor. The face might be otherwise unremarkable, but with those eyes it would take a person of iron self-control even to notice the rest of her. Jury did, however; he was paid to. She was a rather petite, early-middle-ageish woman in a twin-set the color of drabbit. A nice mop of dark curls, apparently untamable.

"Miss Praed? I'm Superintendent Jury, Scotland Yard C.I.D." He flicked his ID.

This seemed to surprise her out of her pose of slinky nonchalance — one hand up the doorsill, the other drooping on her hip. But she said nothing.

"Could I have just a word with you?"

There was a feeble sort of wave of her arm, apparently inviting him in. She cleared her throat, as if to speak, but nothing came out. Jury removed his coat and dropped it on a couch. He looked round the study, or whatever she called it, its small window facing the Green. A battered library table took up what little space there was; an equally battered orange cat was washing its forepaw. Around its neck was a red bandanna, victory flag, perhaps, to mark its hard-won battles with less fortunate cats. "Nice cat," said Jury, trying to put her a bit more at ease.

"Its name's Barney," she blurted out, like an actress cued from the wings.

"Barney looks as if he can take care of himself."

"He's a coward, actually."

Barney seemed to think this estimate called for further explanation and stopped washing. He sat aloof and princely, paws together, tail lapped round them like the robes of state. Barney glared at both of them.

The subject of the cat exhausted, Jury asked: "Could I just sit down a moment? It won't take long."

"Oh. Yes." She turned absently, looking for chairs as if the furniture removers had come and cleaned her out.

"There's a chair just there," Jury informed her. Beside it was a small repast of cheese and crackers on a table. "Did I interrupt your tea, or anything? Sorry." She gave a shake of her head, curls bobbing, and sat down in that chair, nodding him toward another. She offered some cheese and crackers to Jury, who refused.

"How long have you lived in Littlebourne, Miss Praed?" It was going to be rough going with her, he could see. Police did certainly unnerve some people totally.

She bent her head over the single cracker and cheese tidbit she had taken from the plate. How could anyone manage to make a bit of cheese look like a small, dead animal?

"Oh, a long time. Oh, I guess even ten or fifteen years. . . ." A rather lengthy debate with herself followed over how long, exactly, she'd lived in the village. Twelve and one-half years was her final decision. This was submitted to Jury for any possible inaccuracy.

"I understand you're a writer. Mysteries. I guess I haven't read—"

His confession elicited an electric response: "I hope not! I mean, you wouldn't like them at all. I'm sure you'd hate them. I bet most policemen hate mysteries, especially the ones like mine where the lead character's a Scotland Yard inspector. No resemblance to reality—" This rush of words out, she labored over the cracker and cheese again.

"I hope they *are* removed from reality. Police routine's pretty dull, after all." Jury smiled the smile which had once prompted a seven-year-old girl to insist he have the remainder of her container of Smarties. It had the effect on Polly, unfortunately, of making her reach for a pair of ugly, horn-rimmed glasses with which she promptly covered her eyes.

"I interrupted your writing, I guess. Sorry."

"Don't be," she said quickly. "I've just been practicing murders."

"Practicing?"

"Like scales, you know. I practice on the Bodenheims. I'm calling it *The Littlebourne Murders.*"

"Which of them is your victim?"

"All of them. I've killed off each one half-a-dozen times. Guns, knives, faked auto accidents over cliffs, the lot. Right now I'm into poisons. Curare is nice. Cheese?" She thrust the plate toward him. He shook his head. She took another mouse-morsel of cheese and set it atop another cracker. Then she said, casually: "What'd you say your name was?"

"Jury. I'm with Scotland Yard."

"*Are* you? You're a detective?"

He had thought they had got that sorted out long ago. "That's right. I'm sure you heard about the woman found in the Horndean wood this morning."

She nodded. "Beastly, wasn't it?"

"We're trying to ascertain just who she was."

"I'm sure she was a stranger. No one I've talked to ever saw her

59

before. That is, from what we could tell from the Craigies' description."

"Don't you think it odd a stranger would be walking in the Horndean wood?"

They were in her patch now—murder and mayhem—and she relaxed. She even put down the cracker. "Maybe she was killed somewhere else. And taken to the wood." She shoved her glasses back on her nose and regarded him in a getting-down-to-business way.

"We don't think so."

"Where was she on her way to, then? No one goes there except the R.B.W.'s—the birdwatchers."

"Maybe we ought to add a mystery writer to the team. Cigarette?"

She accepted both cigarette and compliment in grand fashion, sitting back, smiling, crossing her legs. Good smile and good legs, he noted. "I've been thinking about it. A lot."

"Tell me what you think."

"Okay. First off, there's the fingers." She held her own hand up, fingers spread. "Why would anyone want to cut off one hand? Couldn't be fingerprints—"

"Some people seem to think it's a psychotic."

"No, no, no." The dark curls shook. "If you were going to dismember a body, you wouldn't stop with five lousy fingers."

Her way of looking at it was refreshingly clinical. "True."

"It *could* be a red herring."

"True again."

"Making people *think* it's a madman. Of course, it could be some sort of odd revenge. Symbolic maiming. Like the Mafia in America. To warn off others." She leaned back and closed her eyes to fix the mental image. "Horndean wood. Early morning. No, evening, wasn't it? Mists, peaty soft ground and her feet sinking in as she walks. Marshbirds. An early owl. And him waiting—or her. I rather like the idea of a woman's doing it, don't know why. The victim stops, hears something. But it's only the owl. Mists close round her. Murderer steps from behind, and—" Suddenly Polly Praed raised her arms and brought the imaginary slasher down with what would have been a deadly crash had she been holding a real one. Both Jury and Barney jumped. "Oh, sorry. One gets carried away." She sighed, puffed on her cigarette, swung her leg. "I wonder if it had anything to do with those letters—" She stopped suddenly, as if she could have bitten her tongue. "You haven't, ah, read . . . ?"

"Yes. Rather silly, they struck me. Someone casting about for things to accuse people of."

She looked a bit relieved. "Well, I wish they hadn't cast about in my direction. Have you thought of blackmail?" It had been Gere's suggestion. Jury shook his head. "Supposing someone finds out you've done something appalling. He threatens to tell the world." She leaned toward Jury, her self-consciousness forgotten in the throes of a fresh plot. "What you do is, you write a lot of spurious letters accusing people of perfectly dreadful things, so that when your blackmailer starts publishing *your* sin, no one will believe him." Her glasses were up on her head now and the amethyst eyes glittered. "Really, it's quite a good plan."

He had to admit he admired the eyes more than the plan. "Hmm. I see what you mean."

She studied her nails. "I guess you're here because you think I wrote them. I bet a lot of people do, because I'm a writer."

"I don't think they're nearly imaginative enough for you."

That flustered her. She asked again, "What'd you say your name is?"

"Jury. And besides, had it been you, surely the Bodenheims would have got several apiece." He smiled. "Do you assume it was one of them who wrote the letters?"

"I doubt they can write."

"Where were you, Miss Praed, two nights ago?"

"Oh. Here it comes. I've no alibi, of course. I was sitting in here, writing." She looked away.

"Did you know Katie O'Brien?"

"Katie? Whatever are you asking about her for?"

"Littlebourne seems to be having its share of bad luck, doesn't it?"

"You don't think she had anything to do with those letters?"

Jury shrugged. "It's doubtful, as they were postmarked the day after she was attacked."

"I admit they are rather adolescent and Katie was awfully put upon by Mary. I mean, repressed. But poison-pen stuff, no. She was too nice. I mean *is* — You see, we're talking about her as though she were dead. It's awful. If you want to know about Katie you really ought to talk to Emily Louise Perk. They weren't anywhere near the same age, but I always saw them about, after school or on Saturdays. It's probably because they're both so good with horses. Though, of course, Katie's not a patch on Em when it comes to that. No one is. She takes care of the Bodenheims' nags, too. Emily knows everything that goes on in this village. Though it's not easy to get things out of her unless you've something to trade."

"Trade?"

"Umm. Bits of information for goodies. You cost me two hot cross buns this morning."

"I did?"

"She knew who you were before you'd had both feet out of the car, I bet."

So she hadn't really needed to ask him twice what his name was. "It's a compliment to know you thought me worth two hot cross buns."

Blushing, she studied the plate of cheese again. "And a cup of tea," she said, weakly.

EIGHT

∞∞∞∞∞∞∞

I

"EXEMPLARY lives, sir. Exemplary lives!" said Sir Miles Bodenheim in response to Jury's question about the letters. And the tiny smile that accompanied Miles's modest evaluation of the Bodenheim family did double duty: Scotland Yard could take it as gospel or Scotland Yard could take it as proof of Miles Bodenheim's ability to have a little joke on himself. Either way, the Bodenheims won the Littlebourne Character Sweepstakes.

From the moment of entering the Bodenheim drawing room, it had been fairly clear to Jury why Polly Praed was writing *The Littlebourne Murders*. Three heads — those of Miles, Sylvia, and the daughter — had turned toward him as if he were royalty's looking glass; the fourth didn't turn much at all. It was too busy looking bored. Derek Bodenheim sat slouched in a chair, his fingers slowly turning a tall glass of something, his expression insolent, as if he were already disagreeing with whatever Jury might say.

Having offered Jury a thimbleful of sherry, Miles Bodenheim sat down and reclaimed his cup of tea. He was wearing a fawn jacket and black ascot with tiny white polka dots and that morning's egg hardening in its folds. When Jury declined the sherry, Sylvia Bodenheim must have felt it incumbent upon her to make an offer of tea. But the voice trailed off so weakly and the hand fell so short of the pot that Jury didn't even bother to say no.

"Who was she, d'ya know yet?" asked Derek, slouching down in his chair. Having inherited what there was of his father's looks,

Derek managed to dissipate them across a face that looked so soft and malleable it could have taken the imprint of a thumb.

"That's what we're trying to establish. No one seems to have seen her here in the village."

"Except for Daddy and that silly birdwatching group, no one goes into the wood," said Julia. She managed to lift her head as if it were quite the handsomest thing Jury would be likely to see in Littlebourne. Ever since he'd got there, she'd been having trouble arranging her expression and her person. She had tossed him enigmatic glances and thrown her long hair about as if he were a fashion photographer.

"Silly? Nothing silly about the Royal Birdwatchers, my dear. Do you good to join it yourself," said her father.

Julia rolled her eyes upwards and tried to find an even more striking pose on the velvet couch, chosen, no doubt, because the blue matched both her shirt and her eyes.

Sylvia set aside her teacup and reclaimed her knitting needles. Her thin hands flew as she said, "There's no earthly reason for the woman to have been in the Horndean wood. None." Ergo (she made it sound), the woman wasn't there.

"It's been suggested this person was on her way to Stonington."

Sylvia gave Jury a smile as thin as the cucumber on the sandwiches. "Why on earth would she be going *there?* And *not* through the *wood*. That's absurd. And not to see Lady Kennington, I daresay. *I* was at Stonington not three days ago to see if she wouldn't do something for our church fête. But as always it was quite useless. The woman's a veritable *recluse*. Now her husband, *Lord* Kennington, seemed pleasant enough. . . . You heard, I expect, about the theft of that jewelry about a year ago."

"Yes. Apparently the secretary came under suspicion."

Sylvia sniffed. "And no wonder. Not a nice sort, at all. You knew him a little, didn't you, Derek?" She turned to her son, who did not bother to recognize her. "Yes, police assumed he must have done it, though they could never prove anything because they never found that emerald. It was extremely valuable. Egyptian, I believe. One of the old ones." Sylvia somehow made it sound as if the Bodenheims had all of the new ones.

"Clever chap," said Derek, determined to say whatever might upset the rest of the family. "Always did think so. It's never turned up, you know. And he's dead. So there's nearly a quarter million quids' worth of emerald gone missing, and the fellow who knows where it is got hit by a car. What an irony."

"Clever?" said Sylvia. "I thought him *quite* common."

"You met him?"

Sylvia sniffed. "Lord Kennington had one small gathering to show off his collection. Egyptology seemed to be his forte. *She* is certainly no hostess."

"How did Tree come to work for Lord Kennington?"

"I understood he'd been employed by Christie's. Now *we* have always dealt with Sotheby's. We find them much more satisfactory." Jury only smiled and looked at the reproductions, the japanned screen, the ornate moldings. They had managed to stamp out elegance without the help of either of the famous auction rooms. She picked up her narrative along with a couple of dropped stitches. "I can't think how the widow runs the place anyway. When I was there no one was about and I was finally forced to tap on panes and peer through the French doors when no one answered to my knock. Finally, *she* appeared. A rather drab person. Of course, we never see much of her because she does her shopping, I expect, in Horndean. I explained to her about the fête and asked her to take the Jumble table. The woman simply has *no* community spirit."

Derek yawned. "Why the hell should she, as she's not right in Littlebourne?"

"She's close enough," said Sylvia, and returned her damp gaze to Jury. Her eyes were the color of fungi one is always afraid of picking in the wilds. "And do you know, the woman had the nerve to open her purse and hand me twenty pounds! As if I were out doing collections! The odious person had the nerve to say that twenty pounds would be as much as the whole Jumble would bring and why go to the trouble of carting dribs and drabs of junk about when here was the case and we could just forego the table. My dears!" Sylvia spread her arms wide, taking in everyone, even "her dear" Jury. "We *always* have a Jumble!"

As far as Jury was concerned, Lady Kennington's reasoning seemed imminently sensible, and he tried to bring them back to the matter of the murder. Sylvia was too quick, though.

"And *I*, who already have too much to do—I'm President of the Women's Institute, after all—I've already the Bring-and-Buy and I suppose now I shall have to take over the Jumble." She looked to her husband for support, but Miles did not appear to be listening, busy as he was with trying to scratch the dried egg from the ascot.

Derek said, "Same thing, nearly. Shake 'em up together and see which falls out first."

"They are decidedly *not* the same, Derek. And remember, you have charge of the Bottle Toss."

"Christ, not again."

"Julia is to take over the phaeton rides—"

"Not *I*. Emily's doing that. I'm not about to do rides for whining kiddies."

"I merely meant to *supervise*, my darling. Just be there to see Emily doesn't get up to something. Polly Praed is to handle the tea tent—"

"Glad it's not the Pennystevens person. She shorted me ten pence last year. And what's old Critchley to do?" continued Miles. "After all it's *his* church. Should think he'd do some work instead of standing about looking holy."

"I hope Ramona Wey isn't to have a stall," said Julia. "I don't think it's right the antiques people from Hertfield just come along and use our fête to do business." -

"Ah, but that's not really why, is it, old girl?" said her brother, hands clasped behind his head. "It's because of Riddley, isn't it? You don't—"

"Shut *up!*" yelled Julia.

"Children, children," said Sylvia, blandly. Jury wondered if she were about to suggest they go out and play. There were times when he was glad he had no children. And then a real one would come along and he'd be sorry once more.

"As to those letters, Superintendent," said Sylvia, needles clicking faster. "I can see why Ramona Wey got one. Calls herself a 'decorator' and has that tarted-up little shop on the Row, but the woman's nothing in the world but a jumped-up little secretary from London. There is talk, too, about her and Freddie Mainwaring, but I'm sure he's got too much sense—"

"I find her rather jolly," said Derek. His soft face split in a mocking smile.

"I have always been able to keep an open mind on such subjects," said Sir Miles, his face turned to the ceiling as if about to receive the angels' blessings. "I suggest you would all do well to follow my example. I do not approve of the woman, no, but at least she does keep herself to herself, even to drawing her shades. Mrs. Pennystevens told me, when I inquired, that the Wey woman must keep a poste restante somewhere, for she receives no mail through our carrier. I'm surprised we any of us get our mail, as he is none too quick either. But we must suffer fools gladly, I expect." He smiled benignly, and opened his mouth to say more.

But Jury cut him short with a smile even more benign, having as it did the blessing of the Metropolitan Police Department. "Where were all of you on the Thursday night? Two nights ago, that is?"

They all looked at one another and then at Jury, as if he were rather a rude child inquiring into his elders' affairs. After a moment of improvised dismay, however, Derek seemed to enjoy the question immensely.

"It appears the Super thinks one of us had a hand in the dirty deed! As for myself—let's see—I was in the White Hart in Hertfield. Must be able to scare up some witnesses, though we were all so pissed—"

"Derek! Really! I'm quite sure the superintendent is suggesting nothing at all. I was at my Women's Institute meeting. We meet at eight-thirty, first Thursday of the month. I was a wee bit late because I had to come back and get my records."

The victim's bus had stopped at 8:05. What held you up? thought Jury, smiling. Sylvia hadn't got the time frame of the murder fixed, or she was innocent of anything. "Alone?"

"Yes, of course. I *do* drive, Superintendent." That was to be listed among her other accomplishments—like knitting and raising children

When Sir Miles saw that Jury's notebook was open, he was moved once again toward speech-making. After all, one never knew what mortal form the recording angel might take. "As is always my custom on Thursday evenings, I have a jaunt down to the Bold Blue Boy. I say it never hurts to have a bit of a laugh and a drink with the locals. One must keep the common touch. You can ask there. Anyone will vouch for me. Ho ho, there's an alibi for you, Superintendent!"

"It closes at eleven, doesn't it?"

Sir Miles winked. "Well, you know country pubs. Cheat a bit. Eleven, eleven-fifteen. Not that Mary O'Brien would keep open after hours—" Since he'd just accused Mary O'Brien of precisely that, the comment seemed irrelevant. "And, of course, since that accident to the girl—"

Julia, apparently seeing a way to get back at Derek, said, "Too bad, Derek. No more grope and grapple in the stableyard." She laughed unpleasantly.

Derek went beet-red. "Sod off!" His soft face hardened.

"Are you talking about Katie O'Brien?" asked Jury. They turned once again to stare, except for Miles, whose eyes were riveted on some point in space, devising or revising his next speech. The others looked uncomfortable, even Julia, who had brought it up in the first place.

"You, Miss Bodenheim. You haven't told me where you were on Thursday evening."

"Out in the stables."

Derek giggled. It was an unpleasant sound coming from a twenty-four- or twenty-five-year-old man. "That's a laugh. You working."

"Well, I *was!*"

"Getting back to the O'Brien girl. Did you know her well?"

"No. She exercised my mare sometimes."

"I was given to believe that this little girl, Emily Perk, took care of the horses at Rookswood."

"She does. Only my mare is nearly sixteen hands and too big for Emily to do properly, so we got Katie to do it."

"She's in hospital," said Sylvia, snipping a strand of wool. "A great pity, but if guhls must be roaming the streets of London ... Not only that—" Sylvia glared at Jury—the streets of London were, after all, *his* responsibility, "she was attacked in an Underground station. Playing her violin, good gracious, for money."

Sir Miles looked over the church steeple of his fingers and intoned, "Really, my dear, we mustn't be too hard on the girl. After all, given she was raised in a pub, and hadn't the advantages of our ..."

Jury listened as the angels looked down.

II

It was after three when Jury got back to the Blue Boy to find Sergeant Wiggins already there spooning up soup.

"Oxtail," said Wiggins. "Mrs. O'Brien gave me some. She just left for the shops in Hertfield. But I'm sure there's more in the pot—"

Wiggins had made himself right at home. "No, thanks," said Jury.

"You don't eat right. You didn't have any lunch. If I ate on the run like you, I'd have no resistance at all. This is good soup."

"Aside from the quality of the soup, what did you learn?"

Unoffended, Wiggins quartered and buttered a breadroll. "Mainwaring didn't know the murdered woman, and couldn't imagine why she'd be out in the woods—"

"No one can. Go on."

"He works part of the time in London, in the City, in insurance. Then he's got a part-time estate agency in Littlebourne."

"He commutes to London some days?"

"That's right."

"He saw the pictures of the murdered woman?"

"Yes. Said he'd never seen her before. Also said he was with the Wey woman on Thursday night. Which she confirmed. You want him to go along and have a look at the body?"

"No more than any of the others. What about Mrs. Penny-stevens? Anything else there?"

Wiggins shook his head. "Just as Carstairs said. She got the packet, thought it was some sort of joke. So did the others. Mainwaring and the Wey woman."

"They'd need to, wouldn't they? Since they were accused of being lovers. Do you think they are?"

For Wiggins, who had shoved his soup plate aside and was in the process of medicating himself, this was a two–cough drop problem. Or, at least, the cough drops were stuck together and he popped both of them into his mouth. "Hard to say. She's good-looking enough."

"What was her reaction to the murder?"

"Same thing. Didn't know anything about it, didn't know why the woman would be out in the woods, et cetera, et cetera. Carstairs had been there before me."

"Has Carstairs called here?"

"No, why?"

"Augusta Craigie thinks the woman might have been on her way to Stonington, the Kennington estate just outside of Littlebourne." Jury looked ceilingward. "Do you know which one of the rooms is the daughter's?" He knew Wiggins would have inspected them all, briefly, to see if he could find a more comfortable mattress.

Wiggins nodded. "First on the right. Lots of flounce and stuffed animals."

"I'm going to have a look."

It was a pleasant room with a slanted ceiling and creaking, crooked floor, white furniture, and, as Wiggins had said, ruffled spread and pillows. It faced the Green; a row of tiny casement windows over a window seat were rolled out, disturbing the climbing roses wandering up the side of the building. Jury looked at the row of books above the window seat: untouched tomes, largely, of classics like *Middlemarch;* very well-fingered Heartwind Romances wedged between and behind them. A poor ruse if the mother were doing a cleaning. But perhaps the neatness here was Katie O'Brien's own. Jury looked in the closet and saw carefully hung dresses. He checked the labels, found two of them were

Laura Ashleys, expensive. The mother would have had to sell a lot of pints to buy them.

There was an album lying on a little desk, which Jury leafed through. Snapshots recording the life of Katie O'Brien and her family. One of them he removed. It showed a pale girl with a heart-shaped, but unsmiling, face. A lot of dark hair had been rolled away from the face, probably collected in back in a bun or plait. It was an old-fashioned hairdo above an old-fashioned dress, a lace-collared gingham. Did the small, beautiful face look so mournfully out at Jury because the hair was too heavy, the collar too tight? Jury took the picture and closed the album.

III

"Cora Binns," said Inspector Carstairs. "It was shortly after you called that we got an identification. Not from Lady Kennington— we're checking that out—but from a Mrs. Beavers. That's the Binns woman's landlady, who got worried when Cora never came home on the Thursday night. Cora Binns told Mrs. Beavers she was off to see someone in Hertfield. Said she'd be back that night and probably get home round eleven. Cora has the upstairs flat in the Beaverses' house and the landlady apparently keeps an eye on her tenants. When Cora didn't show up again on Friday, she was really concerned. Nosy's more like it. She put in a missing-person and a call came through not long ago from 'H' Division. Not much doubt it's the same person. Description, clothes, everything fits. I guessed you'd want to talk to her straightaway. Address—" The voice dimmed as Carstairs turned from the telephone, and then came back again. "Number twenty-two, Catchcoach Street."

"What section's that?" Jury asked as he made a note of the address.

"Somewhere around Forest Gate, isn't it? Wait a tic. . . . Yes, here it is. Well." There was a brief silence. "Wembley Knotts. Coincidence, that. That's where the O'Brien girl got coshed on the head. Odd."

When Jury dropped the receiver back into the cradle, Sergeant Wiggins was studying the photograph of Katie O'Brien.

"Pretty girl."

"Yes. Leave a note for Mary O'Brien, will you, that we'll be back later this evening. Tell her to tell Mr. Plant. I can't think why he's not here yet."

Wiggins looked surprised. "Where are we going, then?"

"London."

NINE

∽∽∽∽∽∽∽∽

I

MELROSE Plant would have been at the Bold Blue Boy, had he not been delayed by Sylvia Bodenheim's gloved hand pointing her garden shears at his lapel. "This is *not* public property, young man. You are trespassing."

As he was forty-two, Melrose appreciated that "young man." For the rest, he said, "I don't know about that. But it *is* a public footpath." With his silver-headed stick, Melrose pointed back along the narrow path. "There's a sign yonder."

Impatiently, she shook her head. The large sun hat, a chartreuse straw unflattering to her sallow skin, cast wavelets of green-yellow across her face, giving her an underwater look. "Whatever the sign says, I should certainly think anyone would understand that the footpath runs *right* across a bit of our property."

"Well, then, you oughtn't to have bought a house on a bit of land with public access, should you?" He smiled.

Sylvia Bodenheim fell back two paces as if he'd struck her. It was abundantly clear that his "house on a bit of land" was not a happy description. "Rookswood is not just a *house*."

Melrose Plant looked to his left toward the imposing if somewhat pretentious facade where stone birds of some sort topped two stunted pillars. "Oh? It's an institution of some sort, then?"

"Certainly not! It is Sir Miles Bodenheim's estate. The family seat. I am *Lady* Bodenheim. Who are you?"

"Melrose Plant." He bowed slightly. "I have just come through a place called Horndean and was wondering if this is the way to

Littlebourne village? I parked my car back there—" He nodded to some point behind him. "And decided to find someone to ask directions of."

After squinting in the direction he pointed to see if the car were also parked on Rookswood property, she turned back to her work, shears snipping. "Just go along and you'll come out on Littlebourne Green, by the Celtic cross. And when you return, please *do* go round our property. Not through."

He certainly wouldn't. He had already determined to use the public footpath as much as possible. "Perhaps you could direct me to a pub called the Bold Blue Boy?"

She tilted her head in the direction in which he was going, but didn't look at him as she said, "That way."

Melrose picked a bit of rose petal from his jacket. "I hear you've had rather an awful crime hereabouts. Imagine it plays hell with estate values, doesn't it?"

She glared at him. "It's nothing to do with Littlebourne. Just some stranger—" Looking a bit flushed, she backed off.

Whether she was about to cut and run, he didn't know. Her exit was interrupted by the approach, across the wide, green lawn, of a glistening chestnut horse on which a young woman was mounted. At first, Melrose judged her to be extremely attractive—and indeed she was—if such assessments can be made on the basis of cheekbones, tilted eyes, and a well-shaped mouth.

But Melrose found her about as unappealing as any woman he had seen in forty years. All of the elegance of bone structure was dashed to bits by the petulant, hard-eyed expression. He could see, beneath the young skin, the hatchet-face of the older woman, who must be this one's mother. The young lady's boots glittered as if varnished; her hacking jacket was a violent, unpleasant plaid that no Scot would lay claim to.

"Who's this, Mummy?"

"No one," said her mother, turning to attack the roses with her shears.

"That is not precisely accurate," said Melrose, who introduced himself, again bowing. "I have the pleasure of addressing—?"

She must have responded favorably to this mild imperiousness, it being a shade less than her own, for she smiled frostily. "Have you just got to the village — or what?"

The Bodenheims were nothing if not curious. "Correct. I am a stranger to town. But not, I hope, for long." He gave what he imagined to be a roguish smile, leering up at her.

Miss Bodenheim dismounted, bringing herself literally, if not figuratively, down to his level. "What are you here for then?" Her fingers played with the reins of her horse. The horse cast a lugubrious eye on the party and Melrose decided it was probably the only one there with any sense.

"To view some property." He had decided on this as a reason that would allow him to poke about without anyone's knowing he was a friend of Superintendent Jury.

The elder Bodenheim woman was snipping her way back round to them and offered her judgment on the matter. "It's that rickety little cottage next the Bold Blue Boy, I suppose. You'll be disappointed, mark my words. I should think twice about buying it; it's been on the market for nearly a year, even though simply *everyone's* coming to Littlebourne and snapping up cottages. Roof leaks, there's dry rot, and the garden's a disgrace. The family who last lived there —" She shuddered. "You'll see how awful it is. You'll need to get the roof rethatched, though, frankly, I would suggest tiles. Thatch simply attracts the birds and sends up one's premiums. Look at the Craigie sisters' thatch if you don't believe me. *I* do not suggest thatch. But if you *must* rethatch, the only person to do it is Hemmings. I will give you his number. Personally, I believe him to be much too dear, but at least he does an honest day's work. You can't say the same for Lewisjohn. You're not thinking of Lewisjohn, are you? Put it right out of your mind; he's a thief. No, Hemmings is the only reliable person in the area. But you should do tiles. You'll regret the thatch." She sniffed and snipped her way down the hedgerow, leaving the roofing of Melrose's cottage to her daughter.

"Willow Cottage," said Julia, "It's just the other side of Littlebourne Green where the Blue Boy is." She pointed her riding crop beyond the hedgerow. "It *does* need doing up. But, frankly, I wouldn't get *anyone* round here to do the work."

Considering the polished nails on the hand which held the crop, it was doubtful the daughter could recommend anyone in the way of work.

Melrose had definitely decided against Willow Cottage. "That isn't the place I'm interested in, actually." He turned his face toward the Horndean Road; along it he had discovered the sort of thing he *might* be interested in. The stone fence must have run both sides for half a mile. The house itself could not be seen from the road, but he judged it to be considerably larger, more formidable than Rookswood. The high iron gate had borne a discreet bronze plaque. There was a For Sale sign, equally discreet, near it.

"Stonington. That's the property I'd like to view." Melrose twitched a bit of old leaf from his coat, idly.

Even the horse shook its mane at his announcement. And somehow, the elder Bodenheim woman had managed to be within earshot. Now there came the general confusion of female voices:

"Stonington! ... Oh, out of the question ... Totally unsuitable for you ... Can't think ... It's so big! ... a bachelor ... You *are* a bachelor?"

"But I find it eminently suitable," said Melrose, breaking in. "Not quite so large as I'm used to. And Aunt Agatha will miss her rookery and the groves of ornamental trees. And the swans. Servants' quarters perhaps a bit small. Stables not quite adequate for my hunters. And ..." He sighed unhappily. "— My sister, ah, Madeleine, needs her separate wing. She's a bit offish, you know." That could mean anything from being in a family way to simple insanity. "But my surveyor can handle the changes. Oh, well, chap can't have everything, can he?" Here he managed a sweet little smile and a deprecating shrug. "It's a jolly old place, isn't it?"

It was quite clear to him from their expressions that Stonington was a good deal jollier than Rookswood. They were — the two Bodenheim women — drawn as if against their wills to follow the direction of his gaze toward the Horndean Road, down which lay Stonington in the blue distance, the manor of manors. When she turned back, Julia was looking at Melrose afresh, reevaluating the situation. But whatever she was about to say was cut off by Melrose's calling happily, "And who's this coming now?"

Miles Bodenheim was stumping across the lawn. Perhaps he had seen them from an upstairs window and could no longer contain his curiosity, or perhaps he had got wind that the first family of Littlebourne might soon become the second and was on his way to scotch that plan.

"Sylvia! Julia!"

Instead of calling an answer, Sylvia said to Melrose, "No, I think you are not serious. You cannot be serious. Lady Kennington has *not* kept the place up. You know he is dead—Lord Kennington. I really don't think they were well-matched. She's most antisocial. True, there is nothing to hold her there. But I think it preferable, if Stonington is to be sold, it had better be sold to some sort of company or used as a Home for some sort of Unfortunate. You don't want to live at Stonington." She turned away and pinched a brown bud from its stalk in a mean way, like a child pinching a cat.

"Plant, Melrose Plant," he said to the latest addition to their number.

"Mr. Plant was thinking of buying Stonington, Miles, but we told him how unsuitable it would be."

"Stonington! Good God, man. You wouldn't want to live there. Big as a barn and cold. No, you shouldn't like it at all. And someone's died there recently, Lord Kennington, that was. You wouldn't want to move in where someone's just died."

"They've got to die somewhere," answered Melrose, wondering if Jury was at the pub, but wondering also how many more there were of this family who might drift toward him like dandelion heads across the lawn.

"I've told him not to buy," said Sylvia, closing the matter for all time. Her large hat bobbed as she moved along the hedge, her expression more set, her face more chartreuse.

"Mr. Plant hunts," said Julia. "You mentioned hunters. You were talking about stables."

Melrose dashed a benighted bud from the path. It landed on the elder Bodenheim's shoe. He had to be careful here; he knew nothing about hunting and found it a perfectly awful sport. "I hunt, yes. But only in Ireland. With the black and tans." Then he wondered if that were hounds or some defunct segment of the I.R.A.

"When do you plan on moving in?" asked Julia.

"A bit premature for that, isn't it? Well, this has been most pleasant, but if you'll excuse me?" Melrose touched his cap with his stick and went whistling down the public footpath, hoping he'd find someone in Littlebourne, besides Jury, more amiable than this lot.

II

Amiable was not precisely the word he would have used to describe the next person he passed, standing hard in the middle of the Green, carefully noting his progress across it. She wore a giant frown. It made Melrose slightly uncomfortable to think he had called up such a look of affliction on the face of one so small.

It so unnerved him he was forced to turn on the other side of the Green and look back. Like Lot's wife, he shouldn't have done it. *She* had also turned and was staring at *him*. The little girl was standing with her ankles turned in; her yellow hair fell in strands round her pointed face. The hacking jacket had seen better days; it was mud-bedewed and too small for her.

As he continued on his way across the High Street, he could sense, rather than see, she was following him. The Littlebourne villagers had precious little to do with their time if he could excite such interest.

The Bold Blue Boy was empty at near four in the afternoon. Although it was not yet opening time, the door to the saloon bar was open. He went in that way and found a long, low room with a huge, cold fireplace. To the right of this room was another, the entrance to which was effected by stooping under its low lintel. It was small and cheerful, full of polished copper, a smaller fireplace which was lit, and snug window seats cushioned in a faded, flowery chintz.

Melrose sat down at one of the tables to wait for the proprietor, who must know Superintendent Jury's whereabouts, and began to make himself at home. He always carried a book with him — Rimbaud, usually, but lately mystery stories had begun to supplant the French poets — and now he drew from his coat pocket his latest acquisition for emergency-waiting-periods, *The Affair of the Third Feather*. Before he began to read, however, he looked through the small casement window, pushing back the flowered curtain to gaze out over the Green. He saw no one except for one old pensioner making his arthritic way towards the post office stores.

As he settled down to read, he heard a popping noise that made his skin prickle. He turned. The little girl was standing in the doll-like doorway, entertaining herself by sucking in her cheeks, bunching up her mouth, and making small, popping noises.

"Mary's over to the shops," she said.

"Mary?"

"Mary O'Brien. She runs the Blue Boy."

"I see," said Melrose, returning to his book. "Well, I shall just have to wait, I daresay." He wondered why the little girl didn't leave.

Far from leaving, she went behind the bar. As the bar was tall and she was short, he could hear rather than see her rooting around. Soon her fair head popped up over the top. She must have got herself a stool to kneel on.

"Want something, then? There's Bass and bitter and Abbot's." She touched all of the enameled beer pulls.

Had he found some pocket of Dickensian England here in Littlebourne where children worked at bottle-blacking and chimney-sweeping and gin-milling? "I really don't think you should be doing that," he said, sounding unctuous, even to himself.

"I do it all the time."

He sighed and shook his head. "Very well, then. I'll have a Cockburn's, dry."

She turned to the optics behind her and measured off the sherry. "That'll be seventy-five p, please," she said, setting it before him.

"Seventy-five? Dear heavens. Inflation has hit Littlebourne."

"Want some crisps?"

"No, thank you." He put a pound on the table. She stood there, sucking in her cheeks again, making the popping sounds.

"Don't do that. You'll ruin the alignment of your jaws and throw off your bite. Your teeth will fall out, too," he added, for good measure.

"They did do, anyway." She pulled back her upper lip and displayed two gaps.

"I told you."

"Sure you don't want any crisps? Bovril's good."

"I don't like crisps. But if we must—" Melrose fished in his pocket for more change.

She climbed up on a bar stool and unhooked a packet of crisps from a circular rack. Tearing open the packet she frowningly ate them. "Want one?" She was prepared to be generous.

"No. Have you a police station in this village?"

"Across the Green." She was sitting on the window seat and hitched her thumb toward the window at her back, sliding down lower in the seat. "Are you part of the police?"

"No, of course not."

"There's one here from Scotland Yard."

Despite his reluctance to question anyone this small, Melrose asked, "Do you happen to know where he is?"

It was rather nerve-wracking, this way she had of beating her heels against the window seat. "Back in London. He had to leave. I guess he came here for the murder."

Over the rims of his glasses, Melrose could see she was waiting for him to be affected. "Murder? What happened?"

She had finished the crisps already and was now folding the greasy little packet into small squares. "I don't know. Want some more crisps?"

"I didn't want those. What about this murder?"

She shrugged. Now the heels were drumming more quickly against the wood.

"Well, *who* was murdered?" As he watched her noncommittal face, he decided he'd sooner open oysters with a matchstick.

She had made a kind of paper plane from the crisp packet and was soaring it through the air. "Mum doesn't want me to talk about it."

He was certain she'd made this up on the spot. Melrose plunked another fifty pence on the table and said, "Let's have some more crisps."

She was up, over and back in a flash with another packet. "It was horrid, the murder."

"Murder usually is. What was this one's special horridness?"

She held up one small, translucent hand, the nails pearly in the dusty light of late afternoon. "They cut off her fingers."

Melrose had to agree. That *was* horrid.

"No one knows why she was in the woods. It was nobody from the village, so they think maybe she was from London. People don't go walking in the woods, except the birdwatchers and they're stupid. *I* go there sometimes to ride Shandy. Do you like horses?"

"No. Yes. Oh, I don't know. Probably."

"You ought to. Horses are better than people." She was looking him up and down as if she knew at least one person horses were better than.

"This policeman from Scotland Yard. Have you seen him?"

"No." She had slid practically all the way under the table, and all he could see was the crown of yellow hair and the arm with another crisp-bag airplane. "I'm thirsty. It must be all the salt."

"What would you like, a Guinness?"

"Lemon squash."

More money changed hands. She did a little sidestep dance to the bar and then started making a racket behind it, clanging bottles and glasses.

"I might have seen him," she said, when she had sidestep-danced back to the table. "They're staying here, I think. Him and the other detective." Carefully, she poured her squash into a glass. They could have lived here for days, he thought, eating crisps and drinking Cockburn's Very Dry and lemon squash without anyone's knowing. He looked out of the mullioned window, where a breeze blew the browned petals of roses. There were no signs of life.

81

"Maybe he'll be able to find out who wrote those letters." She was opening up the window seat, rooting for something inside.

"What letters?"

"Nasty letters," her voice said, coming from inside the seat. This gave Melrose a start. Jury had told him none of the particulars. "Good heavens, but your village is a lively old place."

Settling down at the table again with a coloring book and a box of Crayolas, she said, "I asked Mum what was in them but she told me not to talk about them." She sucked up the last of her squash, making gurgling sounds in the bottom of her glass. "They were all in colors." She opened up her book to what appeared to be a woodland scene and began to color a deer blue.

"Are you saying these, uh, nasty letters were done in *color?*" She nodded. "That's awfully strange." Again, she nodded, filling in the one deer and going on to the next blue deer. He felt vaguely irritated with this flying in the face of convention. "And you don't know anything else about them?"

"What?"

"The *letters.*" She shook her head. Having finished with the two deer, she took a red crayon and drew a thick and crooked line across the forest floor. She looked at it, then held it up for Melrose's inspection. "Does that look like a river?"

"No. It's red."

"It could be a River of Blood, couldn't it?"

"Blood? What a dreadful thought." She was looking down at it now, her pointed chin squeezed between her fists. "What put that into your mind?"

"They said the water was all bloody where they found her. Do you know any secrets?"

He thought he could have planted rows of beans in the furrows of her brow. "Secrets? Well, ah, yes, I suppose so." Was that the right answer?

Sternly she watched him. "Would you tell them?"

Oh, dear, a moral dilemma. He'd have to tread carefully. Playing for time, he lit a cigarette, studied its bright, burning end, and said, "Depends, I suppose." She had slid down in her seat again, and only the eyes regarded him now over the table rim. He could not think of what it should depend on. "If it would do someone a *harm* to keep it, I'd tell."

She frowned. Wrong answer. Suddenly, she was up and tossing book and Crayolas back in the window seat. "I've got to go now. But I could show you round the village if you like."

Well, so much for secrets. Then he remembered why he was supposed to be here. "Have you an estate agent here?"

"Someone that sells houses? Yes, but that's a stupid thing to do."

"To you, I suppose. I myself am thinking of buying property hereabouts."

That she was going to have Melrose as a permanent ornament did not seem to excite her interest. "There's Mr. Mainwaring. I can show you where his office is. It's just along the High next to the sweet shop. There are other shops too. The post office stores, but that's boring. And the Ginger Nut. They sell clothes. The Magic Muffin is nice. And there's Conckles. That's the sweet shop."

As she marched him through the saloon bar, he said, "I suppose this Mrs. O'Brien does meals?"

"Yes. She made tea today for the policeman. Oxtail soup."

"You certainly do keep abreast of the goings on."

"They're coming back tonight, I heard Mary say. You must be his friend."

Melrose stopped at the door and stared. Would none of his ruses work on her? "Not exactly, I just happen to have heard he—"

But she was already doing her sidestep dance down the pavement. He passed the execrable Willow Cottage, which was indeed little more than whitewashed rubble with a lattice of blown roses. Melrose called out to her, three doors down, "Just you mind, we're going to the estate agent!"

But it did no good as she'd already danced her way through the door of the bowfronted shop carrying the legend: CONCKLES— SWEETS AND TOBACCOS.

"And you're wrong," said Melrose, from the doorway of Conckles, "If you think you're going to stick me up for sweets!"

No, she wasn't.

III

Freddie Mainwaring sat comfortably slouched in his leather swivel chair, appearing to regard it as a grand joke that he, of all people, should be caught selling real estate. His manner changed a bit when Melrose mentioned just what piece of real estate he was interested in.

"Stonington?" The swivel chair stopped in mid-turn, and Mainwaring began flipping through a card file. "She'll probably come down in price; she needs the money."

The comment struck Melrose as unprofessional. Who was the man supposed to be representing? Mainwaring set his teeth on edge; he had smooth good looks and a manner silky enough to make women want to touch the goods. The picture on his desk Melrose supposed to be the wife, a woman with a caramelized look: patina of makeup, curls upswept and lacquered. There were no pictures of children.

"It was Lord Kennington's place. He died several months ago, so his widow has been living there by herself with only one or two servants. Two hundred and twenty-five thousand pounds is the asking price."

The dismissive wave of Melrose's hand announced he was beyond money. "I need a largish place." While Mainwaring went on about parlors and public rooms and parquet; about kitchens and bathrooms en suite; paddocks and outbuildings; boundaries and walls—Melrose tried to think of a way to work the conversation around to murder. "Yes, that all sounds fine. I need to be closer to London, and Northants is so far. Business dealings . . ." He wasn't sure how to expand on this. The last actual business dealing he had had was a few years back when he'd exchanged his Jaguar for a Bentley. That reminded him: he'd left his Rolls near the Bodenheim property.

"I could call Lady Kennington now and set up an appointment—" Mainwaring was reaching for the telephone. "When would you like to view?"

Melrose almost said *now* before he remembered he had absolutely no interest in any property, and if he weren't careful, he'd end up buying Stonington and Willow Cottage both. "Let's see. I'm rather busy today. Tomorrow's Sunday, and . . . no, not tomorrow. What about Monday?"

"Well, I go up to London on Monday . . . I don't know if that would be the best day——"

"Not to worry. Tuesday would do admirably." Jury would surely have things sorted out by then. "The, ah, village seems quite charming."

"It's a popular place. So close to London and still country, so there's a real demand for property."

Melrose steeled himself for the bulletin from the Chamber of Commerce. He was surprised when Mainwaring stopped there, giving no further report on Littlebourne's bucolic charms. "Sort of place where nothing ever happens."

"I wouldn't say that." Mainwaring sat back, smiling. "I'm surprised you've been here ten minutes and not heard about the woman found in the woods. Murdered."

"Good God! That's what the police car was doing along the road from . . . what's the next town?"

"Horndean. It was the Horndean wood where she was found. Well, we call it that. It's mostly in Littlebourne. I'm not sure which of us gets her."

A sardonic way of looking at murder, Melrose thought.

"I'm surprised Emily Louise didn't tell you all about it."

"Emily Louise?"

"Little girl who dropped you by here. Emily Perk." Mainwaring seemed to be eyeing him rather more warily. Melrose hoped the man wasn't going to turn out to be awfully clever. After half an hour with Emily Perk, he did not feel up to cleverness.

"Oh, she did babble on about something. But I don't pay much attention to a child's prattle. Imagine she's a trial to her mum— ah, mother."

"All eyes and ears. Seems to pop up everywhere." A shadow passed over Mainwaring's face, as if Emily had popped up at the wrong time, in the wrong place.

Melrose was about to enlarge upon the subject of murder, when the door was quite literally flung open and two women entered. One was thin and mouse-colored; the other was large, square, gray-haired, and, obviously, spokeswoman.

"Ah! There you are, Freddie . . . oh, you're busy." Here followed a vague apology, unfelt. "I just wanted to give you this and make sure you were coming out Monday week." From the bunch in her arms, the woman extracted a paper and put it on Mainwaring's desk. Was she political? wondered Melrose. "And Betsy, too, if she's back. Now don't say you're not able to as I've paired you up with Miles and I want two on each route. That way we should canvass the whole wood." Not political, but some sort of canvasser. Melrose looked at the paper, some kind of diagram of colored lines. "We're to meet at Spoke Rock and then break up into groups. Wear your Wellingtons or, better yet, your waders, because you know how swampy the wood is this time of year and that rain we had might have raised the stream a bit. The Crackle is very cagey and elusive so I've fixed it up so's we cover the whole *if* we stick to our proper groups and go the correct route." There was a distinct warning in her tone, as if groups and routes had got mucked up before through carelessness. "You and Miles are to follow the Yellow Route. It goes from Spoke Rock up over Windy Hill and round the marsh. See, there." She planted a stubby finger on the paper. "We meet at five, and I want everybody there, spot on." Melrose was very much afraid she meant A.M., as no one would be chasing Crackles during the cocktail hour. The woman was tiresomely hearty, voice booming from inexhaustible lungs. The same charge could not be made of her companion who, sunk in timorousness, plied the end of her belt as if she might suddenly hang herself with it. The thin woman's gaze shifted here and there round the room, landed on Melrose, then darted off, guilt-surprised.

"What makes you think the police won't have the whole wood cordoned off, Ernestine?" asked Mainwaring.

"Oh, pooh. They'll all be out in a few days. They can't hang about forever."

"They can do what they damned well please," said Mainwaring, not sounding too happy about it.

"Don't be tiresome, Freddie. The Speckled Crackle won't wait round forever, murder or no murder. Spot on five, then. Should be a bang-up morning. *If* we all keep to our routes." She waved the papers in Melrose's face. "It's not often one has the

86

opportunity of taking on a Great Speckled Crackle." It sounded as if she and the bird were matched in the welterweight championship of the world.

"It certainly isn't," said Melrose, removing his spectacles and polishing them with his pocket handkerchief. "I've seen it only once myself."

Stunned silence. Then she said, "But you couldn't have done. It's been sighted only three times in the last ten years. In the Orkneys, the Hebrides, and Torquay. Where do you think you saw it? Are you sure it was the Crackle?"

Melrose could not have been profligate with news of the bird had he wanted to. "Salcombe."

"Salcombe! That's impossible!" Torquay was one thing. Salcombe was sheer caprice.

"Well, they're not far apart, you must admit."

Mainwaring interceded with introductions. Mr. Plant was made known to the Misses Craigie, Ernestine and Augusta.

Sisters, were they? Odd. But he supposed there was some small resemblance, some shadow-stamp the parents had left on the face of each. He inclined his head politely as he rose to take the hand Ernestine had shot out, like a spanner. It pumped Melrose's own.

"Are you staying here? Visiting? You must join us. You could go the Green Route." She consulted her paper. "Here we are. You'd be with Sylvia and Augusta. Lucky for you, they're seasoned birdwatchers."

Sylvia Bodenheim at five A.M. Serve him right.

"Ernestine, Mr. Plant has simply come to Littlebourne to inspect some property. He'll probably be gone before we meet."

"It's kind of you to invite me. What sort of binoculars do you use?" They were swinging on a strap across her bosom. He thought he recognized them as particularly good ones. There had been a dark patch in his life when he'd entertained himself for a season at Newmarket races. He'd gone the whole binocular spectrum.

"These? Oh, they're Zeiss. Instant focus." Handing Melrose a copy of her map, she said, "Have one in case you're here. We'd soon put you in the picture. Good-bye Freddie!" They departed in a swirl of papers.

"Birdwatching seems quite a serious affair around here if it can supplant murder as a point of interest."

Mainwaring smiled. "Ernestine's got enough enthusiasm for all of us. I doubt there's a quarter-inch of wood she doesn't know. It's no wonder she found the body. She's always out there."

"Did she?" Melrose turned to look at the door through which she had just left. "It didn't take her long to get over the shock."

Through the window, he saw a dark-haired woman pass by, wave in at Mainwaring, pause as if deciding whether to enter, and then turn away. She appeared to be studying the tree outside the door.

"I must be going," said Melrose.

"You'll be in touch?"

"Oh, certainly. Stonington sounds just the ticket."

But as he walked out the door, he was not thinking of Stonington. He was thinking of the Craigie woman. Given her wood-haunting predilections, he wondered that it didn't make her nervous to be walking about with those binoculars for all the world to see.

IV

The dark-haired woman was still inspecting the fruit tree.

"I dislike pollarded trees, don't you?" asked Melrose.

"Umm? Oh—" Her surprise that such a person as he existed was clearly feigned. "Yes. I was thinking it's got some sort of disease."

"Looks healthy enough to me. Do you live here?" Hard to believe a stranger would put herself out to examine the village tree-bark.

"Yes, over there." She pointed across the Green. Then she opened up a notebook and seemed to be making notes about the tree. Littlebourne was full of naturalists.

"Are you Blue, Red, Green, or Yellow?" he asked, thinking this rather a clever introduction to a conversation.

He was totally unprepared for her deep blush and indrawn breath. Then she composed herself and said, "You mean Augusta's telling perfect strangers? She *is* round the twist."

Melrose felt confused. "Augusta? No, the other Miss Craigie."

"Ernestine? She didn't get one."

"One what?"

"*Letters!* Isn't that what you're talking about?"

Then Melrose remembered. The Perk·child had said anonymous letters had been written in colors. "Good heavens, no. I was talking about the birdwatchers' map." Melrose shoved it toward her face like a proof of identity.

"Oh. *Oh!*" As she almost smiled before she blushed again, he took the opportunity to invite her to tea. He hoped the Bodenheims were not dismantling his Rolls.

Once settled in the Magic Muffin at a wobbly table with a view of the High, they introduced themselves. Then Polly Praed said, "Why were you talking to Freddie Mainwaring? Are you thinking of property or something?"

"I'm, ah, interested in Stonington."

"Not really! That's the Kennington place. He died, you know."

Death had apparently not cut a very wide swathe in Littlebourne, given everyone's surprise that one of their number had succumbed to it. Melrose watched a tall, thin woman approach their table. Polly Praed asked for tea and what sorts of muffins she had today.

"Aubergine."

"Aubergine?" Polly looked doubtful. "I've never heard of aubergine muffins." As the woman walked away, Polly lifted her eyeglasses to the top of her head, and said to Melrose, "Do you suppose they're some awful shade of yellow?"

"Probably." He noticed, though, that her eyes certainly were not. They were cornflower blue or violet, depending upon the light when she turned her head.

"Are you trying to tell me Ernestine Craigie and that potty bunch of bird enthusiasts are going out in the Horndean wood after what happened—I'm sure you've heard about our murder."

"Miss Craigie is determined to view the Speckled Crackle. I believe she would step over whole rows of dead bodies to do so."

Muffins and tea were set before them. They seemed quite ordinary muffins, brown and wholesome-looking.

Polly said, buttering a muffin half, "We've even got Scotland Yard here about it." She became silent, pensive, her hand upraised with the muffin unbitten, crumbs cascading down her jumper sleeve. Melrose thought she'd gone into some sort of fugue. Finally, she came back to life and ate the muffin.

"I take it you, ah, got one of these letters."

She nodded. "Green. Please don't ask what was in it."

"Wouldn't dream of it. Haven't the police an idea who's responsible?" She shook her head. "Have there been many?"

"Half a dozen. They all came at the same time." Polly explained Mrs. Pennystevens's parcel.

"That sounds very odd. Hardly the right psychology for poison-pen letters."

"What do you mean?" She frowned.

"Imagine yourself with this queer perversion. You want to make people suffer. Then you'd draw it out as long as possible. Think of poor old Augusta Craigie in an absolute muck-sweat every time she goes to collect her post, or watches it being dropped through the door, or whatever. She's wondering, *Will I be next?* The writer can keep people on a string for ages that way. Finding a letter in an unknown hand. Imagine the letter-writer imagining all that. You see? You wouldn't want just to go and dump the lot all at once. It would take away all of the imagined secret suffering."

"You certainly know a lot about the psychology. You didn't write them, did you?" She buttered another muffin.

Melrose ignored that. "The way this person's done it, everyone knows who else got one and police are called in straightaway. After some initial embarrassment probably no one takes it awfully seriously. And done in rainbow hues. That's even more distracting. Very odd. Do you think there's any connection with the murder?"

"I've been thinking and thinking about that. I'm a mystery writer—"

"*You* are?"

"Yes. But it's not all that fascinating. Pretty routine, really. And it's very discouraging I can't come up with some idea. I imagine that superintendent from the Yard thinks I'm quite stupid." Sadly, she looked down at her muffin half. "Trouble is, if you're clever in fancy, you're not always clever in fact. *I'm* not. I'm even awful at the simplest kind of conversation, as you've probably noticed."

"I've noticed nothing of the sort."

"You must have done. I'm an absolute nincompoop in social situations. I don't go to dinners or teas because I just stand in the corner like a stick trying to think what to say." In blistering detail, and with a mouth full of muffin, she ran down her list of social failings. Then she tossed it all over her shoulder like salt, ending with, "May I have the last muffin?"

"Yes. I think all that you just said is absurd. You might have been describing someone else. I mean, you've been sitting here talking to me sixteen-to-the-dozen—"

"Oh, *you.*" She waved her hand dismissively.

Was it a compliment? Or did she mean they were in the same basket, two nincompoops together?

She shoved her plate and cup aside and leaned toward him. "Listen. I know you're not here to buy Stonington. You'd have to have packets of money. Though it would be nice if you *were* to buy it. That would *kill* the Bodenheims, to have someone else in the area taking over the number one spot. The only *worse* thing for them would be to have someone titled move in—" Polly looked hopefully at him. "You're not, are you?"

Sadly, Melrose studied his cup. "Well . . ."

"You are! Say you are!" Her face was shoved closer to his in her enthrallment. The proximity was not displeasing.

"I'm not." The face moved back and he almost felt he had betrayed her. "But I used to be," he added, brightly.

"*Used* to be? Whatever do you mean?"

"The Earl of Caverness. And twelfth Viscount Ardry, et cetera. But now I'm plain Melrose Plant."

What he was now did not seem to interest her in the least. Open-mouthed astonishment was her response to the loss of the title. "How did you lose all that?"

"Oh, I gave them up."

"*Why?*" She simply glared at him, obviously furious he had given away something that would have come in so useful. Then her expression softened. "Ah, I see. You had gambling debts or did something awful and didn't want to heap disgrace on the family name." Her eyes sparkled, now that she had forged out a history for him. In another moment, she'd have him inside an Iron Mask.

"Unfortunately, nothing so romantic as all that." He wondered what tempted him to justify his action to her. He found her unsettling, though he couldn't understand why, violet eyes or not. There was nothing at all wonderful about the rest of her, sitting there dressed in that unbecoming shade of brown. Her curls were havocking all over her head, and the upswung glasses and pencil stuck there did nothing to enhance the general appearance. "I didn't want them anymore, I guess," he ended, weakly.

She shrugged. "Oh, well, even without the title, Julia Bodenheim'll be prancing herself up and down on horseback before you. You'd best clear off; you're the perfect catch."

Gratified by this, he said, "I'm glad you think so."

"I didn't say *I* thought so," she said, munching the last of the muffin.

V

"I have come," said Sir Miles Bodenheim to Melrose Plant, "to invite you to cocktails at Rookswood."

It was said in what Melrose supposed might have been the tones used by the Angel Gabriel when he made his announcement to Mary. One should only stammer one's grateful acceptance.

Sir Miles apparently inferred why Melrose did not immediately do so. "Please don't think that just because you are a stranger to town you need hesitate about accepting. It is quite true that we are very particular, but I am sure you will find the gathering the sort you yourself are used to. *We* are all there—" Which wonderful revelation was accompanied by his swinging his walkstick over his shoulder and giving a good crack to one of the Blue Boy's Tiffany-style chandeliers. "—Derek is home. You haven't met Derek, our son. He's reading history, you know. Besides ourselves there will be only the Craigie sisters. I just now passed them on the walk and Ernestine was very particular in wanting to include you in one of our jaunts. And as you have our map—she gave it to you—you can see this will be an excellent opportunity to get acquainted. We need to straighten out the details of the fête, which is to be tomorrow. So say no more and come." Sir Miles scratched at the egg on his ascot, and added, "I know you've just been having tea with Miss Praed, but as you probably had nothing decent to eat at the Magic Muffin, I imagine a few canapés would suit you. How did you meet Miss Praed?" Sir Miles seemed clearly put out that this stranger to town was already looking toward fresher fields beyond the boundaries which he himself had so recently erected. "The woman writes rubbishy thrillers. I mean, if you *like* that sort of thing . . . ." He shrugged off the possibility of liking it at all. "I know you will find Ernestine interesting. She's—"

"I wish I were clever enough to write mysteries."

"Clever? I don't see anything clever about it. What's clever about killing someone and then having everyone run about cock-a-hoop trying to decide who did it? Seems an infernal waste of time to me. And as you can see, it doesn't happen in real life that way, does it? You don't see anyone like *her* detective inspector— all that sharp-witted slyness—in on *this* case, do you? Ho ho, not by a long chalk."

"So you've read her books," said Melrose, smiling.

Having given up on the egg yolk, Sir Miles stared at the air above Melrose's head. "Oh, I glanced over one we decided to give Cook for Christmas. Well, if this lot of police comes up with anything, I'll be the more surprised. That Carstairs person seems a bit slow-witted; and the Scotland Yard chap certainly puts himself forward, I must say. But come along, come along, old chap." Sir Miles exhorted Melrose to rise from his chair. "It's already gone five and we might as well go along together."

Inwardly, Melrose sighed. If he meant to ingratiate himself with the locals, he guessed he had better trot along to Rookswood. And Mrs. O'Brien had said Jury would be several hours, so dinner would be very late. "And what is to be the subject of Miss Craigie's talk?" he asked as they left the Bold Blue Boy.

"The molting habits and flight patterns of the Great Speckled Crackle."

"How jolly," said Melrose.

VI

"The molting habits of the Crackle are not at all what one would expect . . ." The voice of Ernestine Craigie droned on.

Funny, thought Melrose, his tepid glass of whiskey sweating in his hand, he had never expected much of anything from the Crackle, including that it might molt.

It was a slide show.

Was there anything *worse,* he wondered, except perhaps pictures being handed round of everyone's vacation or baby? Derek Bodenheim had walked in over an hour ago, poured himself a very large whiskey, invested his "Hullo" to Melrose with as much boredom as was humanly possible, and walked out, bottle in hand: all of this despite his father's assurances in their walk from the Bold Blue Boy to Rookswood that Melrose was to expect only high entertainment from his son.

Augusta Craigie had found herself a chair within reaching distance of the drinks table and was having a marvelous time with the sherry decanter, something that had escaped everyone's notice but Melrose's.

One plate of cardboard canapés had been handed round by a maid — a small, olive-skinned person whose movements were silent and parsimonious.

The only relief from tedium was Julia Bodenheim's trying to engage Melrose in something other than conversation by continuously crossing and recrossing her silken legs and heaving her silken bosom to lean toward glass, ashtray, or canapé plate.

Melrose had simply not been able to keep their minds on murder. From Sylvia's announcement that it should *not* have occurred, so to speak, just beyond their property line; to Augusta's shuddery silence; to the Honorable Miles's brief lecture on police inefficiency and pushiness — their minds could only light on the subject like small blue tits, peck, and flutter away. Even Ernestine, solid and square as a pint of stout in her brown suit, seemed to resist the subject.

There had been, however, an enthralling discussion of the plans for the fête — flinging up tea tents and coconut shies and phaeton rides before Melrose's eyes like an image of Atlantis. The carousel had arrived and most of the stalls gone up.

Could Emily Perk (Miles had asked) really be trusted to deliver the goods and not short the children on time during the carriage rides? *You know how she hates the idea of horses pulling people. Yes, Daddy, but she's the only one who can do it and who's willing,* Julia had replied, flipping through a *Country Life* and, apparently not finding herself in it, flinging it aside. Then Sylvia Bodenheim's knitting needles had flown like twin rapiers over the refusal of Lady Kennington to take the Jumble table.

Thus, from the way they all managed to avoid the subject, a person might have thought, One: the murder hadn't occurred at all; or Two: they were so used to fingerless corpses being flung out in the Horndean wood, what did one more matter?

Or, Three: someone here was feeling rather uncomfortably guilty.

The slide show continued: now flashed upon the projection screen was a pattern of multicolored lines running off from east to west, north to south, and curved variants thereof. The Crackles seemed to be having a right old rave up, flying all over the British Isles from the Outer Hebrides across Manchester and down to Torquay. As Melrose began to doze off, Miss Craigie's pointer was tracing a horizontal red line indicating one of their favorite flights, apparently. He squinted his eyes and tried to remember what it reminded him of. Emily's River of Blood, perhaps? Or maybe just an advert for British Air. . . .

He yawned and wondered how soon Jury would be back. It shouldn't take too long to drive from London to Littlebourne. He wondered if somewhere a Great Speckled Crackle was having a slide show, demonstrating to a roomful of captive and bored Crackles, the British Motorway System. *This is their flight pattern: note this red line ending in a clover leaf. That is the exit to Doncaster. . . .*

Part Two

WIZARDS
and
WARLORDS

TEN

I

IT was clear how Catchcoach Street had come by its name: it was a daggerlike, blind alley, far removed from the fashionable cul-de-sacs of Belgravia and Mayfair. Narrow, rundown houses huddled together, closer at the blade-tip end. The air smelled of fish and brakish Thames water.

Number twenty-two was distinguished from the houses on either side only by virtue of its fresher trim, tidier yard. Nell Beavers, the slum landlady of the street (she had told them proudly that she owned this and both houses on either side) was adding to their store of information on Cora Binns. She had left the house on the Thursday evening, sometime around six, and saying something about hoping she'd get to the Highbury station after rush hour in the Underground.

"I think it was six. I don't keep tabs, do I?"

Jury bet. He could tell she was the type who lifted the lids of dustbins and counted the empties. Cora Binns had the upstairs flat and Jury was sure the landlady knew every creak in the floorboards.

"A bit late for a job interview, wasn't it?" asked Wiggins.

Nell Beavers shrugged. "I wouldn't know, would I? Expect she didn't want to lose a days work. Anyway, she said she was going to Hertfield," continued Nell Beavers, rocking slowly, and proud of her control. She was not one to crumble in a crisis. They knew because she'd told them three times. "She told me the agency— Cora was a temp-sec—rang her up and said someone in Hertfield needed a steno. All you have to do is check with the agency. It's called the Smart Girls Secretarial Service. I'd just hop right round there if I was you."

Jury thanked her. He was often taught his job by the British citizenry. "You told Inspector Carstairs she said she was coming back that same night."

"That's right. That's what Cora said. And then the agency rang up and asked me did I know where she was, and she never did go to the place she was supposed to. Right shirty the woman got about it and all I said was, well, I don't keep tabs, I'm not her mum, am I?" Nell Beavers smacked dry lips. "But after Cora doesn't come back Friday night, I says to myself, Nell, time to call the authorities. Beavers—my late husband, God rest him— always did say a problem don't take care of itself."

"You did exactly right, Mrs. Beavers." She remained tight-mouthed, proof against the compliment she was so well aware she deserved. Her rocking got a bit brisker, though, when she said, "If I was you, I'd ask the Crippses." She hooked a thumb to her right. "Next door. Though why Cora'd want to hang about with *her* beats me. It's disgraceful, it is, landlords ain't got no rights in this country? Just tenants. God knows I been trying to get rid of that one for years. Ash the Flash running around getting up to Lord knows what." Primly she folded her hands in her aproned lap. "I ain't no stranger to police, believe me. Seen enough of them come round about Ash Cripps. Beavers always did say that sort of pervert had a problem." And then to Jury's and Wiggins's infinite surprise, she opened her old blue cardigan and quickly closed it again. "You know what I mean. Been in most of the parks and lavatories in the East End and probably no stranger to the West, I'd say."

"Which Underground station did Cora use?"

"Same's we all do. Wembley Knotts. Cora complained a lot about the tube. Shocking how much it's gone up. Just from Wembley Knotts it's eighty p to King's Cross. But they keep building more, don't they? Still, I guess police don't have to travel that way." She seemed resentful of this. Not only were the authorities keeping her tenants safe and sound, they didn't have to share the Underground.

Outside number twenty-four, a ring of grubby children were holding hands and skipping round a battered pram. They were all coatless, despite the September evening, and one of them was completely stark except for its vest.

In their frolic round the perambulator, they kept to the tune of "Ring-round-the-rosy," but supplied more robust lyrics, dependent largely upon a series of obscenities directed to the innocent occupant.

"Your mum home?" asked Jury, after checking to make sure the baby wasn't smothered or otherwise dead. It lay sleeping on its stomach, tiny hands fisted, with rosy cheeks like small flames not even the soot of Catchcoach Street could extinguish.

Without a break in the tune or the skipping, the children merely exchanged their *fuck you's* to "Mam's home, mam's home, mam's home"—interspersed with high giggles that they could be so resourceful in giving out information without suspending important operations. Thus inspired, they continued their chant, bouncing even higher with feet and bobbed hair, changing now to "Makin' mash, makin' mash, makin' mash." This further commentary on "mam's" doings brought forth fresh peals of laughter and also the opening of the door.

"Shut yer mouths and get yer knickers on. What *you* want?" The last of this was directed at Jury and Wiggins.

A rat-faced dog saw its chance to escape and sprinted through the crack in the door. Through that opening Jury saw half a face and half a figure and doubted the other half would be any improvement over the oily hair, metallic eye and pendulous breast. When she opened the door wider, the extraordinary girth completely filled it. The whole figure sported a cotton frock straining at its buttons.

"Police officers," said Jury, showing his ID.

"Come about Ashley, well, no wonder. Come on in." Before he could correct her misapprehension, she was shouting at the ring of children to come on in and get their mash.

"You were expecting police?" asked Wiggins.

"It's always police, innit? In them macs and blue suits you ain't the Two Ronnies. Come on, come on—" Exasperated by their dimness she motioned them through the door. "So what's Ashley been gettin' up to? Showin' hisself in the ladies again? Stop that!" she yelled to the goblin-ring, climbing all over the pram and nearly upsetting it. "An' come get yer tea."

Two of them had stuffed themselves into the pram with the baby while the others shook it violently. At the mention of food, they nearly toppled the carriage, and Wiggins with it, in their rush for their tea.

"Shut yer filthy mouths and get yer knickers on, Joey." She smacked the child's bald bottom as he darted between Wiggins and Jury.

"Back here." She motioned Jury and Wiggins along like a tour guide.

"Back here" was the dirtiest scullery Jury had ever seen. Crusted dishes, spent crockery and pockmarked pots covered every surface. Icicles of grease hung from the cooker. Sergeant Wiggins stared with perverse fascination at a frying pan which held an inch of hardened lard.

"Mrs. Beavers from next door told us you might be able to help us, Mrs. Cripps."

"You mean Beavers ain't down t' the pub 'avin 'er ten pints and callin' it 'er *ahfternoon sherry*?" She made a primping movement with her hand and then hung over the gas cooker, relighting an old cigarette. At the wobbly kitchen table, the urchins shouted threats and imprecations at their mam, all the while beating their cutlery on its surface. Seemingly oblivious to it all, she spooned out mashed potatoes into their several bowls. They all grabbed for the tomato catsup to douse their bowls. Wiggins stood near the table, fascinated by this red and white mélange.

Her cigarette dribbled gray ash over the pan as she said, "Well, I tol' 'im, din't I? Brings in 'is li'l bit a stray, fer all the world t' see . . ."

She was accustomed, it seemed, to dealing with police, had even achieved a certain rapport with them. Jury smiled his thanks as he refused the proffered pot of mash. Wiggins took a step backward.

Beginning again in the middle of some conversation with herself, she went on, "Right under me own nose and bangin' 'er —" She pointed to some nether region at the rear of the house "— an' I'm not puttin' up wi' that, am I? Got me pride, ain't I? I just takes meself off t' the Labor Exchange. Bloody job only pays three quid a week and the Screeborough gang takes two a that just fer a kip on their bleedin' couch and one quid for me mornin' tea. I ast ya." She circled the table and dropped another dollop of potatoes in each bowl. "There an' that's gone, so shut yer mouths. An' keep yer darty 'ands off Sookey's bowl." Smartly she slapped a hand which had skulked toward its brother's mash with a spoon. She surveyed the ring of grimy faces and said, "Where's Friendly?"

"Over t' the schoolyard. Said 'e was goin' t' show it t' Fiona." Giggles all round and Sookey took advantage of this to flash out a grubby hand and hook up a spoonful of mash from Joey's bowl.

"I'll 'show it' 'im, don't think I won't. Just like 'is Da, Friendly is."

Wiggins was studying the graffiti-covered and faded wallpaper where huge stalks of gladioli had been transformed into phalluses. Following this, he retreated with his notebook to the kitchen doorway.

"Mrs. Beavers said you're a friend of Cora Binns, Mrs. Cripps."

"Cora? Yeah, I know Cora. What's this in aid of? Ashley been at Cora again?"

"Gimme some Ribena, mam," yelled Sookey.

"Shut yer face. Ain't got none, 'ave we?"

"Ah, fuck."

"Cora Binns has been murdered," said Jury.

"*What?* What ya mean, murdered?" The expression on Jury's face told her it wasn't a joke. "Well, I never . . ." The cigarette dangled. The word was drowned in the cacophony of bowls and banging forks and whines. If the Cripps children heard it, they were more interested in their own affairs, and soon were scrambling down from the table. One of them — the girl with the dirtiest face and the stickiest fingers — paused in the doorway to look Sergeant Wiggins over.

"It happened," Jury continued, "in a village not far from London. Littlebourne. Cora was apparently on her way there to be interviewed for a job. Can you think of anyone who might have wanted her out of the way? Or boyfriends, perhaps? Jealousy's a pretty common motive." She could think of no one. She still seemed to be having difficulty in digesting this information. Jury took the picture of Katie O'Brien from his pocket. "Ever seen this girl, Mrs. Cripps?"

She wiped her hands down the sides of her frock, in deference, perhaps, for the dead, before taking the snapshot. "Pretty li'l thing. No, I ain't never seen 'er. What's she got to do with Cora, then?"

"I don't know she has. But she met with an accident in the Wembley Knotts Underground station about two weeks ago. The girl's from Littlebourne, same place the murder happened." Jury pocketed the picture. "Do you know where Drumm Street is, Mrs. Cripps?"

"Sure. That's just two streets over."

"This girl in the snapshot was taking violin lessons in Drumm Street from someone named Cyril Macenery. You wouldn't know him, would you?"

"The fiddler? Sure, we all know Cyril. What you want to do is go along t' the pub at the end of the street, there." She nodded her head to the left. "That's where they all hang out; Ashley, too. Right run down old place it be; you'll see it next the sweet shop."

Wiggins, who was trying to detach the fingers of the little girl who had his trouser leg in a viselike grip, looked as if even a run-down pub would be sanctuary, compared with the Crippses' kitchen. He closed up his notebook, tucked his pen in his pocket. "I can go along there, sir, if you like."

"We'll both go. Thanks very much, Mrs. Cripps."

"If ya see Ashley, tell 'im 'e's wanted 'ere. Bloody fool sits round that pub all day. 'E won't be much 'elp, I can tell ya. Can't even see straight once 'e's got an Abbot's in 'im."

"Okay. Thanks for your time. And I'd appreciate it if you wouldn't mention this to anyone, Mrs. Cripps."

"White Ellie's what they call me." She lay a finger against her mouth. "Me lips is sealed," she whispered.

"Did you see that skillet, sir?" asked Wiggins, as they walked up the street toward the pub. "There were tiny footprints in the grease." Wiggins shuddered.

ELEVEN

∞∞∞∞∞∞∞∞

I

THE sign of the Anodyne Necklace creaked in the rain blowing down the dingy street. Its scabrous paint had once been green, but most of the color and detail were now washed out so that Jury could just barely make out the shape of the crude strand of beads which must have given the pub its name. It was an undistinguished, narrow building of dull burgundy-brown which the dusk turned to the color of dried blood. Windows frosted halfway up glowed yellow and obscured the shadow-life within. The pub shared the narrower end of the street with a tiny sweet shop, in which the only sign of life was a flickering telly, and a dusty-looking news agent's on the right. At one time the Anodyne Necklace must have been a coaching inn, though how coach and four could squeeze through the crumbling arch was hard to imagine. The name of the pub, which had been painted on the stone of the archway, was almost obliterated.

"I think it means 'cure,'" said Jury, to Wiggins's muffled question about the name. No one looked more in need of one than Wiggins. His shoulders were hunched inward against the rain as he sneezed into his handkerchief.

The yellow glow in the windows had come not from the electric lights of the chandeliers but from the gaslight behind sconces on the wall. There were other remnants of a former Victorian elegance: the snob screen at one end of the bar which ran the length of the room; the antique frame of the mirror in need of resilvering. Other than this, there was sawdust on the floor, round deal tables, hard benches lining the walls. An incongruous string of Christmas lights looked either backward or forward to some more festive season. Middle-aged women, clustered in twos and threes, sat with their half-pints, sharp-eyed as overseers watching what their men were up to. Not much, it would appear. Most of them held onto their drinks as if to a past of broken promises. What there was of activity was divided between the dart game at the rear of the room, and one table where a group of some five or six — apparently lorded over by a fat man with pince-nez — seemed intent on some sort of game.

"Slumming, love?"

The girl who addressed Jury actually wore, above the blaze of a very low-cut red blouse, a velvet band round her neck and a beauty spot beneath an eye leaden with mascara and blue shadow. Jury couldn't imagine what custom she could scare up in here Probably she lived in the street as well as on it.

The bartender, who turned from the optics to knife smooth foam from a pint of stout, seemed to know her well enough. "Go home, Shirl, and get your beauty sleep. You could use it, girl. What'll it be, mate?"

"Information," said Jury, watching Shirl move off, having taken the sting without flinching.

The publican cast a bored eye on Jury's warrant card. "It's Ash again, ain't it." He nodded in the direction of the men at the table. "Over there."

"Not him. It's about Cora Binns. Your name?"

"Harry Biggins." His eyebrows danced upwards in mild surprise as he set two pints before a couple of regulars who stared in the mirror behind the bar and pretended not to listen. "Cora, is it? She never seemed to do no harm."

"No. But someone's done her some. She's been murdered. What do you know about her?"

"*Cora?* Well, I'll be." Having just named her, Biggins was soon forgetting all about her, as he wiped down the bar and denied any personal knowledge at all of Cora Binns. Several minutes of questioning by Sergeant Wiggins elicited nothing.

Jury took out the picture of Katie O'Brien. "How about this girl, then?" He could not tell from Biggins's expression whether he was lying or not when he denied even more fervently any knowledge of the O'Brien girl. No, he hadn't heard about the accident in the Wembley Knotts station. That Jury found very difficult to believe, but he let it pass for the time being. "She had a music teacher who I was told comes in here. Macenery. Now, please don't tell me you don't know *him* or I'll have to wonder how you stay in business, Mr. Biggins, given the few people you seem to know. I shouldn't imagine you'd be in business long." Jury smiled.

"Never said I didn't know 'im, did I, now? That's 'im, over there at Doc Chamberlen's table. That ain't 'is real name, Chamberlen; he just uses it for the game. Cyril's the one with the beard."

"What game?"

"Wizards and Warlords, it's called. They're in 'ere all the time. Stupid game, far as I'm concerned. But there ain't no accounting for tastes, is there?" Harry Biggins flashed a gold tooth to let Jury know how cooperative he could be.

"Thanks. Now who in here might have known Cora Binns? Since you didn't." Jury returned the smile.

"Try Maud over there." Biggins indicated a woman whose yellow hair was rolled up on top of her head like a basket of lemons. She was sitting with two others, and all three were coated and kerchiefed.

"You take Maud, Wiggins; I'll take the table."

As he walked up to it, Jury caught a snatch of conversation.
". . . played strip poker wi' 'er. Lost by a 'and." Burst of laughter from the others, all except the portly gentleman in pince-nez who seemed to be intent upon the play. He threw an odd, many-sided, crystal blue die.

From a sallow-faced young man in jeans there came a groan.

"Look at Keith, 'e's getting excited."

Keith looked about as excited as he would in the grave. The one Jury decided must be Ash Cripps had a wide, dented face, as if a car had backed into it. He rolled his cigar in his mouth and looked down at a piece of graph paper. They all had sheets of paper. The table was awash in paper. The fat man had a much larger sheet, creased with many foldings. The game appeared to be something of a spectator sport, if one were to judge from the way people wandered over, pint in hand, watched the proceedings for a moment, and then wandered off.

One of them said, "We're walking along the passageway, checking for a secret entrance in the north wall." This came from the young, bearded man identified as Cyril Macenery.

"You find a door," said the fat man.

"We listen outside the door," said Macenery.

The fat man threw the die again. "You hear a lot of snorting and stamping."

"Gorgon tries to pick the lock," said Ash Cripps with a fatuous smile.

"No good," said the fat one, rolling the die again.

"We bash it in," said Macenery.

"No. The door flies open and two huge stallions appear."

The others were silent, looking at Macenery, on whom they seemed to be depending to get them out of a spot. He said, "Manticore uses silver shield to gather in sun's rays and shield is turned into fire-breather against stallions—"

"Police," said Jury, tossing his card onto the papers like a player anteing up.

Their response was automatic: they all looked at Ash Cripps, who shrugged, tossed down his pencil, and started to take his coat from the back of his chair.

"Not you, Mr. Cripps." He nodded toward Macenery. "You."

Astonishment, stamped on all of their faces, was like a new day on the face of Cripps. "Not me?" He looked at Cyril. "What you been gettin' up to, then, Cy?"

"I'd like a word with you later, Mr. Cripps. In the meantime, you can go." That took the bloom off the day for Ash. "I've just been talking to your wife," said Jury.

"Elephant? Got a big mouth, she 'as. Bugger all." He drank off his pint and left.

"It's about Katie, isn't it?" asked Cyril Macenery when he and Jury were seated at a table out of earshot.

"Partly."

"I told that other cop everything I knew. How many times do I have to answer the same questions?"

"As many times as we ask, I guess. The other man was from 'H' Division, Mr. Macenery. I'm with Scotland Yard. Something else has happened."

"What else?" He seemed extremely wary, and looked now very young and very nervous. Probably, he was older than he looked, but the jeans and turtleneck and extreme blue of his eyes would have put him in his late twenties if one hadn't noticed the small lines of age. His hair and beard were fawn-colored and neatly trimmed.

"You were Katie O'Brien's music teacher for how long?"

"Around eight, nine months. Twice a month. What's Scotland Yard on this for?"

Jury didn't answer. "I've heard you're a fine musician. Good enough, apparently, that her mother, who's pretty protective, let Katie come into London just to go to you. Was — is — she that good?"

"Yes. I wouldn't have bothered otherwise. I need the money but I'm not about to take on every sodding mum's kid to get it. After about ten, fifteen years' practice she'll be able to play all right." He smiled bleakly.

"I guess she can't practice much where she is now," said Jury, trying to break through what he felt to be the man's way of dealing with the violence done to Katie O'Brien. He could feel Macenery's unhappiness as he made little circles with his glass on the scarred table. "There was the matter of her clothes."

Macenery banged the glass down. "Look. All I know is, Katie showed up in jeans. Then this Inspector Hound says they found a dress in her shopping bag. Naturally, the implication being she did her quick change in *my* place. Well, she didn't. If Katie was wearing a dress when she left home, I don't know anything about it. Are you saying she'd come into Wembley Knotts and get herself all tarted up and then go out bashing—"

"I'd hardly call jeans and a bit of lipstick getting 'all tarted up.' I'm thinking she just took advantage of being away from home to wear the clothes she wanted to wear. You didn't know she was raising the money by playing her violin in tube stations?"

A hesitation. "No." Jury looked at him. It was a defensive *no*. "Look, I really didn't. I'd never have let her do it. The thing is, I wonder if I gave her the idea. I used to do it myself. Raised a quid or two that way. A long time ago."

"You walked her from your place on Drumm Street to the Underground, right?" Macenery nodded. "Is there a ladies near by? Somewhere she could have changed?"

"There's a public toilet in the little park across from the stop."

"She must have been changing, for one thing, to make some impression on *you*, Mr. Macenery. Thought maybe it made her look more grown-up?" The young man said nothing. "Is she in love with you?"

His eyes flared up at that. "In love? She's only *sixteen*, Superintendent."

Jury smiled. "I never knew that to stop anyone." Jury studied him for a moment before asking, "Do you know Cora Binns?"

That threw him off balance. "Cora Binns? Blonde who comes in here? Yeah, I know her, but only about as well as I know you. Not my type." Implying Jury wasn't, either.

"She's been murdered. You wouldn't have any ideas about that, would you?"

Macenery seemed totally nonplussed. "My God! Where? When?"

"In Littlebourne. Where Katie comes from. Apparently, you know them both."

"Lucky me."

"Did they know one another?"

"How the hell should *I* know?" The old anger returned.

"Well, did Katie come in here?"

He was going to deny it, Jury knew, and then thought better of the lie. "Okay, once or twice she did."

"Bit young for that, isn't she?"

A huge sigh from the violinist. "For Christ's sakes, we weren't standing her drinks. She just liked to watch the game."

"Did she play?"

"No. Look, she was only in for a bit, honestly."

"Did she talk to anyone else in here, other than you?"

"No. And I can't see how she'd have known Cora Binns; I can't remember her being in here at the same time."

Jury looked over to the table, from which the other players had apparently drifted off, their play rudely interrupted. Only the fat man, Chamberlen, sat there. "It's a strange game."

"Wizards? Passes the time. We've got a kind of club here. Play several times a week. You can really get involved." Macenery looked at his watch. "Look, I've a lesson on in five minutes. Are you finished with me?"

"Where were you on Thursday night?"

"Here." He'd scraped back his chair, but now looked doubtful. "Why?"

Jury nodded. "You can go. I'll want to talk with you later." As Macenery got up, Jury said, "Incidentally, have you been to see Katie?"

The violinist seemed to want to look everywhere but at Jury. "No. She's in a coma, I know that. What good would it do?" On his face was a look of abject misery. "I mean, she wouldn't hear me if I talked to her. What could I say?"

"You'd think of something." He watched Cyril Macenery walk towards the door, as he watched Wiggins coming in his direction, away from Maud and her two companions. Jury thought that if he didn't know what Katie O'Brien's feelings were, he was pretty certain about Macenery's.

III

Dr. Chamberlen sat like a stout idol, hands folded over vest, pince-nez dangling on a thin, black ribbon. "I call myself that," he said in answer to Jury's question, "out of habit. Merely for fun, you understand." To Wiggins, who had taken out his notebook,

Chamberlen said, "I'm a blank page, Sergeant. My real name would be of no earthly interest to you."

"Try us," said Jury, smiling.

Chamberlen sighed. "Oh, very well. Aaron Chambers, number forty-nine, Catchcoach Street. A name very close to 'Chamberlen,' certainly. Have you heard of the famous Dr. Chamberlen? Few have, beyond the portals of the Anodyne Necklace. Dr. Chamberlen swore that a simple necklace of bone — the one represented on the sign above the door out there — that such a necklace as he'd made would cure anything from a child's teething pains to gout to —" He shrugged. "Heaven knows how many he sold, each one in its little airtight packet. Airtight, so that the aura of energy couldn't escape. They were dispensed by an old woman over the confectioner's next door. The shop is still there; the woman long since died. They said it was a hoax. Do you think so, Superintendent?" The question was rhetorical. Chamberlen gestured with his hand, the ash from his cigar sifting over the wash of papers. "You've probably not heard of our game, either. Wizards and Warlords. There's a treasure, you see. We've been looking for it for months, this particular treasure. On paper only, of course. I have made the treasure the necklace itself — the anodyne necklace. Since I'm Wizard-Master, I have that authority. Thus I have decided the necklace can cast spells so remarkable, gentlemen, that it could make both of you disappear right before my eyes." His small mouth pursed in amusement as he snapped his fingers.

"Unfortunately, we'd probably reappear, Dr. Chamberlen, right before your eyes."

Chamberlen shrugged. "You see, to me the anodyne necklace is far, far more than a cure for aching gums. It is an *objet trouvé*, something impalpable, as yet uncreated, until I decide what particular wonders it is to hold. Dr. Chamberlen — that is, the original Dr. Chamberlen" — modestly, he pressed his hands against his vest, "— had many competitors. There was Burcher of Long Acre. There was a Mr. Oxspring at the Hand and Shears who sold necklaces made from peony wood, as I remember, in the seventeen-twenties. Oh, yes, there were many contenders, but I like to think *my* necklace is the one with the true power." He held up the big sheet of graph paper. When Jury reached for it, Dr. Chamberlen pulled the paper back. "You won't tell the others, will you? The map is only supposed to be seen by the Wizard-Master."

"I'd die first," said Jury, taking it from him. It was a diagram of several views of an enormous castle ruin. Enlargements had been made of certain of its rooms — the dungeon displayed in elaborate detail. The towers, the moat, the bridge were all drawn with exceeding care.

"We've been at this particular game for two months now," said Chamberlen. "The anodyne necklace can ward off nearly any-thing—bad luck, illness, all manner of evil, the Manticore's silver shield, ogres, thieves, and even Warlords."

Jury was still looking at the map. "Too bad it couldn't ward off murder."

IV

"I told 'im you'd be back for 'im." White Ellie chuckled. "But I didn't tell 'im nothin' else. Serve 'im right to get in a muck-sweat, the way 'e goes on."

"Shut up, Elephant, and gimme me fags."

From the cooker's top she chucked a packet of cigarettes toward the table, catsup-smeared and still ringed with empty bowls from the kiddies' tea. Except for the now-knickerless girl, who stood, finger in mouth, once more glooming up at Sergeant Wiggins, the urchins had disappeared to the streets. When the little girl once again clamped her catsupy hand on Wiggins's trouser leg, he gave it a smart lick with his pen. The youngster howled but stood her ground. Neither of the parents seemed much interested in crying police child-abuse.

"So whatcha want?" asked Ash Cripps. "Listen, if it's about that li'l bit a mystery says I give 'er one be'ind the Necklace, it's a fuckin' lie—" He pointed his cigarette, like a tiny gun, at Jury.

"It's not about that, Ash," said Jury.

"Then it's them Screeborough gang—" His look darted to his wife, busy over a fry-up. "I tol' ya, Elephant, there'd be nothing but grief, and you goin' fer a kip round there. Listen—" He turned his attention once again to Jury. "I ain't 'ad nothing to do with that bunch, nor no firm since last July and I did me time, so don't be coming in 'ere—"

"Nothing to do with a firm, Ash—"

Ash squinted up at him, confused. If it wasn't sex and it wasn't small-time theft, what could it be?

White Ellie placed a dish towel over a chair seat and said to Jury, "There, sit yerself down. Want some of this fry-up?"

Sergeant Wiggins looked aghast, apparently afraid that Jury might accept.

"No, thanks." He turned to Ash. "It's about Cora Binns. I was telling your wife, here, that Cora's been murdered."

"Cora? That li'l blonde with the big—" He held his hands in front of his chest. "Well, bugger all." His expression was more one of wonder than remorse. Apparently unable to let any unexpected event go by without attaching a sexual meaning to it, he added, "Interfered with, was she?"

"No. What we want is information about her friends, boy-friends, to be more exact. Anyone with any quarrel against Cora Binns. Know of anyone?"

"Had 'er eye on Dick, I know that," said White Ellie, sliding the greasy mess out on a plate.

"Dick, what Dick?" said her husband.

"You know Dick. Dontcha remember, 'e was stayin' 'ere that night and we was in bed and he come along and gimme one?"

Ash's eyes screwed up. "Oh, yeah, *that* Dick. Friend of Trev's, 'e was. Now there was a lad. Best Wizard-Master we ever did 'ave. Though don't let the Doc 'ear me say it." He hooked a napkin under his chin and started in on the sausages. "Matter of fact, Trev and Cora might 'ave 'ad something going for a bit."

White Ellie snorted, wiping another plate with the sleeve of her dress before depositing a chop and some sausage on it, along with potatoes. "Trevor, 'e was one for the ladies. Pity what 'appened to 'im. That's life," she added, philosophically.

Jury looked from the one to the other. "Trevor?"

"Yeah. Trevor Tree. Good lad was Trevor."

Sergeant Wiggins stopped in the act of muscling the four-year-old out of the way of his feet to look at Jury.

Jury nodded, then said to Ash Cripps, "How well did you know Trevor Tree?"

Ash hooked his thumb over his shoulder. "Trevor lived back in Drumm Street, same street Cyril lives in. Smart lad, nicked a quarter million in jewelry. And then the poor blighter gets run down by a car." Ash shook his head ruefully. "Wages of sin."

"You wouldn't have had anything to do with those wages, would you, Ash?"

He stopped sucking his teeth and looked as shocked as if he'd spent most of his life in a monastery. "So that's it, is it? You think I'm at it? In on the snatch, is that it?"

White Ellie hooted, wiping a piece of bread around the plate she'd been standing there eating from. "Ashley ain't smart enough to go in anything like that."

"Did the rest of them at the Anodyne Necklace know Trevor Tree?"

"Not all, I don't think. Some did. Keith, maybe. And Doc Chamberlen, of course. I don't know how well them two got on. At Wizards, I mean. I think maybe the Doc was jealous of Trev. See, Trevor was a real artist. You should of seen some of the maps he did for the game. Finicky, he was, about details. Well, Doc Chamberlen's good too, but not as good as Trevor. Practically a religion that game is to the Doc. He can sit round for hours fiddling with them maps. Treasure maps. Right now we're looking for the anodyne necklace. See, the way it goes is—"

"Shut up, Ashley. The super ain't interested in some stupid game as that. So lemme borrow yer strides, I gotta go to the launderette."

"You don't need me trousers, woman; I'm sick a you using me trousers."

"I *do* need 'em. So's when I sit down they don't look up me legs."

"Well, close yer legs, Elephant."

"Can't. I'm too fat."

Jury rose to leave, apparently to the undying gratitude of Sergeant Wiggins, whose life was now being made hell not only by the girl but by the rat-faced dog who'd got a grip on his heel.

116

"I'll see you, later, Ash. Don't leave town, will you?"

"That's a prayer. If I could do, I'd a done it long ago."

As they walked through the door, the dog slithered between their legs and waited at the end of the walk.

Wiggins gave it an evil look and said, "What do you think, sir? That's very odd about this Tree fellow living round here."

"Yes. Let's leave the car and walk, Wiggins. I want to see the inside of that Underground stop where Katie was attacked, and then go to Drumm Street."

As Jury walked down the pavement, he was amazed to hear his sergeant, whose mouth was as pristine pure as his sinuses, saying—with a kick thrown in to dramatize his feelings about the dog:

"Fuck off, Toto. We're not in Kansas."

V

The narrow entrance to the Wembley Knotts Underground station was almost swallowed up by the lock-up shops on either side. Jury and Wiggins showed their identification to the bored black woman in a kiosk, which earned them nothing but a disinterested nod and a refusal to look them in the eye as she nodded them through.

There wasn't much custom at six-thirty on a Saturday, except for returning shoppers and shop girls, and not many of them were returning to Wembley Knotts. The moving stairs were having a rest, so Jury and Wiggins had to walk down to the tunnels, two of them sloping off to left and right like a wishbone. In the distance a train rumbled.

They followed the curve of the dun-colored, tiled walls toward the train platform. Two punk-rockers passed them, coming round the curve, he with a tomahawk haircut, and she with bright orange hair. They gave the impression of prowling rather than walking up the passageway, threw Jury and Wiggins contemptuous glances, and then passed on.

"They always seem to know police. I have the feeling I'm wearing a badge on my sleeve."

They stopped where, according to Carstair's diagram, Katie O'Brien had been attacked. The train that had disgorged the punks picked up speed and rumbled out of the tunnel.

The spot was not within view of the platform, but near it, just above a short flight of stairs leading downward. Jury looked at the poster, slightly loosened by time and the attentions of graffiti addicts, which advertised the musical *Evita*. One corner flapped in the wind driven their way by the outgoing train. Evita was positioned between a poster of a setting sun going down behind a glass of gin and tonic and one claiming marvelous curative powers for a cough syrup.

"Stuff's no good at all," said Wiggins, appraising this last poster. "Hacking to death I was one night. Didn't do a thing."

Jury made no comment on this, but looked behind him, where the passageway curved. Empty. The stairs too were empty and the platform invisible from this position. In this extremely public place, it would be surprisingly easy to attack someone.

"You think it was the same person, don't you? Then why didn't he try and kill her the same way he killed the Binns woman? Drag her out to the Horndean wood or somewhere not so public? Seems a chancy thing to do, hitting her here."

Jury shook his head. "I don't know, except that he hadn't the time to get at her someplace else. My guess is he was desperate." Jury was staring absently at the *Evita* poster, at the crudely drawn hammer and sickle. "I'm going to the hospital in the Fulham Road to see her."

Beneath them, on a lower level, there was the dull rumble of another train; closer the tightening of brakes taking hold as one stopped at the Wembley Knotts station. It stirred more of the dirty air and blew the detritus of another week's commuting along the bottom of the tiled walls.

"Might as well work down the mines," said Wiggins, coughing.

"Umm. It's nice we have such healthy jobs, isn't it? All that fresh air."

Wiggins, quite seriously, agreed.

"If she could only talk," said Jury, nodding toward the picture of Evita.

"You'd think," said Wiggins, "kids would have something

better to do than to be always mucking up the posters. Looks a treat, doesn't she?"

Diamond points of light sparked Evita's necklace, rings, bracelets, hair — even the microphones bristling around her.

It was then that Jury recalled Ernestine Craigie's remark, the one he had been trying to think of as he left the cottage. Bedizened and bejeweled. Evita certainly was that. *Bedizened, beringed and bejeweled.*

What a mug, said Jury to himself. Why didn't I see it before? "Wiggins, get over to this Smart Girls agency and dig out the manager. Find out about this interview Cora Binns had and call me at the hospital."

"Do you think anyone will be at the agency? It's gone six. If I have to rout whoever runs the place out at home, it might take longer."

"Okay. Why don't you take the car. As long as I'm here, I'll take the tube. Faster, anyway. It goes from here to South Kensington station." They were out on the platform now and in the bowels of the tunnel; Jury could hear the approach of the train. There was an overpass across the tracks, leading to another exit in another street. The mesh had been broken and patched temporarily with a couple of boards. The train pulled in, and Wiggins sketched a salute and left.

Jury settled himself between a couple of *Times* readers. He liked the anonymity of the tube; it helped him think. His eyes traveled across the line of ads over the heads of the passengers opposite. Beside the map of the Underground was a sign warning passengers about pickpockets. It showed the rear end of a body in jeans — the shapely hips making it clear the victim was a girl. There was a hand lifting a wallet from her rear pocket. He especially liked that little touch — the fingernails of the hand were varnished.

As the train swayed through the black tunnel, he thought it was nice that equal rights for women predominated even among dips.

TWELVE

I

As if disease and death were only one more commodity in the Fulham Road, the Royal Marsden Hospital melted into its surroundings. Across from it were the usual shops, launderettes, pubs, boutiques, restaurants.

The nurse who finally led Jury to Katie O'Brien's room could not disguise the fact that she was very pretty, despite her uniform — striped dress, black stockings, a white cap and apron that might have taken a dent, but not a wrinkle. Starched right down to her voice, she said, as she pushed open the door to the room: "Don't be too long, Superintendent." She walked off, uniform crackling.

He was not prepared for the way she looked — porcelain skin, black hair brushed to such a shining neatness it might have been painted against the pillow. Her small, delicate hands were folded across the top of the sheet updrawn over her breast. To one side of her bed stood an oxygen tent, and it made him think of a glass bell on which leaves would drift in autumn, petals in spring, snow in winter. On her face was the memory of a smile.

"Hello, Katie," said Jury.

Against the wall by the night stand rested the black-cased violin. Odd it hadn't been removed, taken home by her mother. He wondered how long it had taken her, standing in some windy tunnel — Victoria, Wembley Knotts, Piccadilly — before she ever could have earned enough money to buy those jeans and that shirt. Months, probably.

Jury walked across to the window to look down at the darkening Fulham Road. Across the street was a pub on the corner whose lights painted its windows with a mysterious burgundy glow. Directly across was a greengrocer's, striped awning rolled in for the night. Beside that sat a launderette. Did Jury really remember this street from the war years, when he was a boy, or only imagine he did?

"Where that grocer's is," he said more to himself and the windowpane than to Katie, "there used to be a sweet shop. I spent most of my time looking through its windows during the war. Long before your time, that was. I remember one of our neighbors had her basement stocked full of tinned stuff, soup and golden syrup and tea. It was just like a shop, her basement, and she even had sweets down there. I used to visit her all the time and she'd take me down and show me all this stuff — shelves and shelves of things. . . ."

Outside the launderette, a little girl stood rocking a doll's carriage to and fro. Waiting for her mother, probably. She picked the doll up from the carriage and held it in the air. There was a pram there, too, waiting for one of the women within to collect it after the wash was done. He could make out the forms of women sitting, probably watching their wash, like little worlds, go round. Momentarily, his vision was blocked as one held up a sheet or blanket like a curtain against the glass.

Jury saw himself again in his room standing with his face pushed up against his bedroom window. The black-out curtains should have been drawn, but since there was no light in his room, he supposed it would be safe to look out. There was nothing to see, though, except a big, pale moon. There had been no noise and no warning before there was no wall and no window. He could remember being thrown through the air, as if he'd been trying to do a high jump. How he had escaped with only a few cuts, he had never understood. His mother hadn't escaped.

A woman came out and collected the pram, pushed it past the covered vegetable bins. Clean clothes and food: life went on in the Fulham Road. In the burgundy light of the pub called the Saracen's Head, a young man seemed to be waiting impatiently. He was carrying a guitar, looking up and down the street.

Not even the air stirred above Katie O'Brien's bed. She lay outstretched like an effigy in a marble dress. The tape recorder her mother had brought in sat on the bedside table. He wondered if the nurses bothered playing it for her. Jury flicked the On switch, and the tinny strains of an old music-hall rendition of "Roses of Picardy" filled the room.

Dusk was coming on in the Fulham Road. The little girl and her doll carriage were gone.

"Good-bye, Katie." Jury left the room.

The pretty nurse, in a vexed tone, said to him, "You've got a telephone call, Superintendent." It seemed to make her cross, the notion that police were not only tramping through her corridors but receiving calls from dangerous places beyond the fastness of the hospital walls.

II

"It's in King's Cross, sir," said Wiggins, who had called Jury to tell him he'd found the Smart Girls Secretarial Service. "And you'll never guess what I found out." Wiggins paused as if he were, indeed, waiting for Jury to guess. "Miss Teague—she's the one who runs it—went back through her files to check on Cora Binns's jobs. It seems the last job was arranged, not by Lady Kennington, but by Mainwaring."

"Mainwaring?"

"That's right. And checking back, Miss Teague found he'd used Cora Binns before."

"Did he specifically ask for Cora Binns?"

"She doesn't know. The call was taken by one of the girls. She's supposed to be on sick leave, but Miss Teague doesn't think she's sick at all. Thinks she's gone off with the boyfriend. Bunny Sweet, her name is."

"See if you can find her. Get some help from 'H' Division. But let's not tell Miss Teague *where* we find her. With a name like Bunny Sweet, I'd say the girl's got enough on her platter."

THIRTEEN

I

"Cora Binns?"

Freddie Mainwaring looked extremely puzzled that Scotland Yard should put the question to him.

"The woman in the Horndean wood, Mr. Mainwaring."

"Was that her name? No, I don't—didn't know any Cora Binns. I've already told that Inspector Carstairs I didn't know her."

"Inspector Carstairs didn't know her name when he talked with you. A couple of months ago you engaged the services of Cora Binns as a shorthand-typist." Mainwaring didn't respond, apparently waiting for Jury to go on. "You called the Smart Girls Secretarial Service and asked for a typist to go to Stonington."

"You're not telling me . . . ?" When it became all too evident that that was what Jury *was* telling him, he said, "I think I'll have a drink."

As Mainwaring unstoppered the whiskey decanter, Jury said, "You didn't recognize her from the picture Carstairs showed you?"

Freddie Mainwaring thrust the stopper back into the decanter, rather careless of its cut-glass elegance, and turned to glare at Jury. "No. Of course I didn't or I'd have said so, wouldn't I?" That the question was not rhetorical didn't seem to occur to him. "For God's sakes, I only must have used her the one time and that was months ago. They all look alike, anyway, don't they? She wasn't important."

Typists being beneath one's notice, presumably. "She was to someone."

Mainwaring flushed and sank into the rich, brocade sofa. He lived in a renovated Tudor house at the other end of the High Street from Rookswood. "All right. So I rang up that agency—"

"The Smart Girls Secretarial Service—"

"Silly bloody name. I rang them up and made the arrangements. It was merely a favor to Lady Kennington. When I was at Stonington one day, going over the details of the property, she said she needed someone to help clear up her late husband's paperwork. I don't know what it was. Debts, most likely. I take it you've heard about the theft of that necklace of Lord Kennington. That and a few other pieces. Lady Kennington would be a rich woman if she had that lot. The necklace is still going missing, isn't it?"

"Lady Kennington is hard up; is that why she's selling?"

"I expect so."

"What time did you tell Cora Binns to appear for the appointment?"

"Look, *I* didn't tell this Binns person *anything*. I talked to some woman at the agency—wait a minute. They asked me who I'd had in the past and I said I couldn't remember the name." He relaxed a bit, pleased with himself. "There you are, Superintendent; just you contact that agency and talk to whoever it was took the call. That should certainly prove this was nothing more than coincidence."

"We have done. The girl's on holiday at the moment."

Frustrated again, Mainwaring said, "Well, why in hell would this Binns person have been going to Stonington through the Horndean wood?"

"What directions did you give the agency?"

"To take the train to Hertfield. And for them to advance her five pounds for a cab and Lady Kennington would make good."

"Cora Binns didn't take a cab. She took the Littlebourne–Horndean bus. She got off in Littlebourne."

"Well, I don't know anything about that, do I?" His face was suffused with blood.

"Your wife's away, Mr. Mainwaring?" asked Jury, suddenly changing the subject.

It unnerved him even more. His drink stopped halfway to his lips. "Away, yes. Visiting her mother." The relationship obviously didn't sit well with the husband.

"These anonymous letters—you have any ideas about that?"

He almost laughed as he said, "I told your sergeant, no. They're all rubbish, of course."

"You seem very sure. Why? I mean, you might be sure in your own case, but as to, for instance, Dr. Riddley or Ramona Wey?"

Mainwaring didn't like that coupling, that was clear. "That's absurd."

"You'd vouch for the character of each?"

"I certainly—"

What he'd do was interrupted by the rather plummy tones of the door chime, dropping its mellifluous treble into the dark hallway. Mainwaring looked toward the door, rather nervously. "Excuse me, will you?"

It was a woman's voice that came to Jury from the hall, first in normal and then in hushed tones.

II

Ramona Wey held out a hand to Jury which was marble-white and marble-cold. She was wearing a very short black velvet cape over a white wool dress and a fall of jet beads. With that white skin and black helmet of hair, Jury imagined Ramona Wey went in for that black-and-white ensemble rather often. She was a woman, clearly, who strove for dramatic effects; she was trying to have one on Jury right now, and not realizing, as she looked him over carefully, that she was failing. Except, perhaps, for the one effect, probably induced by Jury's memory of Katie O'Brien, lying like the princess beneath the glass bell. Looking at Ramona Wey, he could only think of the queen and the poisoned apple.

Despite the presence of Scotland Yard, she seemed to feel right at home. She knew where the cigarettes were and the drinks cabinet and did not bother waiting to be offered either. Jury inferred it was an announcement of proprietorial rights. When she had supplied herself with cigarette and whiskey, she sank into a comfortable chair by the fire.

"I'm glad you stopped by, Miss Wey," said Jury. Mainwaring wasn't, that was clear. He obviously realized how her making free with the house would look to police. "You have an antiques shop in Hertfield, I understand."

"Yes. The Jewel Box. I deal most exclusively in antique jewelry and semiprecious stones. You're here about this murder, I expect?"

"You didn't know the woman?"

"Of course not. I told that inspector from Hertfield everything I did know — which was nothing. I supposed she was some stranger, passing through."

"Funny sort of place to pass through, that wood." Jury waited, but Ramona Wey made no further contribution to Jury's speculations; she simply moved her shoulders in a vague sort of way. "Cora Binns was her name."

"Really?" The tone was flat and rather bored.

Such indifference to a bloody murder on her doorstep could only be studied.

"You're one of the people who got an anonymous letter —"

"Yes. They were all rubbish, of course."

"You were seen as having a liaison with both Dr. Riddley and Mr. Mainwaring."

She laughed. "Obviously, whoever wrote them wasn't very observant."

Mainwaring must have picked up a hint of something to come. "Ramona —" He was trying to check her, but failing.

"Oh, don't be silly, Freddie. All the superintendent has to do is check with Stella."

Mainwaring returned to his gloomy contemplation of the fire.

She looked at Jury, waiting for him to ask. He didn't; she was, obviously, only too eager to tell him. "Freddie and Stella are divorcing. That's why she's gone to her mother's. We're planning on marrying."

"Don't stand there looking so ashen, darling," said Ramona Wey to Mainwaring. "It'd have to come out soon, anyway.

Besides, it does give us an alibi, doesn't it?" She smiled archly, looking at Jury. "All that 'where were you on the fatal night' stuff the inspector was asking. Well, we were together, weren't we? He seemed to think that woman's getting murdered had something to do with these poison pen letters. Do you?"

"Indirectly, yes. How long have you been living in Littlebourne, Miss Wey?"

She considered. "Oh, about a year and a half, I suppose. I was very fortunate; my aunt died and left me a bit of money. So, as I've always been interested in old jewelry, I bought up this little shop. I've done rather well, if I do say it."

"You had dealings with Lord Kennington?" That he would bring this up did seem to surprise her. She reached out her glass to Mainwaring for another drink before she answered. "Yes. He had quite a wonderful collection of jewelry. He bought bits and pieces from me over the months — nothing terribly valuable; I don't deal in things like that emerald necklace that got stolen. I expect you heard about the secretary making off with it?" Jury nodded. "Trevor Tree." She looked off.

Mainwaring handed her drink to her and said, "I didn't know you knew him, Ramona."

"Well, I didn't, not well. He came into the shop once or twice for Kennington. I suppose he was handsome in a common sort of way."

Jury doubted Tree's looks being "common" would really put off Ramona, who had a good touch of it herself. "Did you know him, Mr. Mainwaring?"

"No, no, I didn't. He came into Littlebourne a few times, I heard afterwards. Hung about the Blue Boy with one or two of the regulars. Derek Bodenheim, as a matter of fact, who's no stranger to the place. But I doubt the family knew Tree. Why's all this coming up now?"

"This emerald of Kennington's was quite valuable, I understand." She nodded. "Was it such a large stone, or what?"

"No, not large, relatively speaking. But large for its history and its quality. Maybe six or seven carats, twenty-three or more millimeters, I think. It was Egyptian, you see, and flawless. No defects, no irregularities. It was a saturated, intense green — what they call a 'muzo' green — with a little blue in it. And it was carved. Very old, and very fine. Worth easily a quarter of a million pounds, I'd say."

Jury looked at her. "You seem to have studied it pretty closely."

She returned the look with a cold one of her own. "It *is* my business, isn't it?"

"What sorts of things did he buy from you?"

She thought for a moment. "Several brooches. Mourning pins, mostly. Some rings, several of those over the months. A lapis lazuli bracelet and necklace. Other odds and ends. I can't remember the whole lot. Anyway, what's that to do with all of this other mess?" She smiled at him, her purplish lip rouge glistening black in the firelight. "Shouldn't you be asking us instead, 'Where were you on the night of the murder?'"

Jury smiled. "You've told me that." He looked from one to the other. "Together. Where were you on the Tuesday afternoon, two weeks ago?"

Both Mainwaring and Ramona Wey looked at Jury with surprise. "Whatever happened *then?*" she asked.

FOURTEEN

❧❧❧❧❧❧❧❧

I

JURY looked at his hand, the one which had just shaken Melrose Plant's, and asked, "Why would you cut off the fingers of one hand, Mr. Plant?"

It was nine-thirty in the Bold Blue Boy as Melrose Plant drew his napkin across his lap, and answered, "You've only just arrived, have neither inquired about the menu nor Aunt Agatha, and you're already talking about hacked-off fingers. You certainly do get down to cases, don't you, even when you're two hours late for dinner. Mrs. O'Brien, who seems kindness itself in spite of her troubles, has kept the kitchen open. Molly, our waitress, showed no similar inclination until I crossed her palm with silver. I have taken the liberty of ordering; I hope you don't mind. They do steak and chips, mullet and chips, plaice and chips. An elaborate menu, to be sure, but I was assisted in my choice by Molly, who informed me that they were out of mullet and the plaice had gone off. Thus I plumped for the steak. How are you, Superintendent? Congratulations on your long overdue promotion."

Jury smiled. "Sorry I'm so late. And I'm sorrier yet about the weekend in Northants. My DCS heard I was planning a short holiday and immediately erased all the other names from the frame."

"How *is* Chief Superintendent Racer? Awful, I hope."

"He may not be around much longer. There is growing dissatisfaction on the part of the higher-ups."

"Can't imagine why. Where *is* Molly with our wine?" Melrose craned his neck around at the approach of a heavyset girl with a thick braid and a tray.

Molly had returned with a bottle of wine, which she set, unceremoniously, on the table. "Let's not look at the label," said Melrose, pouring wine into their glasses. "Shall we return to the cut-off fingers? Agatha will be crushed not to have been here. I didn't tell her I was coming, of course. When she finds out, she'll cry all over her fairy cakes. Puts me in mind of the walrus weeping over the oysters just before he devoured them. Now to your question: 'Why would I cut off one hand?' First of all, which hand was it?"

"The left."

"I was thinking, at first, of rigor mortis. That perhaps she was holding something and he couldn't prize the fingers loose. But, then, I gave that up because it would take rigor a while to set in, wouldn't it? And I imagine the murderer would simply have taken it from her. So that doesn't work—"

"On the contrary. There's a thing called cadaveric spasm. Instant rigor. It's not usual, but it has happened at the moment of death, if the death is violent and there's intense emotion. I remember hearing of cases in the war: men still with their rifles aimed. There was one they called the 'tea party'—soldiers in a trench, all caught when the shell exploded, all frozen in the last act of their lives. One had a canteen raised to his lips. There'd be no way of knowing after the real rigor progressed."

"You mean you think she *was* holding something? Something incriminating?"

Jury shook his head. "No, I think she was wearing something incriminating. Something, at least, the murderer didn't want found."

Melrose's next question was interrupted by the approach of Molly bearing down on them, her work-hardened hands apparently impervious to the sizzling platters she carried.

"Steaks up." She deposited the plates and tossed her long braid over her shoulder. "Kitchen's closing, so whatcher want fer afters?"

Melrose snapped his napkin into his lap. "Soufflé Grand Marnier, please."

Molly's expression remained placid as she said, "We only got bread-and-butter pud."

"I'll pass, thank you."

Jury also declined the sweet.

"Suit yerself," she said with a shrug that suggested only the most dim-witted would turn down the pud.

When Molly had shuffled off, Jury said. "Let's back up a moment: for starters—as Molly would say—we've got these anonymous letters. For afters, the murder of Cora Binns. It's the main course I'm especially interested in: Katie O'Brien, together with a chap named Trevor Tree. I don't suppose you remember that story. It didn't make headlines, but it was an interesting little fiddle he worked on one Lord Kennington. As you've been here a whole half a day, you've probably heard of his estate, Stonington—"

"Indeed I have," said Melrose. "I'm buying it, it would seem." Melrose smiled brilliantly. "Well, I had to have *some* reason for hanging about Littlebourne."

"That's resourceful of you. Anyway, this Tree made off with a quarter-million in jewels. A necklace was the chief booty. But over the months he worked for Kennington, it seemed the lord of the manor was missing the odd piece here and there. Nothing of extreme value, some antique stuff. And apparently Tree was such an amiable, trustworthy chap, Kennington never suspected him. Indeed Kennington apparently thought he might have misplaced the stuff himself. I think perhaps Tree was at it to see how much his employer *did* trust him."

Melrose shook his head. "It's all I can do to hold on to my own valuables. My mother's jewelry keeps turning up on Aunt Agatha. She was wearing a moonstone on her finger this morning. God knows how she does it."

"That's what made me finally twig it."

"Agatha's finger?"

"No. Cora Binns's. Ernestine Craigie found the body and, in her words, the dead woman was 'bedizened, beringed and bejeweled.' Cora Binns was wearing a necklace, bracelets, ornate earrings. But no rings. Not on the right hand, at least. The ring, or possibly rings that I think she might have been wearing also might have been part of Kennington's collection. Not the good stuff, but some of the antique jewelry not easily identifiable."

"But why go to all the trouble of murdering the woman if the police wouldn't attach any importance to it?"

"The police wouldn't. But *Lady Kennington* might have. Cora Binns was on her way to an interview. Whoever met up with her somewhere along the way recognized that ring. And certainly might have wondered how much Cora Binns knew."

"What was the woman doing in the woods, though?"

"She was given five quid by her boss at the secretarial agency to take a cab from Hertfield station to Stonington. But she pocketed the money and took a bus. She got off in Littlebourne, apparently thinking Stonington was in walking distance. It's two miles away, though. But if you cut through the woods, it minimizes the distance considerably."

"How would the Binns woman know that?"

"Whoever she asked directions of must have told her."

Melrose, wrestling with the tough steak, finally put by his knife and fork. "And that's the someone who followed her, having, I take it, seen this ring and knowing . . . But wouldn't that mean this person might have been in on the whole theft of the Kennington stuff from the outset?"

Jury nodded. "That necklace has never surfaced. Tree got rid of it somehow and my guess is he let someone know — an accomplice, perhaps — something about where he'd stashed it. That's what I can't figure out. It's been a year since Tree got run down by a car."

"But what's all this to do with the O'Brien girl?"

"Katie was attacked in the Wembley Knotts tube station. Trevor Tree was from that section of the East End and so was Cora Binns. They both frequented a pub called the Anodyne Necklace. Katie went in there a few times with her violin teacher. All of those people coming together under the same roof, even if at different times, could hardly be coincidence. Someone is looking for that emerald; someone wants it very badly — not surprising, considering its value."

Melrose pushed his plate away. "I hope to God you sort all this out before I'm forced to put on my waders and go looking for the beastly Speckled Crackle."

"You've met Miss Craigie, obviously."

"Yes. I really feel on intimate terms with this bird. I'm sure I could pick it out of a police line-up. Frankly, though, were I Ernestine, I don't think I'd feel very comfortable walking round the village with those high-powered binoculars of hers swinging from my neck. A garroting might be in order. And I'll tell you something else. If you think the O'Brien girl might have been attacked because she knew something, there's a little girl who was a good friend of hers who I think is keeping something back from police. . . ."

II

The little girl in question was coming through the doll-like doorway of the private bar, all oblivious of Jury and Plant, directly in her line of vision. Quickly she disappeared behind the bar. Thence ensued a great commotion of glasses rattling and papers rustling. In a moment she reappeared, a box of crayons and a coloring book firmly in hand. These items she pretended to be inspecting closely.

"Isn't it a bit late for you to be up canvassing the public houses? It's nearly ten. Oughtn't you to be home with your mother?"

Turning upon Melrose with an air of abstracted concentration, Emily Louise said, "Oh. It's you." She went back to counting her crayons.

"Surprise, surprise. I said, oughtn't you to be home? Your mum must be very worried."

She was mouthing the names of the colors silently: *blue, yellow, purple*. "Mum's at the pictures in Hertfield."

"That's no reason for you to be doing watchman's duty. But since you're here, why don't you sit down for a bit? Superintendent Jury would like a word with you."

The frown extended from the box of crayons upwards and came to rest on Jury's face. "Who?" She squinted myopically, as if trying to make out something on a far horizon.

"This gentleman seated directly across from me."

All unconscious of the formidable gentleman to whom she was being introduced, Emily Louise grudgingly climbed up on a chair beside him, opened her coloring book, and selected a crayon.

Melrose could not help inspecting the picture. It was another awful scene, this one a barnyard. She was aiming an orange crayon at a duck. He tried to control his annoyance.

"Pleased to meet you," said Jury, holding out his hand. Her small hand lay in his like a cold petal. "I understand you're a friend of Katie O'Brien."

She was going at the mother duck with a vengeance and merely nodded.

"Katie was a pretty good rider, I hear."

"Kind of." Having filled in the duck with orange, she began to color the webbed feet blue. Plant stared at it.

"Nice to have friends," said Jury. "Too bad when something happens to them."

Emily nodded and started coloring the line of ducklings blue, to match the mother's feet.

Jury went on: "Friends sometimes tell us things. . . . I remember when I was a lad, I had this great friend. Jimmy Poole, his name was. We were always together. Jimmy Poole and I used to tell one another secrets, and sometimes we'd even stick pins in our fingers and swear on the blood we'd never tell—"

"Don't talk about blood."

"Okay." Jury lit a cigarette, tossed the match in the ashtray. "Jimmy Poole and I used to go out in the woods and smoke fags and stuff like that, which we weren't supposed to. We did a lot of things we weren't supposed to—"

"Like what?" she asked without looking up from her book. But the crayon had stopped moving.

"Oh, you know. Swimming in water too deep. Staying out after dark. We used to put pillows in our beds to make our mums think we were asleep and then crawl out of our windows. Jimmy Poole was really clever when it came to finding places where no one could find *us*. He left false trails. There was a cave where we liked to go and where we hid stuff we didn't want our mums finding. I remember once I stole a comic from a news agent's." He watched as both Emily Louise and Melrose looked at him in mild astonishment. "Oh, yes, I did things like that. Honesty came to me late in life, I expect. I swore Jimmy Poole to secrecy." Jury looked at Emily. "He didn't tell, so I was safe." He noticed Emily was scrubbing away at the line of ducklings with deep concentration now. "That cave was a good place to get away from our mums."

"Didn't you like them?" Emily had laid down her crayon and was frowning horribly at the book.

"Sometimes, I guess. Sometimes not. We used to have to make up incredible stories to explain where we'd been and what we'd been doing. I mean, if we came home with our clothes muddy or torn we'd have to make up stories."

"Who made up the stories, you or Jimmy Poole?"

Jury considered. "Jimmy Poole. He was smarter."

"Why doesn't he work for Scotland Yard, then?"

"I don't know."

She was looking at him now, hard. "I wish I had a lemon squash."

"I'm sure Mr. Plant would be happy to fetch one."

Melrose, who had been feigning a light doze, opened one eye and said, "I might miss an installment." Sighing, he got up.

"Go on, then," said Emily Louise, prodding Jury's arm.

"Well, Jimmy Poole told me lots of strange things and made me *swear* I'd never breath a word to anyone. But then something happened to someone in the village." Emily Louise had clasped her hands over the top of her head as if she meant to push herself under the table. "This one person had an . . . accident."

Emily slid down in her seat. "A bad one?"

"Pretty bad. She fell downstairs. That is, *maybe* she fell. Some people thought she might have got *pushed* downstairs. We were never sure, though, who did it." Jury studied the coal-end of his cigarette.

"Well, didn't the *police* come?" Emily frowned mightily at Jury, apparently much irritated at this dereliction of duty on the part of England's finest.

"Not the Yard, no."

Emily shook her head sadly, disappointed that Jury's villagers hadn't had the foresight to call in the Yard.

"Of course," said Jury, "they might have done. If only Jimmy Poole had told what he knew."

There was a deep silence on the part of Emily, a silence interrupted only by Melrose's rattling three glasses onto the table. One lemon squash and two brandies. Emily took a sip of her drink and then said, "But he didn't tell."

"No. But I did."

"*You!* But it was a secret!"

"I know. Believe me, I thought about it and thought about it. See, the trouble was Jimmy Poole was sick and I couldn't ask him if it was okay to tell."

"What was wrong with him?"

"Mumps. He couldn't talk, his throat was so bad."

"Did he die?"

"No. But you see, as long as he couldn't talk, *I* couldn't get him to *agree* to letting me tell the secret. I had to decide for myself, and that's what always makes it hard. Deciding for yourself. You know why I finally did?"

Emily shook the head beneath the clasped hands, but kept her eyes riveted on Jury.

"Because I was afraid that someone else might get pushed downstairs. Or maybe even the one that they pushed might get pushed again."

"Didn't she die?"

Jury shook his head. "No."

"That's good. Who did you tell?"

"The rector. He seemed the right sort of person."

"Well, why didn't you tell the constable, then? Didn't your village have one?"

"Yes. Only, I was afraid of police."

"*I'm* not!" Her answer rang out.

"*You're* not, I know."

She rolled her blue crayon back and forth. "Was Jimmy Poole mad at you?"

"No. He was glad. He said he'd have told himself, finally, only he couldn't talk."

"He had mumps." Jury nodded. Emily Louise blew out her cheeks, then poked them with her fingers, one on each side. For a long while the three were silent — Melrose with eyes narrowed to slits, Jury staring out of the casement window, Emily Louise puffing out and collapsing her cheeks. Finally, she said, "Did Jimmy Poole ever give you anything?"

Jury thought for a moment, stubbed out his cigarette and said, "Yes."

Another silence. "Did he tell you not to give it to anyone else?"

"Yes."

"Was it before he got sick?"

"Yes."

"What was it?"

"A tin box."

"What was in the box?"

"Money. Some letters. Some jewelry. A strange message."

"What sort of message?"

Jury shook his head. "I never figured it out."

Now, only Emily's eyes appeared above the table rim, contemplating Jury. Then, suddenly, she jumped up, gathered her crayons and book together, and said, "I've got to *go* now." It was as though she'd suddenly remembered ten previous appointments.

As she disappeared through the doorway, Melrose said, "That was absolutely fascinating—"

Jury interrupted. "Keep an eye on her, will you? You were right, I'm sure. She knows something, all right."

"Well, she'll never tell *me!*" When Jury didn't respond to this, he went on: "She's to do the phaeton rides tomorrow. There's a fête tomorrow, didn't you know?"

Jury shook his head. "First thing I have to do is talk with this Lady Kennington. Right now, I think I'll have a kip. Christ, I'm tired."

"It's all that mucking about with Jimmy Poole."

Jury smiled and yawned as he cranked open the casement window, disturbing the brown-edged climbing roses.

"I seem to remember," said Plant, "that you told me you were born and bred in London. There never was that village, was there? There never was a Jimmy Poole?"

Jury thought of the bluish-cold lights coming on in the Fulham Road, the girl with the doll, the mum with the pram, the boy with the guitar standing in front of the Saracen's Head. The blurred outlines of rose petals drifted by in the dark.

"There's always a Jimmy Poole." He drank off his brandy and said good-night.

FIFTEEN

∽∽∽∽∽∽∽∽∽

As Melrose stood breathing in the heavily scented air of the roses which had escaped Sylvia Bodenheim's ministrations, he heard a shrill yell coming from some point beyond the privet hedge. The stable block was back there, so he cut through the hedge, much to the distress of the gardener who craned his neck to see what this stranger was doing to his topiaries.

Melrose wasn't sure what had woken him at first light, but as he hadn't been able to sleep again — perhaps sharing Jury's unease regarding Emily — he'd got dressed and fiddled around for a bit over a pot of tea and finally made for Rookswood. He knew she would be there, grooming the horses in preparation for the fête.

The voice was definitely hers, and it was now yelling, *Give it back, give it!* The rather unpleasant laugh, in answer to this demand, was male.

As Melrose rounded the stables, he glimpsed the white sweater-sleeve of Derek Bodenheim raised on high and holding a book. Neither Derek nor Emily saw Melrose, as he was standing to the side of the stable door. Anyway, they were too engaged in their game of grabs — although it didn't appear to be a game to Emily.

Derek's back was to Melrose as he stepped forward, raised his silver-knobbed stick, and brought it down smartly, catching Derek just in the crook of the arm. "Really, old chap. She asked you nicely, now, didn't she?"

"What the bloody hell — ?" said Derek, rubbing his arm and glaring at Melrose.

Emily had moved swiftly to collect her book. Her face was very red with all of the exertion.

"Stupid," said Derek to her. Then he turned his temper on Melrose. "You oughtn't to go about hitting people with that stick on their own property, you know. What are you doing here, anyway?"

Melrose didn't bother answering. He was very curious about the sort of man who could possibly get pleasure out of teasing a ten-year-old. "Why don't you just run along, there's a good lad."

"Run along! Who the hell do you think you're talking to?" Then he turned to Emily: "I'll tell your mother, see if I don't, you've been reading dirty books."

"Go away! It's not dirty. I never read it anyhow."

Derek, furious, crunched across the gravel of the stableyard.

Emily looked from the silver-knobbed stick to Melrose. "Did you ever kill anyone?" She seemed hopeful.

"Only in the Foreign Legion. What the devil was that all about?"

Holding the book firmly under her arm, she went about retrieving her pitchfork. "He's horrid." She then dragged pitchfork and book into the stable where stood a magnificent golden horse, apparently being made ready for the carriage rides.

Melrose sat down on a convenient bale of hay and lit up a small cigar. "Is he always like that?" He wondered what the book was and why she seemed intent on keeping it so near her person.

"Yes." Now she was stamping out of the stable block over to the bins of feed. Half of her disappeared into one of them, and the remainder of her speech about Derek's horridness was lost in the echoing bin. As she got out the bucket of feed and once more entered the stable, she said, "All boys are horrid."

"Oh, I don't know. They can be rather fun. After all, they grow up to be people like me."

Her eyes appeared over the stable door to regard him with distaste.

"Did Katie O'Brien have a particular boyfriend?"

"I don't see why we have to talk about boys. It's stupid." She tramped out of the stable and back to the barrels. The one she was drooping over now was so large that she had to drape herself over its rim to reach what was left of the oats at the bottom.

"Look here, do you want some help?"

"No." Her legs dangled down, toes missing the ground.

"Derek Bodenheim acts very strange for a young man of twenty-odd." Back with another bucket, she went into Shandy's stall, making a retching noise in her throat at the mention of Derek. "Do you think he's quite right in the head?"

"No. He was horrid to Katie, too. She hated him."

"Did he tease her, too?" Melrose's interest quickened.

"*You* know. Sneaking up on her and grabbing her and trying to kiss her." Small shudder as she raised a forkful of hay to Shandy's hayrack. "She said he had a wet mouth. . . . I'd rather not talk about it."

There was a lengthy silence, broken only by the scrape of the pitchfork. But Melrose sensed she was interested, although she didn't want to admit it. He knew she was hiding something that had to do with that book. "Let's pretend something."

No answer came from the occupants of the stable except for the sound of the pony chewing.

"Let's pretend we live in a magnificent country — a kingdom, say. Full of green fields and amethyst skies." That made him uncomfortable; how had amethyst got into it? "And you are a beautiful princess." He noticed the sound of the scraping pitchfork had stopped. "And I—" Oh, heavens, what should he be? Why hadn't he thought this through? Something unattractive, he knew, to make the story more acceptable to her. "*I* am a stupid, ugly, nasty gnome."

A velvet cap and eyes appeared over the stable door. Behind her, her pony chewed its fodder, unmindful of princesses and gnomes.

"Indeed, I'm a perfectly *horrid* dwarf who's always going about the kingdom doing mischief. I pinch cakes and tarts and muffins straight out from under the nose of Cook. I am so small — and ugly, of course — they hardly know I'm around." He paused to reflect and to relight his cigar. "Now, *you* are the gorgeous princess of this kingdom of, ah, Nonesuch." Warming to his tale,

Melrose started pacing the small enclosure. "Your gowns are magnificent. One of them is a violet color, studded all over with amethysts." Melrose flicked her a glance to see if she was attending closely to this baroque and colorful tale. She was. "The dwarf—that's me—is very conceited. I have a brother who is even a worse gnome than *I*—" Did that sudden snort come from Emily Louise or the pony? "*He* is even more conceited; he thinks, despite his silly behavior and evil, horrid ways, he is a handsome gnome. Even though he's no higher than a table leg and his head is flat and his cheeks stick out—"

"Maybe he's got mumps."

Melrose stopped pacing, annoyed. "Gnomes don't fall prey to human diseases. They've got their own. He's—"

"Like what?"

"Never mind. He's not sick; he's just—horrid." Now she'd made him lose the thread. He was working Derek in. Ah, yes, vanity. "So because he was so vain and because his mum and dad would let him do anything . . . did I mention his family? His family—mum, dad, and sister—all perfectly *awful*. They treated the other villagers—subjects, I mean—as if they didn't amount to a hill of beans. So one day this horrid gnome went straightaway to the palace stables where the princess was walking to and fro in her jewel-studded gown and *reading a book*." He looked at her. She stared back. "And he sneaked up behind the princess and grabbed her and tried to kiss her." She obviously didn't like that part of gnome behavior. Her expression was fierce. Melrose rushed on. "He was trying to find out what was in the book, the stupid, clumsy lout. But it was a royal secret, and the princess didn't want him to know. He was a spy, she decided. So you know what she did?"

She stared at him blankly.

"She went to the royal guard!" That was a clever way of bringing in the police, thought Melrose, pleased with himself.

"Is Jimmy Poole going to be in this story?"

"Jimmy Poole? Of course not. What the devil's *he* got to do with it?"

The small face disappeared from over the rim of the stall door and he heard the pitchfork again.

What was the matter with her? It was a whale of a good story. "You see, the gnome—"

"I don't wear dresses and I don't kiss gnomes."

"Well, I haven't got to the end. You'll *love* the end." What *was* the end?

"I don't want to hear it. It's a stupid story."

Oh, devil take her. He might just as well be direct. "What was that book Derek was trying to get away from you, and why'd he call it 'dirty'?"

Brief silence. "Because it's about men and women."

"That takes care of ninety-nine percent of the world's literature. Anyway, why do *you* want to read it? Since you don't kiss gnomes."

"I'm *not* reading it. I'm giving it to that Scotland Yard person."

As if, he thought, the name Jury weren't engraved permanently on her heart.

"Superintendent Jury said he was going to Stonington. When you've finished with the horses, why don't we go along to the Blue Boy? With your book. I'm sure, though it's barely nine, there's always a lemon squash about." Two could play at this game, though he suddenly realized he was playing it wrong. He'd have to get the book *before* she held him up for drinks and crisps. "As a matter of fact, I think you ought to give it me now, and then we'll go along to the Blue Boy."

She was stroking the mane of the golden horse, stalling for time. There was an incongruous blue ribbon on its mane, which she undid and flung to the ground. "I'm not giving rides if it's got to wear *that*." She hazarded a glance at Melrose and, seeing him adamant, said, "Oh, *all right!*" She stomped over and dropped the book in his lap.

It was, he realized, a burden she was only too happy to palm off on someone else. "It's Katie's," she said.

"Katie O'Brien's book? What's all the secrecy about?"

"I don't know. She told me to get it out of her room in case anything happened."

"Was she expecting something to happen?"

Emily shrugged and looked over his shoulder at the book.

It was covered with a piece of white graph paper on which the word *GEOMETRY* had been printed, angling down the front. He removed the cover and saw it was a standard, neo-Gothic bosom-ripper, titled *Love's Wanton Ways*. "Was she hiding this from her mother?"

Obviously thinking Melrose quite dim, Emily said, "It's not the *book*, it's the cover." She took it from him, unfolded the homemade cover and held it up. "See. It's a kind of map."

It was a very strange sort of map, meticulously drawn in pencil and ink, bearing the legend *THE FOREST OF HORNDEAN*. Thick woodland surrounded a central picture consisting of small figures, a castle down in the right-hand corner, and numerous trails and roads. There were bear's tracks, a footpath, a grotto, a trail left by a giant snail. All of these were partially enclosed by a moat and a yellow brick road.

The Church of St. Pancras sat above a small bridge.

And running right through the center of everything was the River of Blood.

THE FOREST OF HORNDEAN

THE KINGS ROAD

TRAIL OF THE SILVER SNAKE

TRAIL OF THE BLACK BEAR

ST PANCRAS CHURCH

THE BLUE GROTTO

RIVER OF BLOOD

ANODYNE NECKLACE

THE YELLOW BRICK ROAD

YE OLDE MOATE

THE FOREST OF HORNDEAN

SIXTEEN

∞∞∞∞∞∞∞

I

THE woman who ran out of the front door of Stonington just as Jury stopped his car in the circular drive was carrying something wrapped up in a blanket. As he crunched up the gravel toward her, she called to him, "Would you please go with me to the vet's? I can't drive and carry the cat, too."

Drooping out of one end of the blanket was a black, wedge-shaped face, a tiny ribbon of blood matting the fur between nose and mouth.

"Sure, only let's use my car. You hold the cat and I'll drive."

She was silent as he held the door for her. He backed up and started down the long gravel drive, passing a squat gatehouse on his right. When they got to the Horndean Road, he said, "Which way?"

"Left. Toward Horndean." She turned her head then to look out of her window, cutting off conversation. A square of paisley lawn tied at the base of her neck held back her oak-colored hair. He knew Lady Kennington had few servants—just a gardener and a cook. This was certainly neither, so it must be the lady herself. Jury was disoriented. He had got a picture firmly fixed in his mind of an imperious, elderly woman, perhaps thin and gray-haired, wearing a dress of lavender silk adorned by a cameo. The reality was substantially different.

"What's the matter with the cat?"

"I don't know. I think it was hit by a car, but I don't know. I saw it running up the drive an hour ago and didn't think anything was wrong." She looked out of her window, rather than at Jury, as she said this.

He turned to peer at the cat, which looked back, glassy-eyed, and made a sort of weak sound, as if it and Jury shared some secret knowledge of what happens to cats in this condition. The speculations of the woman beside him were probably just as sad.

"It's another mile or so," she said, her attention still riveted on the misty-morning fields and hedges that flew by. He could not see the face now, only that square of Liberty lawn, but what he had seen he thought to be a fine face. Pale, green-eyed, intelligent. The last word he would have used to describe her was Sylvia Bodenheim's word—"drab."

"This cat feels cold." Her hand had slid inside the blanket. "I bet it's dying." She sounded utterly forlorn.

"That's only because of shock. The temperature drops a little." Jury had no idea how cats reacted to shock, only people. He looked at the cat's eyes, now closed. "It's just sleeping." Actually, it looked dead.

She did not reply. Even the air that moved between them seemed abject. He felt he was letting her down, her and her cat. It was irrational. She was just one of those people who could make you feel guilty without even trying to.

"Is that your favorite cat?" What a stupid question. He cursed himself as he negotiated a sharp curve that seemed to have flown toward the car from nowhere.

"No. It's just an old cat that wandered onto the grounds one day."

Jury looked again out of the corner of his eye, furtively, almost as if the look might kill the cat. The head hung limp as a shot gamebird. He resisted the strong impulse to poke the cat to see if it was alive.

In her voice was a note of defiance as she added, "I don't even like this cat."

"Of course."

Quickly she looked at him and just as quickly looked back through her window. "Oh, just shut up and drive."

*

148

He had offered to go in with her. He felt she needed, if nothing else, the moral support; but she had asked him only if he would mind waiting. She had still not bothered to introduce herself or ask him who he was.

Finally, he had got out of the car and walked aimlessly about in the damp of the barnyard. The veterinarian's surgery was in a tiny cream-washed building on what appeared to be part of a large farm. Jury leaned against the fence and looked at the distant line of ash and oak, which marked this side of the Horndean wood, disliking the idea of asking her all of those questions.

It wasn't more than fifteen or twenty minutes before she emerged, looking even sadder, but it seemed an age. "It's got a broken jaw, a compound fracture, and its pelvis is dislocated, or something. Can you ever understand them? It's going to be awfully expensive. A hundred or more pounds it could run to, he said, and then he kept saying it was my decision." Standing beside him at the fence, she gazed off into the distance at the sheep and the cows this side of the line of trees. She frowned, as if they might be called on to explain this matter to her, as if the entire animal world had let her down.

"Well, you could have it—put down. Wasn't that what the vet was implying?"

"He made me think *he* wanted to save the cat."

"But it's your cat. What's its name?"

"Tom or something. And it's not 'mine' in that sense." She still did not look at him; it was as though she were disappointed or angry with him, as she might have been at a relative who'd gone off and left her and only just turned up on her doorstep with no excuse and no explanation for his erratic behavior. "It's not mine in the sense I should decide it can die. Especially since I don't like it. That makes it worse. You see—" And now she did turn to look him squarely in the eye, as if it were important he should understand this theoretical point. "You see, you can't go killing things off just because you don't like them." Her tone was instructive, as if Jury were the type who might go carelessly disposing of whatever he didn't like.

They were back in the car now, splashing through standing

pools collected in the ruts of the dirt road. He turned to look at her again, and again saw only the scarf with the light hair curling beneath its edges as she faced determinedly away from him. She seemed only to want to commune with the hedgerows and fields, and her voice was as misty as the fields as she said, "I don't even like that cat."

Jury made no comment.

II

Stonington's square, gray facade reminded Jury of a prison. Its stark front was broken only by monotonous oblongs of leaded glass, which managed to give the impression of windows narrowly barred. It struck him as rigorously medieval. The wide steps were flanked by an urn on either side, empty. An untidy row of trees lined the drive. From what he could see, there were no ornamental gardens, no sculptured lawns, nothing to break the monotony. And no sign of life, animal or otherwise. Directly across the road was the Horndean wood, dark, thick, and impenetrable.

They had, on the ride back, introduced themselves. She did not seem unduly concerned about his position; once inside the house she hung his coat on a brass coatrack with some care, shaking beads of water from it. The light drizzle had stopped, finally. It was very cold in the enormous entry-room of the house, which struck Jury as almost cloisterlike, with its stuccoed walls and small embrasures for statuary.

"I should have lit a fire," she said, looking at the cold hearth. "But it's not so bad once you're out of the hall." Her tone was apologetic, as if the cold of the day were her personal responsibility, something from which she should protect visitors. She led Jury into a much smaller room, but only a few degrees warmer, where the fireplace looked as unused as in the entry room. This room was all cold leather and floor-to-ceiling bookcases. There wasn't a piece of furniture here that looked comfortable. Weak sunlight spread through the panes, sickly, like a promise of winter. Beyond the window was a sort of cloistered courtyard or piazza, surrounded by the outer walls of the house. It surprised

Jury, somehow: the look of the prison gave way to the look of the abbey, even to the colonnaded walks on either side of the courtyard. He almost expected to see abbés or nuns prayerfully walking there. The center of this court was dominated by a large, dry pool and a statue of a cloaked woman, head bent. It was not a very good piece of statuary, but in its surroundings, it was affecting.

"Do you mind if we talk somewhere else?" asked Lady Kennington. "I've always hated this room."

The "somewhere else" was an even smaller room with a French window at one end through which he caught another glimpse of the statue from a different angle. Here, a fire had been lit. The room was bare except for some packing cases in one corner and a chintz-covered chair draped with a shawl. Beside the chair, sitting on the floor, was a teacup.

"I was sitting in here when I saw the cat." She gestured toward the window on the other side.

Jury was looking at the blank places on the walls where pictures had clearly hung.

"I just had Sotheby's in to take the furniture. Except for the chair, which they didn't want. You've come about that woman they found in the wood, haven't you?" Jury nodded, and she looked at him mutely before she turned away as if trying to divine the answer to a difficult puzzle set for her. She dragged the square of paisley from her head and ran her hand, like a comb, through her hair. "I think she was coming here to see me."

"Didn't you wonder when she didn't turn up?"

"Yes, of course. But I supposed that you just can't depend on people ... well, you know. I rang up the agency Friday, finally. The woman in charge there was surprised, but, again ... she just put it down to irresponsibility on the girl's part. Apologized profusely and offered to send someone else. I told her not to bother, what I wanted done wasn't all that pressing. I'd call her later. ..." Her voice trailed off as she shook her head in wonder.

"When did you hear about the murder?"

"Not until early this morning, really. I was out last night. I went to the pictures in Hertfield and when I finally got back I found a message from Annie — she's my cook — to call Hertfield police straightaway. I guess I was expecting some sort of police car; I guess you think it's pretty odd getting into that state about a cat, after there's been a murder." She'd moved over to the French window and what little sunlight there was bathed her loose, gray sweater so that it glinted like metal. "I really didn't connect you with the police. Sorry."

"No need to apologize. And, no, I don't think it was odd — about the cat, I mean." Jury felt it had all happened, that ride to the veterinarian's, a year ago, rather than only fifteen minutes. "Mr. Mainwaring says he arranged for this girl to come here."

"Yes. Freddie was doing me a favor. He said he'd used the agency and they seemed good. Listen, won't you sit down?" Vaguely, she indicated the single chair.

"That's okay. Sit down yourself." She shook her head and shoved up her sweater sleeve. "Wouldn't it have been easier just to get someone local to do the secretarial work?"

"Yes, certainly. I couldn't find anyone. And Freddie said this place was quite reasonable."

She seemed on good terms with Freddie. "Did Mr. Mainwaring seem, well, to be pushing this idea?"

"'Pushing—'? I don't know what you mean." But she was quick enough to figure out what he meant. "Are you suggesting that Freddie Mainwaring knew the girl in some other way?"

"It's possible."

She looked at him, considering. As the sunlight died, her gray eyes darkened. "You seem to be saying he had something to do with her death."

"It's a coincidence, at the very least."

Smiling slightly, she shook her head. "I seriously doubt he was involved. Freddie's much too shrewd to go about murdering women. I'm sure he'd get what he wanted more easily than that."

"As with Ramona Wey, for instance?" She merely cocked her head at that and made no comment. "Your late husband had some business dealings with her." She nodded. "Antique jewelry." She nodded again, giving him the awfully uncomfortable impression she was looking straight into his mind. "Lady Kennington, I'd really like to get some information about the theft of that emerald necklace a year ago."

That did seem to surprise her. "What's that got to do with it?"

"Trevor Tree, you remember, was run down by a car after he was released by police. That necklace has never turned up. And it must be somewhere."

Her hand went to her throat as if the mention of it had triggered some tactile response. "Yes, I suppose it does. John was extravagant about jewelry. It was some sort of obsession with him. Stonington was mortgaged up to the hilt to indulge it. You'd think he'd have been wise enough to insure that necklace, after all that, wouldn't you? But he said insurance for jewelry cost the earth. Can you imagine such reasoning? You know, I think John — my husband — had a sort of gambler's nature. Self-destructive."

"So you have to sell up in order to pay for that. You don't seem very bitter about it."

She seemed puzzled, as if bitterness had nothing to do with it, as if it were an alien emotion. "I'd have sold up, anyway. I should have done, a long time ago." She looked off. "I've never much liked jewelry, myself."

The woman, he thought, was a master of understatement; she made that emerald sound like something from Woolworth's. "It was a very rare sort of emerald, I understand. Egyptian?"

"Yes. John was especially interested in Egyptology. It was a carved stone. It was carved with a crow, and beneath that what appeared to be a crab, or something. The carvings were supposed to ward off 'disturbance, dreams, and stupidity.'" Her smile was fleeting. "It didn't. I'm no smarter than before. And my dreams"—she clasped her hands behind her and looked off— "are just as bad.'

"And the case Lord Kennington kept this jewelry in? Has that been sold too?"

"No. It's in the next room." Once again he followed her to a door on the other side of the room.

The immensity of this next room gave Jury a shock, both its size and its emptiness. Here, the furniture was also gone. At one end of the room—dining room, it must have been once—was a phalanx of French windows facing the courtyard, showing once again the mournful statue in different terms. They were now in another wing of the house, the one he had seen before with a walk screened by tall columns. He felt as though he were seeing the statue through round bars. There was nothing in the room except for heavy green drapes at the windows and a glass-topped display case shoved into a corner by the marble fireplace. This strange circumnavigation of the house — with only that stone statue as some sort of compass point — disoriented Jury. As he bent down over the display case, empty now, he asked, "Did you like Trevor Tree?" He looked up at her.

"I didn't mind him, I suppose. I wasn't that often around him. We were not on intimate terms." There was a flicker of temper — or was it really humor? — in response to his unasked question.

"What happened that night, Lady Kennington?"

Again, that fleeting smile. "I'd rather not be called that, really. Just Jenny Kennington. John kept the family name, said it was much easier. He was a very sensible man in some ways. I don't think I did very well as a Lady."

Jury looked at her for a moment. "I imagine you did fine. Tell me about the night the necklace was stolen."

She told him exactly the same story Carstairs had. "Of course, when we found Trevor had gone, we knew. And we wouldn't have known so soon if our cook hadn't got up so early."

"I see. There were a few other pieces of jewelry that had gone missing over the time Trevor Tree worked for your husband — apparently also taken by him. Would you remember them if you saw them again?"

"Oh, yes. There was a cameo brooch. It was unusual and quite beautiful. Then there was a small diamond, in what they call a European cut. Not a brilliant and not really valuable. And a gold ring, coiled like a serpent. I liked it." Quickly, she looked up at him. "You're not going to tell me you've found those things, are you?"

Jury shook his head. "No, but I think possibly Cora Binns knew Trevor Tree. I even think she might have been wearing a ring — perhaps the one you described — taken from Lord Kennington's collection. Maybe he took the stuff just to see how much he could get away with. What sort of person was he, from your point of view?"

"Terribly shrewd. But that's rather obvious, the way he had the whole thing planned out."

"How did your husband meet him?"

"At Sotheby's. Or was it Christie's? John had dealings with both. That's probably how Trevor knew about this emerald. John was looking for a secretary and this Tree was recommended as very reliable. He was an employee at one of those places. Of course, he was very knowledgeable. Had to be, didn't he? John trusted him." She shrugged. "Maybe it was the gambler's instinct coming out again. Why should he have trusted him? I thought Trevor was too shrewd by half, frankly."

The sun had come out again and shown in wide bands across the polished floor like light on water. He could see her eyes were silvery, even though they were standing a great distance apart, he by the case, she by the windows. She pulled the long sleeves of her sweater down, the metallic thread in the loose knit glinting like chain mail. "I'm awfully cold," she said. "I'd like a cup of tea. Would you?"

"I wouldn't mind," he said.

"I'll just get it then." She walked across the expanse of oak floor and through a door at the far end. It closed behind her.

He missed her the moment she walked out of the room.

SEVENTEEN

∞∞∞∞∞∞∞

"WHY are you making that dog purple?"

"Because I like purple." Emily Louise did not look up from her coloring book.

The Bold Blue Boy was empty, save for Melrose and Emily Louise, which was not surprising, as it was barely nine o'clock.

Looking at the bizarre colors in her farmyard scene, and from there to the map, Melrose was reminded of Miss Craigie's dreadful slide-show presentation. Something rankled. He felt he should be able to dredge it up from his unconscious.

"Do you know the Misses Craigie?"

"Yes. Ernestine's the one that's always doing boring things with birds. She goes into the woods with those binoculars and stands about." Intent upon coloring a gaggle of geese pink, she wetted the crayon with her tongue.

"Don't chew on crayons. You'll get Crayola poisoning." Melrose looked down at the map, smoothed out on the table before him. All of those lines running and crisscrossing. Lord, would he be forced to ask Ernestine for a repeat performance of the migratory patterns of the Crackle? Wasn't there just so much the human organism could stand in the pursuit of clues? His eyes slid over to Emily's coloring book. Unable to stop himself, he said, "Those geese are pink."

"Yes. They're quite *lovely*." She fluted this, throwing down her crayon and holding up her artwork. A barnyard scene of rainbow animals. Except, Melrose noted, for the horse. The horse was good old horsey-brown. This irritated him almost beyond endurance. "All of the *other* animals are totally ridiculous colors and the horse is brown."

"Of course it's brown. Horses *are* brown, some of them. Anyway, it's supposed to be Shandy."

He refused to discuss it. "Might I have a piece of paper from that book?"

She stopped in the process of outlining a crow she had left out. It was going to be lemon yellow. Suspiciously, she looked at Melrose. "Well . . ." She leafed through her book, came upon a picture of a Cinderella-like young lady about to have her tiny foot shoved into a glass slipper by a young man with a page-boy. "Here. You can color this one if you want. I don't like it, anyway."

"Color? I don't want to *color*, for heaven's sake. I want the *back* to draw some lines on."

"You mean tear it *out?*" Sacrilege.

"I'll buy you another book!"

She looked down at the prince holding the foot and back at Melrose. "All right. He looks stupid, anyway." Carefully she folded, creased, and tore the page from her book.

"Thank you," said Melrose frostily. He then took a red crayon and drew a line across the back of the picture. This he crossed at an angle with a blue crayon.

Emily was interested. "What are you doing?"

"The migratory patterns of the Great Speckled Crackle."

Forgetting her lemon crow, she clamped her chin between her hands and watched as Melrose bisected the red line with a green one, swooping upwards. In a moment lines were going every which way. "That's not it," he said.

"It looks stupid."

"Don't fight kiddies."

It was Jury's voice behind them.

"Make him get his own coloring book," said Jury, who sat down beside Emily and immediately had her undivided attention. "What've you got there?" Jury slid Melrose's brightly lined paper across the table. "Influence of Jackson Pollock, I'd say."

Emily shoved her barnyard scene in his face. "Isn't this nice?"

"Very nice. I had a purple dog once."

Wonder glowed on Emily's face. "You *did?*"

"It wasn't born purple, of course. But one day in the alley it liked to ramble in, someone had set out some tins of paint. My dog was always into things and he got it all over him. There was some green in one can, and that overturned and splattered him. Just on the tips of some of the hairs."

"He sounds lovely. Did he die from it?"

"No. But I could never get it out."

"When he did die, was he still purple and green?"

"Yes. Faded, but still rather colorful."

She had picked up a green crayon and was putting spots all over the purple dog.

Melrose shoved the map from Katie O'Brien's book toward Jury, frustrated that the answer he'd been hoping for hadn't flashed into his mind, dazzling him with its brilliance, like sun on the wings of gulls . . . there he was, back with the ornithological metaphors.

Jury studied the map for a few seconds, his face blank. "Where'd you get this?"

Emily told him about Katie.

"In case anything happens? That's what she said?"

Emily nodded and started to gather up her crayons and book. "I've got to be to the fête at ten-thirty." It was clear that, once having delivered her secret to the Yard, she wanted no more to do with it.

But Jury had hold of her wrist. "Is that *all* she told you?" Emily nodded. "Didn't you think it very strange?" Again, Emily nodded, her brow creased as she looked at Melrose, as if it were all his fault. Jury went on: "She didn't mention anything about London or her music teacher? Or a game called Wizards?"

"Once she did, but not then."

"Once she did what?" asked Jury, patiently. But he was not letting go of her wrist.

"Wizards. She said it was a game she saw in London and it seemed ever so much fun."

"Didn't she tell you anything else? About the pub in London where she saw it?"

Emily shook her head hard. Her little look was now piteous,

and as contrived, Jury thought, as the frown. "Please, I've got to go see to the horses."

Jury released his grip. "Okay. Thanks."

In the light of Jury's smile she now seemed somewhat ambivalent about leaving. There was some scuffling of feet before she finally made for the low lintel of the door, brushing by Peter Gere, who was stooping under it.

"What's all this 'Wizards' business?" asked Melrose.

Jury put the map in front of him. "This is the sort of map they do for a game—hullo, Peter."

Peter sat down with a sigh. "Thought I saw you come in here. The Bodenheims are driving me daft over this fête. They seem to think I'm at fault just because the carousel broke down. How d'ya do?" he said, when Jury introduced him to Melrose Plant.

"Have a look at this, Peter." Jury put the diagram before him. Gere studied it for a moment, frowned, turned it this way and that, finally said, "What's this in aid of?"

"Katie O'Brien for one thing. And for another, maybe, that necklace stolen from Lord Kennington a year ago."

Peter stared at him, disbelieving. "How?"

"You said you'd seen Trevor Tree and Derek Bodenheim in here a few times playing a game called Wizards." Peter nodded. "Doesn't this make you think of one of those diagrams?"

"It could be, yes. Where'd you find it, then?"

"I didn't. Katie O'Brien did. Whether she found it in London or Littlebourne, I don't know. Tell him, Mr. Plant." Melrose gave Peter Gere an account of that morning's activities.

"Are you really suggesting Tree hid that emerald somewhere in the Horndean wood?"

"I don't know. But it's a bit too much of a coincidence—Katie O'Brien, Cora Binns, Trevor Tree, the Anodyne Necklace—"

"What's the Anodyne Necklace when it's at home?"

"Pub in the East End where Tree was a regular. A place where they play Wizards."

Gere tried to get his pipe going, sucking in his cheeks, finally tossing the matches on the table and dropping the pipe back in his pocket, bowl upwards. "I guess he could have done. It *looks* like somebody meant to draw the Horndean wood. There's the stream, and the church. . . ." He pointed. "But what always puzzled us was how he nicked that emerald in the first place. There wouldn't have been time to get out and secrete it anywhere. And it wasn't on him. I searched the bastard. That could be Spoke Rock, right there." Again he pointed to the map, to the Black Bear's Cave.

"There must have been someone, an accomplice, or at least someone who knew Tree had that emerald."

Peter Gere looked upset at Jury's implicating one of the villagers. "That's eyewash. Although Derek Bodenheim might just be low enough—"

"I don't think it's eyewash, Peter. Katie's in hospital and Cora Binns is dead."

EIGHTEEN

≈≈≈≈≈≈≈≈

I

THE graveyard looked very gay. Balloons had loosened from their moorings in the field beyond to float and bob in the breeze across the old graves. A gentleman in a clerical collar, whom Melrose presumed to be the Reverend Finsbury, was standing with his hands behind his back looking pleased with himself. Sylvia Bodenheim, who had come along a while ago to argue with Emily about the horse, was now arguing with a young man, one of the workers with uprolled shirt-sleeves, about the setting up of the coconut shy.

The fête was scheduled to begin at noon, and Melrose saw off to his left that the fun-seekers were already paying their fifty-pence admittance fee to Sir Miles, who then herded them through the gate with full instructions as to how they were to disport themselves. His other aim was to make sure they did not stray from the public path and onto the adjoining grounds of Rookswood.

Melrose could not actually hear whatever exchanges he was having with those whose fun he sought to spoil even before they started having it; he merely deduced this from the elder Bodenheim's waving about of his walking stick. Still they paid up and were allowed to enter the grounds made more holy by virtue of his standing in them.

Already the spirited cries of what Melrose knew would be entirely too many children were reaching his ears, children who would soon be advancing upon the small plot Emily had staked out for horse and carriage, the side just at the edge of the

Horndean wood. Melrose was here supplying unasked-for (and, she had made it crystal clear, undesired) aid to Emily Louise, who was readying horse and carriage for what Sylvia Bodenheim insisted on calling the "phaeton ride," although it was a closed carriage. Some few minutes had already been given over to haggling between Emily Louise and Sylvia over the loss of the ribbon from the mare's golden mane. Emily denied ever having such a ribbon. After Sylvia beat a retreat up the grass, Emily and Melrose continued their job of decorating the phaeton, Emily losing no opportunity to tell him he was getting all the bows and loops wrong. The carriage was an impressive, if funereal ebony, its high doors outlined in gilt and looped about with golden ribbon. All in all, it was quite a sight, fit for a royal wedding or funeral. The golden ribbon almost matched the elegant horse that had been entrusted into Emily's hands by the farmer whose pride and joy it was.

This had become another sore point. Emily had insisted the horse have its rest periods. She would ride the children round for no longer than twenty minutes at a time, and then horse and phaeton were to be parked here by this stand of ash on the edge of the wood where it could crop grass. All of that the Bodenheims insisted was nonsense: the phaeton ride was the most popular item every year at the fête and the biggest fund-raiser. To have it going only two-thirds of the time meant a loss to church funds.

To appeal to Emily Louise Perk's religious instincts was about as effective as requesting the dead to rise and have a go at the coconut shy. Naturally, she won the day. She always did, so far as Melrose could see. (He wondered how her mother stood her.) No rest, no ride, she had said stoutly. She had them by the throats, and she knew it, for the owner of the horse would allow no one to touch it but Emily Louise.

She had picked out this pleasant, shady spot for the horse and carriage and had managed to erect a sort of crude barricade of logs and boards on which she had hammered a sign: *Nobody Beyond This Point.* Melrose, having finished with his rococo decoration, turned away from her discourse — not one she was holding with him, but with the horse, some tedious longueur about barley and blowflies.

He looked off into the Horndean wood and thought about Ernestine Craigie and her field glasses. Ernestine knew every inch of that wood — every leaf, feather, marsh, pebble in the stream in which the body of Cora Binns had been lying, face down. He wondered about that stream: How far did it go and in what direction? The River of Blood? He frowned.

The trouble with the map, which Jury had taken off to London, was that it made no sense in terms of simple logistics: even in terms of fantastic and imaginary treasure maps there was some sort of sense in the relationship between details. Even the gnome, after all, had some sensible relationship to the princess . . .

. . . who was at that moment glowering at the little line of hopeful kiddies who had lined up to be first for the ride. She would take, she said, only three at a time (though there was easily room for six), for the horse oughtn't to pull any more weight than was necessary. All down the line there were groans and blighted little faces. By now there were at least a dozen children lined up and Emily was collecting tickets as if they were tickets to a funeral. The three allowed through the barrier were quickly admonished for bouncing the carriage as they scrambled up to their seats.

Melrose watched Emily mount up into the driver's seat, look glumly around at the children inside the carriage, and then click her tongue to move the horse out and away.

He bet it would be a short ride.

Melrose leaned against the nearest tree, looking out over the wood where sun slanted through coppery branches. He drew from his pocket the copy of Ernestine Craigie's map. It was crude, concentrating only on vantage points from which the Crackle might be expected to launch its next attack on the Royal Birdwatchers' Society. Here was Coomb Bog, here a specially large rock with an indecipherable name, here a stand of ash and clump of laurel. And, of course, the stream. That cavern Ernestine had marked up toward the top of her map. Possibly the Cave of the Black Bear? He wondered about the bear tracks. Why was the bear going across the moat, the stash of gold, and the grotto? Hell of a gauntlet for a bear to run.

Katie's map ran against reason. The moat seemed to be protecting nothing. No castle, no fortress, only a meeting of river and grotto and bear's track. And the Church of St. Pancras—Melrose turned to look at it, perched on its small hill—overlooking all.

As he stood there thinking about Cora Binns, he saw in the distance a flash of a dark suit disappearing into a clump of trees. One of Carstairs's men. They were going about the business now of searching the wood not only for clues to the murder, but clues provided (or not provided, he was more inclined to think) by the map. If a murder had been done in the Horndean wood and there was a cache of priceless emeralds in that wood, it would not be at all surprising to think the two of them were related. Cora Binns could have been murdered because she was after the same treasure as the murderer. But the circumstances of her coming to Littlebourne did not seem to support that theory. She had been summoned here—hadn't she?—by the prospect of a job. It was hardly likely that the woman had stumbled on this necklace in the bear's cave and got her fingers cut off for her trouble. . . .

There was another figure moving out there. Coming toward him was Peter Gere, wiping his face with a handkerchief. Melrose could see, as Gere got closer, that he was shaking his head as if to say *No luck*.

They shouldn't expect any, thought Melrose. . . . Why did Katie O'Brien's map seem familiar to him? God knows *he* hadn't been out in the Horndean wood in waders and field glasses.

As Peter got within hearing distance, no luck was indeed what he said. "Nothing. No luck at all. God, he" (meaning Jury) "doesn't really think we can turn up every inch of ground and look in every goddamned hole and cave, does he? Does he think that emerald necklace is hanging from a branch, or what?"

"He doesn't know. But if you were Superintendent Jury, wouldn't you have a go at it?"

Reluctantly, Peter agreed. "I'm just an old crock of a village bobby. The most I'm used to doing is hauling Augusta's cats out of trees and trying to find Miss Perky Perk for her mum. God." Peter spat a tiny stream of tobacco juice toward a clump of bracken. "Hell, I don't know. Maybe I'm just jealous Scotland Yard's mucking about in our patch. . . ."

They had to step aside, for the phaeton was returning, hell-for-leather. Emily drove through her homemade barricade to the general displeasure of the three within, whose small faces, one bright red with anger and tears, were popping out of the carriage door demanding more of the ride. Emily looked as if she might gladly grind Melrose and Peter into the dust beneath her wheels, her disgust with her charges being quite palpable.

"*Twice,*" the red-faced one screamed. "You was to take us two times round the grounds and we only went round once." The other two sent up a similar roar of protest and nodded their heads in agreement.

Mums had strayed back from whatever they'd been doing, looking almost as unhappy as the children, but probably only because they'd got them back so soon. Now they'd have to collect the kiddies and be yanked about the churchgrounds in search of other treats.

Emily was out of the driver's seat now and jerking open the carriage door. They were still rabbiting on and refusing to move, so she got hold of the skirt of the fat girl and pulled her stumbling down the single step. "You were rocking the carriage," she said. Melrose waited there with Peter Gere for the rest of the Sermon on the Mount as she helped each roughly from the carriage. The worst of their sins appeared to have been spitballs aimed at the rump of the horse.

The mothers were now getting into it, in a mild way, but they backed off as they observed the Jovian frown of the driver. Nobody argued with Emily Louise Perk, it seemed. The three children were led away in a landslide of tears.

Three others replaced them. Very quietly they marched, single file, to the carriage door.

"Twice around *if* you behave," was the driver's instruction.

The three chastened faces looked at her and nodded angelically before climbing sedately into the carriage. Once more it pulled away.

"Right little monster, isn't she?" said Peter Gere, accepting a cigarette from Melrose's gold case.

"She'd give the Black Bear a good mauling, I'm sure. Did you know this Trevor Tree, Mr. Gere?"

"Not much, except, you might say, in a professional way.

Seemed a right villain to me. Smooth as silk. Well, he'd have to be, wouldn't he, to get Lord Kennington to take him on. Kennington, the little I knew of him, was no fool. Poor sod." Gere sighed. "I made a proper cock-up of that one, didn't I?"

"It wasn't your fault."

"Letting Tree make off with that lot. And now all this—" He nodded in the direction of the wood.

"You seem to be taking an inordinate amount of blame on yourself." Melrose felt some sympathy for the policeman. He regarded Gere as neither especially bright nor especially dense, but the man had more conscience, apparently, than was good for him. Or perhaps it was a sense of protecting, as Gere had said, his "patch."

"I was there, man, straightaway when it happened. *How* could Tree have got rid of that necklace? It's been bothering me ever since." Gere ground the stub of his cigarette with his boot. "I saw him in Littlebourne a couple of times, at the Blue Boy, with Derek Bodenheim, playing that damn-fool game. I often wondered . . . well, no matter." Melrose assumed his wonder was about Derek's connection with all of this. "Trevor Tree was a type, you know. He put me in mind of those card sharks in old American films that sit facing the door so's they won't get pumped in the back."

They stood there for ten minutes, talking and staring into the wood. Melrose wondered if the Horndean wood was just the right metaphor for the whole puzzle. Too dense to see into or through. There were only transitory glimpses of Carstairs's men, and outlines cast by the sun dropping bright coins through the leaves onto a carpet of needles. The colors were thick and dim, figures melting into it. "I don't think you're going to find—"

Melrose's remark was interrupted once again by the arrival of the horse and carriage, more quietly this time. Obviously the three passengers had outdone themselves in hewing to the line set up by the driver. They made their way, wordlessly and uncomplaining, back to their mothers.

Emily Louise jumped down from her seat, checked the inside of the carriage and yelled to the waiting line that it was rest time for the horse and that the rides would commence again in twenty

166

minutes. A general air of mourning hung over the assembled group as she released the horse from the carriage, tethered it to a tree, and said to Melrose, "Time for tea." She jingled some coins in her pocket. Emily had struck a bargain with Mr. Finsbury, allowing her to keep one-quarter of what she earned. She had turned in the ticket stubs, and he had produced the coins. The Bodenheims had been shocked beyond belief.

"Well, back to work," said Peter Gere, moving off through the wood. Coming the other way toward Melrose was Miles Bodenheim, like Moses parting the Red Sea. No wonder Peter's departure had been precipitate.

"Rude and loutish bunch this year," said Miles, without preamble, as he came up to Melrose. "I see that awful Winterbourne brood is here." He looked off over the crowd. "Well, old chap! What do you think? A bang-up job we've done this year, and so long as they stay away from Rookswood, I think it should be a tolerable success. Old Finsbury stands about with his hat in his hands—if we had to depend on him there wouldn't *be* a new window. Same thing every year. We do the job; God gets the credit. Julia's over in the tea tent, in case you're interested." He winked broadly.

Melrose wasn't, until he saw Polly Praed carrying what looked like a great load of napkin-draped plates into the tent. She was swallowed up by darkness on the other end. "Considering what's happened in the Horndean wood, Sir Miles, I'm rather surprised people mightn't find its proximity to the church a bit off-putting."

Miles looked rather blankly at Melrose, as if murder had its place, after all, and, like the Winterbournes, should keep off when it wasn't absolutely wanted. "Oh, well . . . I imagine it'll be sorted out. . . . Derek's over there, doing an A-one job at the Bottle Toss. Clever boy."

Melrose wondered how clever one had to be to stand up rows of bottles so people could throw hoops at them.

". . . And Sylvia's already sold at least fifty pounds' worth at the Jumble." He pointed toward a clutch of women squawking like chickens. Sylvia was probably knocking up the prices on everything.

As they strolled through the gathering crowd, Sir Miles took a swipe with his stick at a child whose fingers were sticky with cotton-candy and who had had the gall to get too near to Sir Miles's plus-fours. With his argyle socks and plaid beret, he was looking quite jaunty. The effect of this bit of Aubrey Beardsley in Littlebourne was somewhat dashed by the dab of crusted egg yolk on the cashmere sweater. "So, where are you off to?" he asked Melrose, as if they'd only just met on a railway platform.

"Thought perhaps I'd try the tea pavilion."

Again, Sir Miles winked. "Thought you would, my boy, thought you would."

II

"I was just thinking," said Polly Praed, her violet eyes alight as she handed over a cup of tea to Melrose, "of the most *marvelous* way to murder Derek Bodenheim."

"Join me for tea and tell me all about it."

She shook her head. "Thanks, but I've got to serve. But just listen: you see, Derek, the oaf, is in charge of the Bottle Toss, isn't he? Everyone brings a bottle full of something, but no one knows what. There's only the name on each of the bottles to tell you who brought it. Well, of course, the murderer simply puts a sham name—excuse me ..." Polly moved down the table to help some children—or hinder them—who were trying to get at the cake plates. Having disposed of them, she came back, and picked up the thread of her story. "... a sham name. Now, *that* bottle contains strychnine. Derek tosses the hoop and it lands on that one and Bob's your uncle. Can't you imagine—?"

"Wait a minute, how do you know he'd land the hoop on *that* bottle?"

"... imagine him lying there, writhing on the ground. Strychnine does such ghastly things to one—excuse me." Happily she poured out three cups of tea, which were collected by three ladies who looked at them with disapproval.

"That's a quaint way of going about it," he said, drinking his tea and trying to ignore the beckoning hand of Julia Bodenheim, sitting at one of the tables.

"Quaint? I thought it excruciatingly horrible, myself. I like the image, you see. All of the bottles neatly lined up, all different colors. And then the innocent-seeming church fête where one would hardly expect anything like that to—excuse me." Farther down the table went Polly, and Melrose could no longer ignore the fingers of Julia, diddling at the air as if she were practicing scales.

When he appeared at her table, she said, "Please do sit down, Lord Ardry."

"Just plain Melrose Plant. I don't have a title."

Her smile was conspiratorial, as if that *Melrose Plant* were like the fake name on Polly's bottle. "Of course. It's all rather hideously boring, isn't it?"

"The fête? I've always found them interesting. One could make quite a study of human nature here."

Julia sighed. "Perhaps *you* haven't been subjected to them every year. I can't think why Mummy *will* insist on taking charge of the damned things, as it puts me and Derek in the most awful position . . ." She rambled on as Melrose wondered what position she could be talking about since she seemed to be nothing but sitting here drinking tea and smoking Balkan Sobranies. As Julia talked herself blue, Melrose let his mind wander off to Katie's map. Where had she found it? Through the open flap of the tent he saw that the phaeton had started up again and was moving out of the pool of shadow at the far end of the churchyard. Emily would certainly die with her boots on, since she never took them off.

Ten more minutes was about all Melrose could endure of Julia's life story, the only interesting part of which was a fall from a 'chaser which had broken her jaw, rendering speech impossible. He tried to extricate himself by saying he was going to have his fortune told.

"By old Augusta, you mean? Whatever for?"

"To see if some mysterious woman is going to enter my life." He tried for an enigmatic smile. She loved it. As he turned to go, Melrose asked her suddenly, "Tell me, Miss Bodenheim—did you know Lord Kennington's secretary very well at all?"

"Trev—?" She stopped before the name was completely out and he thought a shadow passed over her face. "No. No, of course not. We had very little to do with the Kenningtons, and certainly not with the secretary."

Melrose considered. "Your brother did, though, didn't he?"

She frowned. "What on earth's all that to you? How do you know about all that business?"

"Oh ... chitchat, chitchat. Since I'm thinking of buying the place, well ... you know."

It was doubtful she did. But the slight flush left her face as she regained her composure — or, rather, the Bodenheim arrogance which was supposed to pass for it — and said, "I hope you'll be more sociable than *she* ever was."

Melrose hoped he wouldn't.

III

Madame Zostra, with her crystal ball, jeweled turban, and redoubtable accent was not much like that same Augusta Craigie who followed her sister about like a lapdog. Perhaps the costume permitted her to reveal some cutthroat self, for she had no compunction about grinding all of Melrose's hopes for the future into the ground. Fortune-tellers (he had always thought) were there to make one feel happy and hopeful: beautiful strangers and money and exotic ports-of-call were supposed to fall into one's lap as easily as autumn leaves. But having crossed Madame Zostra's palm with silver, all Melrose could look forward to was a life of ravaged dreams. He wouldn't make a fortune, but lose one, very probably at the hands of a dangerous (not beautiful) stranger, who would fall across his path, not like a scattering of leaves, but like a dead tree.

Melrose left the tent and did not wonder at the lack of customers outside. Word must have got round that to enter this tent was truly to abandon hope. If the fête's fortune were left to Madame Zostra's fund-raising abilities, the church window would have to wait until hell froze over. That appeared to be where all of her clients were headed, anyway.

Sylvia Bodenheim was in her métier at the Bring 'n Buy, haggling with a thin woman over the price of a ratty-looking shawl knitted by Sylvia's own hand. As Sylvia was also manning the Jumble table, set up in a booth next door, she was having the time of her life flying betwixt the two like a great scavenger bird.

The Bake Sale was lorded over by Miss Pettigrew of the Magic Muffin. Ramrod straight she stood, arms splayed either side of her wares. They all looked pretty much as if they'd come from the same batter. There was a decided muffin-y scent in the air, a strange mixture of carrot and cinnamon.

The small carousel of four horses, two pigs, a lamb and a goose was grinding out some unidentifiable tune as it circled very slowly, and the tots on the faded painted animals whipped them along with imaginary crops. Aside from Emily's phaeton rides (which Melrose observed circling the outer edge of the church grounds), the carousel was the most popular of the attractions. Melrose watched the golden horse, glowing in a shaft of sun, trotting the carriage along. He saw two small heads poke out, apparently yelling something to friends on the carousel as they passed. Almost as quickly, they pulled their heads back in when the driver, whip in hand, turned toward them.

IV

Derek Bodenheim was gathering up the small plastic hoops used for the Bottle Toss as Melrose approached. Ignoring Derek's surly look, Melrose said happily, "Think I'll have a go. How much?"

"Three for twenty-five."

He handed over the money and received in return three hoops. He missed all three and requested three more. By the time Melrose had missed his twelfth shot at ringing a bottle, Derek's surly attitude had changed to his more familiar, supercilious one.

"Guess I'm not exactly a dab hand at this sort of thing," said Melrose, modestly. In truth, he was a dab hand at anything like quoits, horseshoes, darts—whatever demanded judging distances. But he had managed to put Derek more in the mood for a bit of a chat.

"It's quite simple, really, if you've any coordination," said Derek, with his usual nobility of spirit. "Mainwaring got three in a row."

Melrose expressed astonishment at Mainwaring's prowess and asked, "What's in the bottles?"

"Wine, whiskey, hair tonic—"

Strychnine, thought Melrose, smiling. "I'm not any good at games demanding physical dexterity. Chess, now. That's more my game." Melrose hadn't played it since he was ten years old. "Something that requires concentration . . . and a little imagination." He looked off toward the Penny Toss and saw Emily squandering her newfound riches. Away across the churchyard, the horse cropped grass. Rest time. "Someone was telling me about a game that's all the rage, called 'Wizards.' Ever play it?"

Derek's expression didn't change as he said, "When I'm up at Cambridge. It's quite fun. Very complicated. Takes a lot of imagination and you sort of make it up as you go along."

"No one around here to play it with, I suppose? I might like to learn." He hoped he was right in assuming Derek would hardly offer to teach him.

He was. "The last person I played with here was that secretary of Kennington's. The one who stole a quarter-million worth in jewelry. Heard about that, I expect?" Melrose nodded. "Tree was really good. Used to play with him in the Blue Boy. Of course, I'm sure it was a set-up straight from the beginning."

"How do you mean?"

"That's why he took the job in the first place. Wouldn't be at all surprised if she were in it with him."

"'She'?"

"The high-and-mighty Lady-bloody-Kennington. Tree was an attractive bloke, I expect. Wouldn't trust him out of my sight, of course. He was too sharp. Somehow, I always ended up standing drinks."

Tree must have been sharp, thought Melrose, who had put the younger Bodenheim down as one of the world's great borrowers.

"He was a Wizard-Master." At Melrose's questioning look, Derek said, "The one who controls the play. What rules there are are set by the Master."

"What I heard was there was talk he had a partner to bring it off. Someone in the village."

Derek was perhaps not quite so stupid as his vapid eye and slack face suggested. "Don't look at me, chum."

"Was I?"

Heatedly, Derek asked the same question as Julia: "What the devil's your interest in this? Did you hear about it when you were looking at Stonington, or something? Afraid it's got a curse on it? That girl was on her way there, I hear. Poor bitch. Hell of a way to snuff it, face down in the mud."

V

For a few more minutes, Melrose moved among the crowd which seemed to swell and thin out by turns. The smell of popcorn combined with the sickly sweet smell of cotton-candy: the very air seemed pink and sticky with it. He saw that the tea tent was even more crowded, and that Miss Pettigrew still stood guard over her baked goods: not much change in the pieman's wares. The voices of the children grew, like the sun itself, bright and coppery. To get away from it, Melrose decided to walk up to the Church of St. Pancras to have a look at the window that had inspired all of this activity.

It was after he'd got to the church and turned on the rise of ground that he saw, at a distance, the woman in white and black standing at the gate, exchanging a few words with Peter Gere as she dug in her bag for change. Peter was apparently doing his stint, taking Miles Bodenheim's place. The dress was quite striking, its black-and-white zebra stripes running diagonally from short silken sleeves to the bottom of the skirt. And the pallor of the skin was highlighted by the coal-black hair. She moved through the gate and through the crowd with a queenly bearing that seemed as inappropriate to the gathering as was the dress on this cool September afternoon. He wondered who she was, as she picked things up and put them down in the various stalls. He watched her having a rather long conversation with Derek Bodenheim, erasing some of the slack look from Derek's face and replacing it with an intensity unusual for him. Then he watched her at the Bring 'n Buy table being cut dead by Sylvia Bodenheim. Watched the woman in black and white, in turn, say something to Miles which did not make him at all happy. Finally, he watched her loop an arm through the arm of Freddie Mainwaring, who looked this way and that, obviously uncomfortable. Melrose got the impression that quite a few people could have dispensed with her presence.

He went inside the little church, where the air was deliciously cool and free from the mingled odors of lemonade, iced lollies, and cotton-candy. It was also deliciously quiet. He looked round at its pleasant plainness. It was no wonder that the Reverend Finsbury was pleased with the idea of stained glass. The window, though small, was quite beautiful, catching the sun as it did right now.

The church had been the one thing fixed on Katie's map like a star, looking off — if one used one's imagination — toward the River of Blood. Melrose stood at an easterly window, looking off and down. A policeman seemed to be drawing a stick through the stream quite a long way away.

He spent some time in the church, staring out of the window, and more time walking about, not expecting to find anything, but still looking for possible hiding places. He was surprised when the bell tolled four o'clock.

It was then that he heard the screaming.

People were rushing in waves, yanking children along, and for a moment he imagined they were converging on the Bottle Toss. His mind was so full of Polly's strychnine-in-the-wine, that it took him a minute to see they were moving, rather, in the direction of the carriage, parked in the shadow of the wood. And even as he looked, he thought he saw Emily Louise fall from her driver's perch.

VI

But Emily Louise Perk was too used to keeping a firm seat on a saddle to fall out of anything. She hadn't fallen; she'd jumped.

The screams were issuing from some children, Melrose saw,

once he'd cut through the crowd — their two white faces looking out of the carriage and one yelling and fumbling at the latch, all butterfingers. Emily Louise, always master of the situation, yanked it open, and children seemed to tumble from everywhere — though there were only the requisite three — arms and legs flailing, pointings of fingers, tears and tremblings all round as they rushed into the protecting arms of their respective mothers.

From what he could gather, there was a Thing in the phaeton.

He could not really get a good view of the proceedings, as he had come up near the end of the crowd and was circling it and looking over shoulders. Peter Gere had managed to hack his way through and was trying to hold back the wave of people. As Gere managed to create a path for himself, Melrose caught a glimpse inside the carriage: from the rug which was rolled up on the floor of the black carriage dangled an arm, marble-white and (he guessed) marble-cold. There was a red-lacquered hand, the edge of a black-and-white sleeve.

What a short time he had known her.

NINETEEN

⸻⸻⸻

THE fête was a shambles. Fear, confusion, and shock had resulted in trampled shrubberies, trippings over headstones, upset booths, runaway dogs, and screaming children as their parents tried to drag them out of the path of the Hertfield police.

There was, fortunately, no dearth of police. The forensic crew seemed to spill out of the wood. Nathan Riddley had been the first medical man on the scene and had pronounced Ramona Wey very dead indeed. Except for the thin trickle which had run down her arm and caked in a dark ribbon, there was very little blood.

From what Melrose could gather in the general confusion that reigned, the weapon was a small, silver awl-like thing used, back in Victorian days, for punching holes in canvas for needlework.

It had, apparently, come from Sylvia's Jumble table. It had been donated by Sylvia herself. She was none too pleased, now, with her generosity. The sterling hole-puncher had come home to roost on her doorstep.

Melrose marveled at the nerve of the murderer, killing the woman with the whole Hertfield constabulary back there in the wood. The position of the carriage had effectively masked any maneuver—opening the door, shoving the body in, and covering it with the rug. The murderer had taken advantage of one of the rest periods.

"What godawful nerve," said Riddley to Carstairs, who had arrived at the scene in nothing flat from Hertfield. "Can't believe anyone would be that reckless."

"Or that desperate," Melrose heard Carstairs say as he walked off.

Melrose was rather enjoying watching the Bodenheims being ground exceeding small in the mills of the Hertfield constabulary. D. I. Carstairs had commandeered Rookswood for questioning, and Miles Bodenheim had had a time of it, trying to herd people like sheep to the public footpaths.

"Disgraceful," he said to Melrose as they stood in the hallway of Rookswood. He seemed to think the murder had been done to ruin the festivities. "It's given Sylvia a sick-headache and Julia is simply overcome with nerves." Melrose seriously doubted both. "That such a thing could happen in our village — *twice*, mind you —" (as if Melrose had forgotten the first murder) "and now here's police simply tramping about our drawing room, and all of those *people* . . . Ah! There's the Craigie sisters come in . . . I must speak to them at once . . . Ernestine! Augusta!" He sailed off.

Most of the visitors to the fête had been questioned briefly by police and been permitted to leave. A handful remained in the drawing room of Rookswood — the Craigies, Mainwaring, the Bodenheims, Polly Praed, and, of course, the children who had made the grisly discovery and their mums, one of whom was being quite vocal. "Disgraceful," she announced to anyone who would listen, echoing the opinion of Sir Miles. "Disgraceful, I calls it. Here's little Betty, and her only nine, being questioned by police." Little Betty's mother heaved a giant carryall up to her lap and looked as dour as one of the Bodenheim ancestors hanging about in portraits on the walls. Little Betty was a moon-faced child with eyes like brown buttons who enjoyed inspecting the tacky blood on her shoe.

Sylvia Bodenheim, sick-headache or not, had been brought down from her bed for questioning. Under her eyes were dark smudges, and her complexion had a distinctly greenish cast as she sat wrenching a handkerchief. Melrose thought her reaction was owing less to the object taken from her Jumble table and the consequent tragedy in the wood, than to the tragedy in her drawing room, now overrun with unwanted villagers and, worse, actual strangers.

It was a room filled with ruby velvet, cream brocade and gilt, a room that looked straight out of a decorator's album of Elegant Country House Drawing Rooms, right down to the portraits and paintings, a combination of awful Bodenheim ancestors and awful views of the Versailles gardens. The room had been chosen by the police because it had the advantage of adjoining Sir Miles's snuggery, which was the place Inspector Carstairs was using for the questioning of witnesses. A constable stood guard at the door. Thus, the pride of Rookswood had been turned into little more than a railway waiting room, to be sloughed off as passengers moved toward their trains.

Melrose watched as Sylvia moved quickly to admonish one of the three squalid kiddies who had been in the carriage. This one had decided the brocade bellpull would make a nice plaything. Its mum grabbed it back with a *Come 'ere, lovey,* and a dirty look at Sylvia's retreating figure.

"Lovey" pretended to bury her face in her mother's front, but was, instead, sticking out her tongue, either at Melrose or, more likely, Emily Louise beside him. She gladly returned the gesture. This continued until Lovey's mum gave her a smack and nearly hurled her onto the brocade loveseat.

Around the room, the other Bodenheims registered various attitudes of outrage and ennui; the Craigie sisters sat like stumps against the wall; Miss Pettigrew kneaded her brows as if she were making muffins in her mind. A few villagers, such as Mrs. Pennystevens, who had tended the other booths had been questioned and permitted to leave.

The door opened and Freddie Mainwaring came out of the snug, looking like a pile of ashes, from his gray slacks to his gray face. Next to enter the snug was Derek. It was rather like waiting to be called up before the headmaster.

The star of this occasion, although she took it with as little grace as she usually took anything involving her precious time and presence, was Emily Louise Perk. It was her carriage, after all, her golden horse cropping the woodland grass, and, by implication, her body. She had had her little stint with Detective-Inspector Carstairs, and if Melrose felt sorry for anyone, it was Carstairs. Melrose wondered how much information the poor man had got from Emily Louise by using that syrupy "little lady" approach. From what he could gather, Emily knew no more than what had happened after the children had started screaming. Lacking her own mum (for whom many calls had been put in, but none of them effective), she had wedged herself into a gilt armchair beside Melrose and now sat, arms folded across her chest, hunting cap over her eyes.

"Your mother should be here," said Melrose. "Where is she?"

"At the pictures, I expect."

"Why wasn't she at the fête? Everyone else was."

"Doesn't like fêtes. Anyway, she isn't here. Where's that man from Scotland Yard? He's supposed to be seeing about things."

Melrose liked that way of putting it. "He's in London. I'm sure he's been contacted, though. What happened?"

"*I* don't know, do I? I just heard the nasty Winterbournes screaming and I drove straight back."

He started to ask her another question when he saw the constable beckon to him.

That Melrose was in Littlebourne to buy property seemed scarcely a satisfactory answer to Inspector Carstairs, since he had been in no hurry to look the property over. Still, Mainwaring had confirmed that Plant had been to his estate office, so the inspector took the explanation with as much grace as possible, which wasn't much. "You say you were watching the dead woman as she was walking about."

This question had been put to him in at least half-a-dozen different ways. "She wasn't dead then, Inspector."

"Please don't be flippant, Mr. Plant. This is a murder investigation."

They always said that in books, thought Melrose, sighing inwardly. With the blood running down the walls and the bodies sprawled all round, someone invariably mauled in and said, *This is a murder investigation.* "Sorry. But you seem to be thinking I had some particular reason for keeping this woman under observation."

"Did you?" Carstairs snapped.

"No. She was someone I'd not seen before and I found her rather remarkable looking."

"Meaning?"

"Oh, I don't know . . . white and dark and deadly."

"Why 'deadly'?"

"I told you, Inspector. It was merely an impression. She was walking about the place, but didn't seem part *of* it. As if she hadn't come for the festivities at all, I suppose—"

"And you saw her at the Jumble table."

"Yes."

"Talking to Mrs. Bodenheim."

"Not precisely 'talking,' from what I could observe." He almost felt sorry for old Sylvia, who had had possession of the silver puncher at just the wrong time.

Carstairs looked at him for a long moment and then said, "Thank you, Mr. Plant, that'll be all for the moment."

Melrose stood up and ventured the question, "Has, ah, Superintendent Jury been informed of this new development?"

Carstairs's look was dark indeed, and Melrose was surprised that he answered at all. "We're trying to locate him." He returned to his sheaf of papers.

Trying to? wondered Melrose, as he looked round at the gilt and brocade, empty now except for the clutch of policemen smoking in a corner and a thin woman with cotton-candy hair sitting stiffly upright in a chair. Trying to? Could a superintendent of the C.I.D. simply slip through a crack?

The hell with it, he thought, reclaiming his stick and his coat. If the Hertfordshire constabulary couldn't put his finger on Jury, he bet he could.

TWENTY

○○○○○○○○○○

I

SLIPPING through a crack would have been an appropriate description for finding oneself in the salvage depot of the Crippses' front room, where Jury was at the moment as far removed from gilt and brocade as one could be who had not actually hit another galaxy.

He had made two other stops first, however, upon returning to London. One had been on the other side of Chief Superintendent Racer's desk.

The question at New Scotland Yard was not whether the chief superintendent was mad, but whether he had gone madder. If Racer would not give way to God, he certainly would have had to give way to the commissioner, who had, along with everyone else, wondered when Racer would go down for the last time.

Jury was about the only one left who would listen to him with something resembling patience, a response not motivated so much by altruism as by curiosity: he wondered how often Racer could bob up again before the waves finally sucked him under. Although Racer seemed to think the collapse of the Empire was imminent with his resignation, he also believed it would rise again out of the ashes of his memorable accomplishments. He had just expended some few moments outlining one of his early cases to Jury in filigree detail, a case which bore, as far as Jury was concerned, little resemblance to the one he was now working on.

He said so. "I don't see how that's relevant, sir."

Racer, who had got up, apparently to twitch his Savile Row lapels into smoother place, sat down again. He shook his head, a bit sadly.

"Do you know the difference between you and Sherlock Holmes, Jury?" Racer was having a go at the game map, which Jury had produced for his inspection.

Jury pretended to think this question over seriously before answering, "I could think of quite a few differences, yes."

Racer shook his head violently. Even when Jury agreed with him, Racer assumed he was disagreeing. Once a mug, always a mug, the look leveled at Jury said. "Imaginative grasp!" Racer grabbed for a fistful of air. "You're a plodder, Jury. Always have been."

"You've always accused me of being a corner-cutter before."

"You're that, too," said Racer crisply. Would Moses have taken back one of the Commandments even if the good Lord had come along with an eleventh that punched holes in the first ten? He looked up from the map. "So you've got the Hertfordshire police turning over every stick and stone in this godforsaken wood looking for a necklace?" Racer shoved the cat Cyril off his desk. The cat had been discovered one day walking through the halls of New Scotland Yard; no one knew how it had got in. But it had seemed determined on reporting something. Jury considered the cat had an ulterior motive in attaching itself to Chief Superintendent Racer, probably because Racer couldn't stand it. It liked to sit on Racer's desk with its tail wrapped around its legs like an ornament, part of a matched desk set.

Now it sat the same way on the floor, waiting its chance.

"The necklace," said Jury, "is only part of it. They're out there searching for clues to the murder of Cora Binns. What would you have me do, sir?"

It was apparently just such an opening that Racer had been waiting for. "What would I have you do?" He smiled slightly and shoved himself back from his desk to get up and walk about the room. He could not resist talking down to Jury, literally as well as figuratively. "To sum up: what we have here is: One, a bundle of anonymous letters; Two, a girl coshed on the head in a tube station; Three, another woman murdered in a wood outside this one-eyed village; Four, a necklace worth a king's ransom stolen by a small-time dip a year ago—"

"I wouldn't call Trevor Tree a small-time anything—"

Racer ignored the interruption. ". . . And, Five, this damned map thing. Diagram, game plan. Whatever the hell you call it. So we are dealing with several disparate elements." Racer had stopped somewhere behind Jury's chair. The cat Cyril flicked its ear, as if warning Jury.

"Disparate elements," he repeated, fond of the phrase. "You have lined up these particular ducks, Jury, and simply assumed they all belong in the same row, right? But . . ."

Was Racer going to take him back to square one? Apparently.

". . . But what if they don't? Isn't it just possible that this O'Brien girl's case has nothing to do with the rest—?"

"They do and she does," said Jury, bored with this catechism. Coming into Racer's office was more and more like walking into a confessional with a divvy priest on the other side of the grille. Jury watched the cat Cyril plotting his next assault on the desk. He was slinking round the corner. As Racer droned on about the disparate elements, Cyril made a four-point landing on the desk and started washing.

". . . and what does forensics have to say about this?" Racer was back at his desk now, holding up the map.

"Nothing yet. They're sending round a report."

Racer shoved Cyril off the desk as he switched on the intercom and asked Fiona Clingmore if the report had come up on the Littlebourne case. "Well, bring it in, for God's sakes, girl!"

Fiona entered, all in her own good time. She cracked her wad of gum at her boss as she put a folder in front of him, at the same time giving Jury one of her high-voltage smiles. She was wearing a long-sleeved, high-necked black dress which strained across the bosom. It was held together by what seemed a hundred little jet buttons and tiny loops running down the front. Almost together, that is. Two or three of the buttons had popped their moorings disclosing a bit of black lace beneath. Jury watched Racer's eye travel the length of the button-row. Then he tossed the folder over to Jury. "Nothing here we didn't know before. If you two are through making eyes at one another, get out. And take this moth-eaten cat with you! I'm busy!"

All three were happy enough to leave. Only the cat Cyril would make it a point to come back.

Twenty minutes later found Jury at the hospital, where the pretty, cross little nurse was at her station writing up reports on a clipboard. She nodded to Jury, curtly. When he asked for Sergeant Wiggins, she said, "I think he's down to the canteen. He asked me for some tea, but after all, I don't have time to be forever getting tea, do I?"

"Sorry we're upsetting routine, and you don't have to get him tea, of course not. Nor diagnose his ailments." With an entire hospital at his disposal, it would be hard to believe Wiggins hadn't tried to take advantage of it.

Her mouth twitched up; she was trying not to smile. But the starched bosom heaved a bit. Starched women had never in-timidated Jury; he figured it would always come out in the wash. She clasped her clipboard to her breast as if to keep everything under control and said, "It's all right, I expect. It's just having police all over makes me nervous. As if something horrible were going to happen."

"That's not doing a thing for my ego." He smiled and tapped the clipboard. "Katie O'Brien's report in there?"

She nodded, flicking over pages and turning it toward him. "There's been no change. You keep seeming to think there will be." She looked sad.

"Oh, you know the police. Eternal optimists. Anyone been in to see her?"

"Her mother, this morning. And her music teacher."

Macenery? Jury was surprised. So he'd finally worked up the nerve. "When?"

"He's there now, I think." She nodded toward the corridor behind her.

The room was empty, though there were signs of Sergeant

Wiggins's recent occupancy — a bottle of nose drops and a box of cough drops.

Jury went over to the window. Across the Fulham Road the pub was shut up. A gust of wind ruffled the scalloped edge of the greengrocer's striped awning. A woman, scarved and huddled against the wind, dragged a shopping cart across the road. Sunday or not, the launderette lights were on, and he could see someone turning the pages of a magazine.

He turned from the window and looked at the still form of Katie O'Brien. It startled him afresh, the thought of the mangled brain inside this perfect body. She lay, hands still clasped on the white sheet, legs outstretched, a perfect sculpture, something one might find on a medieval tomb. She only lacked a little dog at her feet.

Jury switched on the tape recorder, and the tinny voice of the old music-hall singer scraped through the room with "Roses of Picardy."

They were sitting together in the canteen, Sergeant Wiggins and Cyril Macenery. Jury punched the button of the coffee machine and got in return a stream of muddy-looking stuff and took it over to their table.

Wiggins started in immediately apologizing for having left the room. Sometimes Jury thought he was his sergeant's conscience. "It was my head. Killing me, it was, sir. I should've brought a thermos of tea. The nurse doesn't seem to like me much."

"Us," Jury corrected him. "The whole M.P.D. is what she doesn't like. Nothing personal. Hello, Mr. Macenery. I'm glad you decided to visit."

Macenery's blue eyes glinted for a moment before he looked away. "There doesn't seem much they can do for her, does there?"

The three of them looked down at their several flimsy cups of machine-brewed tea and coffee.

"Her mother was in this morning," said Wiggins. "She talked to her. That's supposed to help, the nurse told me. She talked to her about what was going on in the village. There's a church fête going on today. And about her school chums, and how school would soon be starting. . . ." Wiggins's voice trailed off. Seldom a man to comment on emotional rather than physical distress, he added, "Depressing, isn't it?"

These remarks were made, these questions asked without her really looking at one another, as if each were addressing some invisible fourth sitting at the other end of the table, some person who could come up with answers that none of them could.

Finally, Macenery rose. "I guess I'll go back to her room for a minute."

Jury hesitated. "Okay."

As Macenery left the room, Wiggins started to get up. "Did you want me to —?"

Jury put his arm on the sergeant's sleeve, pulled him down again. "No." Jury was thinking of what Riddley had said. Irreversible. This chilling thought crossed his mind — of Katie O'Brien never waking, or waking with a brain so damaged that even death might be preferable. "In a minute. I wanted to tell you I had one of my talks with our D.C.S. Superintendent Racer seemed to feel I'm spending too much time in Littlebourne, in London, everywhere. That's what comes of reporting in."

Wiggins smiled bleakly. "Better you than me."

"Yes. At any rate, he thinks we should have this tidied up in another day or so, or he might have to put someone else on the case." Jury smiled.

Wiggins, who Jury thought might have had his mouth washed out with soap once too often as a child, was seldom given to obscenities. He muttered one now.

"He lined up all the — what he likes to call 'disparate elements' — like dominoes and wonders why I can't tip one and have all the others fall neatly on top. So let's see how they do fall." Jury moved the salt and pepper shaker, two empty cups, and a napkin holder into a row. "The first one, the letters, weren't important in themselves. What they did do was to take everybody's mind off Katie O'Brien. There was scarcely a person I talked to who wasn't surprised when I brought up her name. Of course, there'd been a murder by then, but her mother made a point when she said the letters made people forget. The attention of the Hertfield police was directed elsewhere. Domino number two—" Jury overturned another cup. "The murder of Cora Binns. I think she met up with the murderer who saw a ring or rings on her hand that would bring the whole business back to the Kennington emerald. Something he or she'd been looking for for upwards of a year and must have felt close to finding."

"But don't you think it's strange, a bit of almost too-bad luck, that the person she'd meet by accident would be the murderer? It's odd nobody else in Littlebourne saw her, isn't it?"

Jury thought for a moment. "No. I don't think so." Wiggins frowned, but Jury went on. "Whoever tried to kill Katie and succeeded in killing Cora Binns was afraid the police would start snooping around again. And what if they found the map? Katie obviously found it somehow. Was she going to the police? We don't know. That takes care of domino number three. Number four—" Jury overturned the other cup. "—The mutilated hand. I can only think there of instant rigor. Maybe he could have broken the fingers, but with Ernestine Craigie's little hatchet so easy to hand—" Jury shrugged.

"It seems Miss Craigie has more to do with this business than's good for her."

"She your favorite suspect, then?"

"A tough old bird. Excuse me. No pun intended." Wiggins turned over the pepper shaker. "Well, then, you've done it, sir. The dominoes. All except for the napkin holder. The murderer—right?"

Jury looked at it. "Right." He started to turn it over, then set it upright. "There's one person all of this fits like a glove."

Wiggins was astonished. "You mean you *know?* Well, for God's sakes, why—?"

"I *think* I know." Jury got up heavily.

"You don't look too happy about it."

Jury wasn't happy about it, not at all. "I don't have any evidence, Wiggins. Not a shred, not a hope, unless we can catch someone dead to rights. Which probably means finding that necklace." He pulled the map from his pocket, folded in half like an open book, and stood it against the napkin holder. "Trevor Tree's mate, accomplice, or whatever must now know where that necklace is. And is going to trample anyone who gets in the way. I hope no one else does."

As they rose to leave, Wiggins swept some of the spilled salt into his hand and tossed it over his shoulder. "You never know, sir."

When they were halfway down the long, cool corridor, Jury knew why the cross nurse was steaming toward them, skirts crackling, clipboard anchored against her bosom. It was the music.

If Jury had a tin ear — and in this case, even he was stopped dead — Wiggins didn't. Music was one of his passions; he certainly had few enough of them. "My God, that's beautiful."

Apparently, some of the patients felt the same way. They stood in open doorways, sat in wheelchairs, leaned on canes. Cyril Macenery was playing the violin — Katie's favorite song, "Roses of Picardy." It had seemed to Jury, up to then, a quaint old song; now it was unearthly.

And the nurse was not so much cross as worried: "Really, I don't know whatever Matron will do." She shook her head; her white cap bobbed. "I just don't know. I suppose he picked up her violin and started playing. . . ."

She had the authority to stop Macenery, of course; only, she hadn't. She was probably as much beguiled by the wonderful sound of that music in this white, dead corridor as anyone else. Jury's estimate of what lay behind her starched exterior seemed to have been pretty accurate, after all. He clicked his pen and wrote on a notebook page, tore it off, and handed it to her. "I realize it's your patch and not mine. But if you have the M.P.D. behind you, maybe that would help. Tell Matron — if she comes along — the C.I.D. thought it would be a good idea. And nobody's complained." Jury looked down the corridor. One or two of the women seemed to be mouthing the words or dancing in their heads. The nurse took Jury's note. Apologetically, she said, "I'll have to stop him soon."

"I know. Sergeant Wiggins will take care of it."

"But not," said the nurse, looking up at Jury with one of the starriest looks he'd ever seen, "until the song's finished." She smiled.

Thus, when the call came through from Scotland Yard to the hospital, Jury had left for the East End.

And now, Ash Cripps, dressed in a faded bathrobe and rolling a cigar in his mouth—plucked from the box Jury had had the foresight to bring with him—was strolling about the parlor, one hand holding the map Jury had handed him, the other with a bottle of White Shield. He was being none too careful about the sediment in the bottom as he took a pull from it. He set the bottle on a mantel over a fake fireplace which would glow, in colder weather, with fake coals. Bits of paper and a tin ashtray full of old butts cascaded from the mantel. He shoved them with his foot into the tiny fireplace.

The Crippses' children were half in the kitchen eating mash and half outside having a war with sticks and the tops of dustbins.

Ash continued his map-study and his stroll. He wore his old robe like the robes of state, the cord dragging the cabbage-rose carpet. They were waiting for White Ellie to get back from the launderette with his trousers.

"Aye, it does look like something Trevor could of thought up." He scratched his head. "Only it don't make no sense."

"Do they usually? I thought the whole idea of Wizards was to confuse and mislead."

"Yeah, only . . . look." Ash was rummaging through the drawers of an old bureau, stopping now and then to yell through the door to the kitchen at the little bleeders to stop screaming. Finally, he slammed the door, dampening the noise only slightly.

He handed Jury a map. "This is one Trevor did a couple years ago. Make-believe village where there was supposed to be treasure stashed. Turned up in the blacksmith's shop." The village was intricately drawn, with all of the shops, the church, an inn, farms and barns in the outlying areas. Trees looked like cotton fluff. There were a pond and a lake. It was like an aerial view, very neat and tidy. "He could make up adventures that'd 'ave us going for months."

Certainly, the two maps bore a marked similarity; the art work seemed identical.

"I seen others he did, like one of the Necklace itself. That was a town adventure. Trevor 'ad it all down, just like the pub looks — table and chairs and so forth. Then there was the castle ruins one 'e did. That was good. Good on giant rats and ruins was Trevor." He poked Jury's diagram. "That's what I say, this one's odd. It don't look like anyplace real. I mean, even real *unreal*."

Jury let that pass for the moment. "How about women, Ash? Was Trevor good with them?"

There was a burst of laughter from Ash, and his robe fell open. Elaborately, he closed it and retied the cord. "Trevor'd give it t' anybody walked on two legs. Bits a stray, old drippers, for all I know. Elephant says 'e give 'er one, but she was only braggin' is my guess. I mean, a man's gotta draw the line somewheres."

"I've seen pictures of him. He was handsome."

"Aye, Trevor was that, all right. Wi' them looks and them brains, Trevor could of gone somewheres. Too bad."

"Was one of his girls Cora Binns?"

"Well, Cora hung around, yeah. They all hung around Trevor. But Cora, she wasn't 'is type. I mean, Cora's one that'd go for the life sentence. Stupid." As if on cue from Ash to make sure Jury understood just how marriage could soothe the soul, there came the sound of crockery breaking in the kitchen and a window flying up behind Jury.

The face of White Ellie appeared, shouting above the din of dustbin covers, "Whyn't you watch the bloody kids? Sammy and Sookey's out 'ere stark and Friendly's 'avin' a piss on Mrs. Lilybanks's roses again." Then she saw Jury, and turned an even more thunderous brow on her husband. "You been at it again?"

The panes rattled as the window was flung down. Ash rolled his eyes heavenward as White Ellie, true to her name, stampeded into the parlor, shoving the pram before her. Atop the baby lay a huge mountain of clothes. Jury once again had the impulse to check and see if the baby was breathing.

"No, I ain't been at it and me and 'im's got business down at the Necklace, so if you'd kindly gimme me trousers—"

White Ellie was layered in clothes: a gingham wash dress was topped by a blue jumper, which, in turn, covered Ash's trousers.

As she started to take them off, he said, "Wait a tic. I'm puttin' on me new strides."

"You ain't! Them's for church!"

As he walked into the dark of the back room, he said it again: "Puttin' on me new strides."

Fred Astaire couldn't have said it better, thought Jury five minutes later, as they promenaded down the street toward the Anodyne Necklace.

II

They seemed to be sitting just where Jury had left them the day before, caught up in the vaporous yellow lights of the gaslights like flies in amber. The kerchiefed women sat on the benches; their menfolk sat round the tables or leaned against the bar.

"Well, an' if it ain't Ash," said the one called Nollie. "All got up like a dog's dinner. What's the occasion?"

"No occasion. Just 'elpin' out police. You know me."

Jury spread the map on the table. "This look familiar to any of you?"

Keith frowned, shook his head and passed it on to Chamberlen. He took some time studying it, polishing up his pince-nez like a jeweler's lupe. Finally, he said, "A very good job, very nice."

"What's this 'ere bleedin' bear's track?" asked Nollie, the next to get it. "Where's this 'Orndean forest?" He looked up at Jury.

"Thought maybe you could tell me."

Nollie turned on Ash with a look of suspicion: "This a fit-up, Flasher?" He started pulling on his coat.

"No, it ain't. What do I know I'd not be ashamed for me old Mum to 'ear?"

Keith hooted. "Considering yer auld Mum, 'twouldn't make no difference. Right old dripper, weren't she?"

To insult Ash's old mum was, apparently, going too far. He began to remove his coat. Jury clapped him on the shoulder and pushed him back down in his chair. Dr. Chamberlen merely sighed and shook his head. He tucked a large white napkin into his collar as Harry Biggins set down a plate of jellied eel before him.

Jury said to Chamberlen, "Does this look like Trevor Tree's work?"

Squeezing lemon juice on his plate, Chamberlen pulled the map toward him with a fat forefinger and looked again. Jury liked the way he studied a situation before committing himself. "Could be, yes. Trevor always did go in for the cunning detail. Very imaginative, was Trevor."

"Meaning?" Jury watched the glutinous eel being stuffed into Dr. Chamberlen's mouth. No wonder Wiggins didn't like the stuff.

"The various details done to throw one off. But what is all this about, Superintendent? Are *you* looking for the anodyne necklace?" Chamberlen looked owlish. The lenses of his spectacles flashed.

"No. Something more concrete: the emerald Trevor Tree took from the Kennington place about a year ago. Quite a treasure, it was. I understand Trevor used to hang around in here."

Chamberlen nodded. "Tree was a Wizard-Master. As I am." He held up the large sheet of grid paper. "Oh, yes, I heard all about that emerald necklace. Never found it, did they?" Chamberlen wiped his fingers. "Trevor was a very shrewd lad."

"Trevor was a right villain." Jury thought of Jenny Kennington, standing alone in that empty room. "The lady in question is having to sell up her house because of that loss."

Chamberlen drew a finger across his cheek, chasing an imaginary tear. "Oh, my, oh, my. That's 'Lady' with a capital L, I believe. Out into the snow with her poor, tattered children clinging to her skirts."

"No tattered children. She may be titled, but I think she's as much right to her possessions as we have."

Dr. Chamberlen picked up his empty dish. "Nollie, get me another jellied eel, will you, there's a good chap? The superintendent's untempered moralizing is increasing my need for sustenance." Obediently, Nollie took the dish.

"You can't tell me anything about Trevor Tree that would help, then? He's dead now. You'd hardly be grassing on a mate. And it's pretty obvious Tree *did* have a mate."

"Not I, if that's what you're thinking." Daintily, he wiped his mouth with the corner of his napkin.

"I suppose you were in the pub here last Thursday night?"

Chamberlen nodded. "Witnesses, Superintendent, witnesses."

Jury looked round at the lot of them. They all nodded solemnly.

"And I suppose all of you were here and can supply each other with alibis."

They all nodded solemnly.

"And none of you has any idea why Cora Binns should have been murdered?"

Solemnly, they all shook their heads.

TWENTY-ONE

⊂⊃⊂⊃⊂⊃⊂⊃⊂⊃

I

BY the time Melrose Plant had got into the environs of Wembley Knott, he had picked up two traffic tickets, one on the A10 and another for running a red light while he was getting lost in Chigwell, an area with which he was grossly unfamiliar. An old woman he had nearly grazed at a zebra crossing delivered herself of some well-aimed epithets as Melrose tipped his hat and drove on.

The sight of a Silver Shadow sliding down Catchcoach Street elicited varying responses from the few onlookers who happened to be on hand. The women assumed it must be Princess Di come to succor the East End poor; the men—at least the two emerging from the Three Tuns at the top of the street—assumed the vision had something to do with the ten bottles of Abbot's they had downed between them on a bet. To correct what they thought must be an hallucination, they turned back into the Three Tuns for some hair of the dog.

Twice Melrose stopped to ask which of the terraced hovels down the street was the Anodyne Necklace and twice received only gaping mouths in return. He was wondering where to park when he thought he sighted Jury's police-issue Ford. He managed to fit the Rolls between it and a rusted-out Mini lacking a windscreen.

He saw, when he emerged from his car, that Jury's car was parked in front of a house like a mirror-image of the houses to right and left except for its being in a state of even graver disrepair. Peeling blue paint was the only reminder of a door and trim which might have looked quite gay at one time. Behind the curtainless window, a dark shape moved like something inside a fish tank. The most wretched group of children he had ever seen, five of them — no, six, for a small one was popping out of the center of the crowd — had been manhandling an old perambulator, but stopped to watch the intricate maneuvering of the Silver Shadow into the spot beside the curb. Melrose made sure he locked the door.

"Could you tell me where the Anodyne Necklace is, please?" A walleyed child started to answer, but he was immediately given a sharp jab in the stomach by the largest of the group.

This large one said, "Ah could do. What's it t' ya?" He looked up at Melrose, with as much challenge as his moon-face could muster, his eyelashes so pale that the eyes looked lidless.

Melrose flicked a fifty-p piece to the lad, who caught it with the sure instinct of a frog snapping at flies. The boy pointed toward the end of the street. "Down there it be."

Melrose saw at the narrower end of the street what looked like a couple of shops flanking a thinnish building with an unremarkable facade from which he could now observe some sort of sign hanging. He looked then at the house behind him. "Is that where you live?"

"Mebbe," said the moon-faced boy.

"And have you seen the gentleman who drives this car?" Melrose pointed to the Ford with his walking stick.

Another sly whip of a smile was his reward. "Mebbe."

"Mam's home!" piped up the only girl in the crowd who had been noisily sucking her finger and who now got a shoe in her shin for supplying Melrose with this morsel. In the meantime, the other four, having inspected Melrose's car first from a respectful distance, were now crawling all over it like slugs.

He managed to lift the smallest one off with his stick and deposit it on the sidewalk. He then lined up the six of them and passed out coins to each. "There could be more where that came from. And if *that* doesn't keep you away from my car," he added with a winning smile, "I shall have to break all of your little arms and legs."

This threat seemed to amuse them far more than it frightened them. The moon-faced one, who answered to the name of "Sookey," opened his mouth to answer this vile outrage, but Melrose had already pushed the line with his stick, collapsing them like dominoes, as they giggled all the while. They then danced off down the street toward the shops, Sookey trying to snatch the coins from the smaller ones and getting kicks in the groin for his trouble.

Melrose walked up to number twenty-four.

The woman who filled the doorway, having opened it to his tap, was the fattest Melrose had ever seen. Her voluminous frock floated above trousered legs. An interesting ensemble, he thought. But she had apparently gone to some trouble to dress up, for her hair was tied back by a shiny green ribbon and lip rouge bled into the lines round her mouth.

She looked him up and down. "If you come about Friendly, there ain't nothin' we can do. I didn't know the social services worked on Sunday. The lad takes after 'is divvy Da." She pushed past Melrose, moving toward the pram. It was filled with what might have been either clean or dirty linen, Melrose noted. And there seemed to be a sleeping baby underneath. As she chugged back with it and rolled through the doorway she said, "But Ashley's Da was even worse, I can tell you. What was I supposed to do, then, and 'im lyin' on the landin' makin' them 'orrible noises? Well, wouldn't you a got out?" She glared at Melrose. "Was I suppose to know 'e was dead, then?"

"I don't see how you could." Melrose cast an eye about what must have been a parlor, hoping this was not the last place to see Jury alive.

His reply seemed to satisfy her immensely, as she pulled a pile of laundry—no, it was the baby—from the pram, shook it a bit, and put it back. "Down all them steps 'e fell. Well, I wasn't goin' to bloody stay in the 'ouse, was I?" Her glance was as challenging as Sookey's. Melrose could see where the boy got his looks. "Well, then, come on back."

Fascinated, Melrose followed. A mean-looking, thin-faced dog with bandy legs looked up at him as he surveyed the kitchen. A spoon was sticking up in a bowl of something that seemed to have life of its own: bubbles sprouted, erupted, burst along its surface. She applied herself to this restless mixture, and, then, seeming suddenly to realize she was in her kitchen with a perfect stranger, she said, "Who are you, then? Come walkin' in 'ere nice as ninepence."

Melrose bowed slightly. "Melrose Plant, madam. I'm a friend of Superintendent Jury, and, as I saw his car outside the house, I thought he might be here."

"You ain't from the social services, then?" She seemed quite surprised. "Well, then. Me name's Cripps. Friend of the Super's is ya?" Jury might have been one of the family, thought Melrose. "Gone over to the pub with Ashley. Just missed 'im. I'm on the way there meself, soon's I fix the kids' tea. Just set awhile."

In for a penny, in for a pound, thought Melrose, as he swept the crumbs from a chair. "It's very important I see him, Mrs. Cripps."

"White Ellie. Just you wait a tic and we'll go along to the pub together." No one, her tone said, could refuse such a tempting offer.

Melrose wondered what could be in the bowl which would do for a meal. She pulled a skillet across the cooker, gave it a wipe with a towel, lit the burner and poured more grease from a jar. Out of the corner of his eye Melrose thought he saw something scuttle from behind the sink and make for safer digs in the shadows behind him. He kept his eye off the floor and opened his cigarette case. "Care for one?"

"Ta very much," said White Ellie, taking a cigarette and lighting it from the gas ring. The cakes sputtered in the pan as dollops dropped from her spoon. "'Ave one?" Melrose declined politely. "Wonder where them kids got to."

Before he could tell her they'd made for the shop on the corner to spend his money, whoops and hollers and feet announced the return of the Crippses as they swarmed into the kitchen with sticky faces and paper screws of candy, which they deposited along with themselves on the assorted chairs and stools around the table. One of them was missing, Melrose noticed. So did White Ellie as she handed round the plates. "Where's Friendly?"

Sookey, who seemed absolutely set upon ruining the visitor's day, sweets or no sweets, said, "Friendly says 'e be 'aving a piss all over them 'ubcaps."

The rest of them giggled, traitors all.

Melrose smiled and rose, at the same time pressing a button on his walking stick and drawing a thin-bladed sword from the shaft. "If I were you, I would scamper off and tell Friendly that the gentleman inside strongly suggests he find another outlet for his interests."

They dropped forks, spoons and catsup bottle. Sookey turned even whiter than his naturally pallid complexion warranted. "Cor!" he whispered, sliding from his chair and shooting like an arrow out the door.

Only White Ellie remained unmoved. She dropped her cigarette on the floor, stepped on it like a bug, and picked up the swordstick. "Ain't that quaint. Wish't I 'ad me one. You ready then? I'll just slip off me strides and we'll go t' the Necklace."

While he waited, Melrose inspected the wallpaper.

He decided he had lived too long with his aunt Agatha to quail before any malfunction of the universe. Given a millennia or two, he could sort out this little lot.

II

If Jury had kept a memory book, the first entry would be the sight of White Ellie on the arm of Melrose Plant, outlined in the murky light of the door of the Anodyne Necklace.

He had just hung up the telephone as they entered and then separated, White Ellie to join the benchsitters (and upsetting a pint as she squeezed between tables); Plant to join Jury at the bar.

"Buy you a drink, Superintendent?" He nodded toward the phone. "I take it you've heard about Ramona Wey."

Jury nodded. "That was Wiggins. They called the hospital. What in hell happened?"

Melrose told Jury about the circuit around the fête grounds. "She didn't seem to be the most popular woman in town, from what I could observe." Plant put a note on the bar and beckoned to Harry Biggins. "I've been wondering about the connection. If

Ramona Wey sold Lord Kennington that jewelry — is it possible *she* might have recognized a ring Cora Binns was wearing? Assuming she'd seen her, of course, in Littlebourne." Harry Biggins came down the bar and Melrose directed that Mrs. Cripps was to be kept happy with whatever kept her happy for the remainder of the evening. He was a bit surprised that the publican took in his stride Melrose's request for a bottle of Old Peculier and moved off to get it.

"That mention of Ramona Wey and Cora Binns reminds me of something. While you buy me a pint of mild and bitter, I'm going to use the telephone again."

"All right. But while you're making your call, I'd like to have a try at the game. Is that the table, over there?"

Jury smiled. "It's a very complicated game, Mr. Plant. The fat one is called Dr. Chamberlen. That's what he calls himself. He's Wizard-Master and he calls the shots. Or, to be more literal, throws the dice. I don't think you're going to get much out of him, or any of them, for that matter."

"We'll see. May I borrow your copy of Emily's map, Superintendent?"

"Be my guest."

Melrose ordered Jury's pint and then gathered up his gloves, his stick, and his glass of Old Peculier.

These he deposited on the large, round table. All of them looked up at him with, he was sure, feigned surprise, as if they had not been keeping track of his every movement.

All of them except for Dr. Chamberlen, who was either too smart or too vain to bother with this pretense.

"Which of you gentlemen is Wizard-Master?" asked Melrose.

Dr. Chamberlen held up a plump, pink forefinger, and said, with a certain amount of irony, "And I have the honor of addressing who, sir?" The glance that grazed Melrose's cashmere coat made it clear that the honor was questionable in the Anodyne Necklace.

From his inside coat pocket Melrose took a visiting-card case which he kept for emergencies. On the table he dropped his card.

Dr. Chamberlen stuck his pince-nez on his nose, leaned over and read it, and then sat back, having difficulty in effecting the same indifferent manner.

The rest of them were not at all indifferent. "A bleedin' earl? In the Necklace?" said Ash Cripps. "And where'd you meet up with Elephant?"

It took Melrose a moment or two to realize he was talking about Mrs. Cripps. "At your house. She was kind enough to direct me here."

"And Superintendent Jury," said Dr. Chamberlen, "appears to be a friend of yours."

"True. But I'm not the police masquerading as the peerage, if that's what you think."

Chamberlen picked up a single die, shook it in his hand. "What's your concern with us?"

"Wizards," said Plant, smiling. As they all looked at one another, Melrose poked his stick among the scattered pages of graph paper. "I'm a thirteenth-degree Wizard-Master myself."

The rest of them all turned to Chamberlen, who looked rather unhappy. "Cor!" said Keith. "They only go up to fifteen, Doc."

Melrose was glad he hadn't succumbed to the temptation to say twentieth.

"That's very interesting," said Chamberlen, who was now concentrating—or pretending to—on a plate of jellied eel set before him by Biggins. He tucked his napkin in his collar. "But I repeat: what's it to do with us?"

"I'm interested in this." Melrose put the map on the table.

"You mean the same map Superintendent Jury is interested in?" Chamberlen squeezed a triangle of lemon over the dish of eel and peppered it. "It's of no interest to me."

From his wallet Melrose took some notes and spread them on the table. "Five hundred pounds. Will that get me in the game?"

Except for Chamberlen's, whose own mouth was busy with eel, all of the others' fell open.

There was a moment's reflection, a quick look at the money, and then Chamberlen said, "We don't play for money."

A man of principle, thought Melrose, knowing how fragile were such principles. "We don't play for anything else. What I propose is that if you can work out what this map means before I do, you keep the five hundred. All of you, of course."

"That's not much of a bargain for you, is it? I'm afraid you have caught us at a moment of financial embarrassment. We none of us can cover five hundred pounds."

Melrose shrugged. "That makes no odds. If I win, you'll count me in on the game whenever I'm in town." To keep Melrose out of the game would be more attractive to Chamberlen than the money, he imagined.

"I'm not sure I understand: if you're a friend of the Superintendent, why didn't he come to you in the first place?"

"Oh, he did." Melrose picked up the map. "I don't know what it means."

That obviously made Dr. Chamberlen happy. "I would have to make one stipulation."

"Go ahead."

"This place" — Chamberlen stubbed his finger at the map — "is probably imaginary. And you can't expect me to read Trevor Tree's mind. Therefore, I think we would have to let the wager stand on breaking the key."

What the hell was the key? wondered Melrose. "Very well, I accept."

For the next fifteen minutes, Melrose, seated with his piece of graph paper and his pencil, and not knowing what to do with either, was subjected to the most inane or bizarre or mysterious conversation he had ever heard. Occasionally, he doodled something on his paper, since he noted the others were all going at theirs hammer and tongs. Money on the table had attracted most of the customers in the Anodyne Necklace.

". . . pick up twelve pieces of gold from Black Bear's Cave."

At this point Jury had come to stand behind him. Melrose looked at the message he had written: *Ramona Wey worked at S.G.S.S.*

When Keith and Nollie found themselves stuck in the Black Bear's cave, Chamberlen put down his pencil and looked across at Plant. "You surely must see it by now." His perky little smile told Melrose that Chamberlen had won, or thought he had. When

Melrose said nothing, he went on, pleased with himself. "The key: the repetition — usually names, places, numbers. You're a thirteenth-degree Master. I surely don't have to tell you *that* elementary rule. The key here is obviously colors."

"Perhaps you'd like to explain that," said Melrose, laying his stick across the five notes toward which a hand was moving.

Dr. Chamberlen folded his hands on his stomach. "The River of Blood would obviously be red. Hardly a startling deduction. The Black Bear is rather clearly named, as are the Yellow Brick Road and the Blue Grotto. The footpath I'm uncertain about — brown, perhaps? The moat would be green or blue, probably water-green."

"What about the King's Road?"

"Surely, purple." Chamberlen shrugged, looking from Plant to Jury. "Really, gentlemen, if I knew more I'd tell you. But that's the key. I'm quite sure of it."

Melrose removed his silver-knobbed stick from the bills which Chamberlen collected and, with surprising generosity, divided among the players.

Catchcoach Street was not often enough visited by peers and police superintendents that the patrons of the Anodyne Necklace cold allow them to leave so easily. Especially after Melrose Plant had stood drinks all around. It was difficult to watch such a benefactor go, and for White Ellie, who had been more than the rest at the receiving end of such largesse, it was to be met with an equal show of hospitality. "'Ere now, 'ow's about you two comin' back to the 'ouse for a nice fry-up?"

III

They stood beneath the sign of the Anodyne Necklace looking down Catchcoach Street. In the blue evening light, the lamps had come on and the narrow houses cast tall shadows across the pavements. A band of children up the street were playing some rough game.

"Colors," said Melrose Plant, lighting a small cigar. "What in the hell does that mean? If we only had Emily and her crayons. . . . Anyway. Was your telephone call fruitful?"

"Yes. What I remembered was, Ramona Wey had been described to me by Sylvia Bodenheim as a 'jumped-up little secretary from London.' Granted, there are plenty of little secretaries in London. But it would appear that only a few of them work, or worked, for the Smart Girls Secretarial Service in King's Cross. According to its manager, Ramona Wey was one of them, until she left over a year ago when an old auntie died and Ramona was able to chuck the typewriter."

"You mean she must have known Cora Binns?"

"Oh, yes. Well, I can hardly blame her for not wanting to admit it in the circumstances. Better if she had, though. And I think the main reason was to set her own little plan into action. Blackmail, I suppose. Poor, stupid woman."

For a moment they were both silent. The silvery voices of the children playing splintered the otherwise quiet street. Everyone else was in the pub.

"You say this secretarial agency was somewhere near King's Cross?"

Jury nodded. "Why?"

"I just wondered: where's this Wembley Knotts tube stop?"

"Not far. A few minutes away."

"Could we have a look-in, do you think?"

"Sure. I have to be getting back to Littlebourne, though."

"Yes. Just for a minute." Melrose dropped his cigar in the gutter and looked up at the sign of the Anodyne Necklace. "Sawdust, gaslights, Chamberlen and Cripps. This place could live off chic for the rest of its life."

They had come abreast of their cars. Plant's walking stick must have done its job: the Silver Shadow was unscathed, untouched by either human or Crippses' hands.

But Jury sighed. Across the windscreen of the police car was soaped a large PRAT, followed by a smaller direction to sod off.

Melrose shook his head. "Can't they even teach them to spell in school?"

As Melrose piloted the Rolls with great care down the street, Jury saw the Crippses stop their game and dance along the pavement after it, waving.

Friendly was waving too, but not with his hand.

IV

The black woman was leaning over the small door of her kiosk, practicing impertinence on a family of wizened Orientals, when Jury showed his card and she grudgingly let them through. Of the Orientals she was demanding another thirty pence.

A train pulled out in the distance and wind like a hand pushed at them as they walked through the tunnel. From its other end, amplified by the curve of the tiled walls, came the sound of a guitar and a voice singing some melancholy song about going home, as if he had no hope of ever doing so. Jury had a strange sense of *déjà vu*. They rounded the curve and Melrose dropped some coins into the open guitar case; without stopping his song, the guitarist nodded his thanks and upped the volume as a reward for generosity.

"They found her here," said Jury, stopping in front of the *Evita* poster, now further defaced by a long rip from the loose corner down through the center. One glittering arm was upraised; the other was off at the shoulder. Mustached and maimed, Evita still clung to the wall as, in real life, she must have clung to power.

Footsteps echoed near them and two teenage girls came around the corner. They were mirror images of each other — same long hair, deep eye shadow, jeans, gum.

"It's such a public place," said Melrose. "Taking a hell of a chance, this person, attacking her here."

"I think maybe whoever it was had to. Didn't want to be seen in the vicinity of Wembley Knotts and the Anodyne Necklace."

They walked down the steps and out onto the train platform. Giant hoardings lined the wall across the tracks. Crystal-clear gin; a skirt blowing up over a rounded rear end packed neatly into tights; the eyes of an old woman imploring one to give to a home for destitute widows; the even more desolate eyes of a spaniel who would not (according to the RSPCA) last much longer. Jury turned away. The girls were down at the other end of the platform. A couple of boys in leather jackets and old-fashioned ducktail hairdos came through one of the archways. The kids all frisked one another with their eyes.

Jury turned to look at the wall behind him where Melrose Plant was pointing with his walking stick.

At that moment, their thoughts might have been packed together in one mind. Plant had directed his walking stick to a dark spot on the Underground map, one of the largest interchanges on the London tube. "King's Cross St. Pancras."

Each line was a different color, making it simple for even the dimmest passenger to find his way through the maze. Plant's stick traced the narrow red bar which split central London in two. "The River of Blood, wouldn't you say? The Central Line. Blue, Victoria Line; black, Northern; green, District — let's have a look at your map."

Jury drew it from his pocket. The Church of St. Pancras had been drawn at the spot Plant had first pointed out. "He drew this little replica of the necklace directly above the approximate spot where we are now. Wembley Knotts."

"If you shut your eyes a bit it looks like one of Ernestine Craigie's maps."

How many times had he seen that map in the last two days alone? wondered Jury. Riding the tube and looking up at the varnished fingernails of the female pickpocket — and this map right beside it. Repeated endlessly, in every car, at every tube stop. He'd seen the map of the London Underground every day of his life.

"You mean," said Melrose, "Tree hid it *here?* In a tube station?" He looked around as the first train thundered in, disgorged several passengers, picked up the girls and the boys in leather jackets.

The guitar player walked onto and down the platform carrying his black case. Jury's mind only now absorbed the fact that the music had stopped. The guitarist lit a cigarette and waited, leaning against the wall.

Jury looked at him and said to Melrose Plant, "You know, if

you thought there was a chance, as Tree must have done, of police waiting for you outside or back in your digs, and you had an accomplice on this end—" The rest of the words were lost in the rush of wind as the train picked up speed and pulled into the dark patch of tunnel at the end.

"—you might wrap that necklace up in a pound note and just toss it in the case with the coins. But it sure as hell would have to be someone you trusted."

Jury turned from the map of the Underground to look again at the miserable dog, whose eyes trusted no one. Could he have been dead wrong? It was difficult to believe it was Cyril Macenery. Difficult or not, he was at the hospital, alone with Katie O'Brien. "Drop me at the hospital, will you, on your way back to Littlebourne?"

Plant was trying to keep up with him; they were nearly running back through the tunnel now. "Am I going back to Littlebourne?"

"Yes. To keep an eye on Emily Louise Perk. She was the one Katie gave the map to."

"I'd feel," said Melrose, running up the moving stairs behind Jury, "a lot safer if Emily Louise Perk would keep an eye on *me*."

TWENTY-TWO

I

EMILY Louise Perk was sitting in the Littlebourne police
station, her coloring book open before her, and wishing that
Superintendent Jury would come back. True, Peter Gere *was* a
policeman, but he was only the village bobby whom she'd seen
every day of her life, nearly, and anyway, he was so busy on the
telephone and that crackling box of his linked up to the Hertfield
police that anyone could have reached in the door, hit her over
the head, and bolted without Peter's even knowing.

Emily Louise would almost rather have needles stuck in her
fingernails than admit the happenings of the afternoon had made
her extremely nervous. She felt she needed police protection.
And Peter did not seem too enthusiastic about giving it. Twice he
had told her to leave, that he was very busy.

He was telling her again. Clamping one hand over the receiver
of the telephone, he said, "Emily, I've got a lot to do; you'd best
be off." And before he took his hand away from the receiver to
answer the voice on the other end, he added, automatically,
"Your mum wants you home. Yes, this is Gere . . ." He turned
away.

Why were they always telling her that? You'd think God had
pushed a button on that box of Peter's and a huge voice had come
over it saying, *This is your mummy speaking.* Peter knew her mum
was in Hertfield; she'd already told him; grown-ups simply never
listened, except for a few, like Polly and Superintendent Jury.

She looked at the last picture in her coloring book with distaste.
Snow White was patting Dopey on his polished head and wearing

a smile that looked dipped in goo. Emily stuck out her tongue at the picture, slapped the book shut, and let her eye rove the room.

What it was drawn to was the map — several copies of it — stuck to Peter's bulletin board with a drawing pin. With every policeman round about having one, the map was hardly a secret anymore.

Peter Gere's back was turned, and she slid off her chair, hastily took down a copy, and went back to her crayons. It would make a wonderful picture, colored. She lined up the stubs of crayon and started in on the grotto, coloring it blue. After working for two or three minutes, she looked at the result, dissatisfied. Because her crayons were so dull, the grotto, river, moat and highway had come out thick and straight. She put her chin in her hands and studied it. What did it remind her of? She frowned. Then, when she saw Peter move to take his coat from the back of the chair, she snatched it up and stuck it in her coloring book and slid down and pretended to be asleep. He would kill her if he knew she'd been at his bulletin board. She had strict orders never to touch it.

"I've got to go Hertfield, Emily, so take yourself home, there's a good girl."

She yawned. "I'm supposed to feed the horses."

"Well, go do it then, though for you to be running around this late . . ." He mumbled something about her mother. "It's gone eight already. What's this in aid of?"

Fatal. When she'd picked up the book the map had slid out.

"Emily! This is police evidence. What do you mean going and using it for coloring?"

She tried to distract him from that particular line of questioning. "It reminds me of something, I can't think what." She frowned. "It looks different colored, doesn't it?"

Peter turned the map this way and that. "It doesn't look like anything to me except like some fool treasure map. What do you mean it reminds you of something?"

Emily screwed up her eyes and studied a moth floating above the ceiling light. "I'll think of it in a minute."

His face was like a thundercloud. "Don't you go playing that game with me, now. I'm not about to fill you up with crisps and sweets."

When he turned away to ball up the paper and chuck it in the dustbin, she stuck out her tongue again at his back. It wasn't a game. She *would* think of it.

Peter herded her out the door, flashed her another dark look, got in his car, and sped off down the High. When he was out of sight, Emily sneaked back into the station, rescued the map and smoothed it out.

On the way to Rookswood, she stopped in at Polly Praed's and was much more satisfied with the response there than at Peter's. It was Polly who had taken her to the London zoo and let her ride all over the city on the Underground.

To say nothing of the response — amounting to several fresh cream cakes — this latest revelation earned her in the Rookswood kitchen.

II

"You're *crazy!*" said Cyril Macenery, half-rising from his chair before Jury pushed him back down.

Jury had run the gauntlet — literally — of the cross little nurse, several aides, a medicine trolley, and a woman who looked quite capable of tackling him and dragging him from the hospital by his heels. Matron, surely. But when he flashed his warrant card in her face, she could only clamp her mouth shut and accept the situation.

Katie was as he had left her. He resisted the temptation to hold a mirror to her lips before he led Cyril Macenery from the room.

At the moment, they were in a room reserved for mourning families. Wiggins had his notebook open, sitting beneath a hospital lamp. He had taken down everything.

"Listen, I was here in this hospital — you saw me. I could hardly have been in Littlebourne murdering somebody."

"I'm not talking about that at the moment. We're on the subject of what happened to that necklace. The police knew Tree took it, no matter we've never found it."

Macenery looked absolutely wrung out. "To think Trevor would have trusted me enough to toss a quarter-million-quids' worth of jewelry into my violin case and walk away is ridiculous. He didn't trust anybody."

"He must have done, in some way. Somebody else was in on that theft with him. The somebody to whom he sent or left that diagram of the Underground."

Wiggins had stopped writing and was turning his pencil over and over in his fingers, tapping it on his notebook. "The thing is, sir, it just doesn't fit Macenery here. Tree was taken in by police and then watched all the while until that auto accident. He knew he was under surveillance. So since he couldn't get to the necklace himself, he got this Wizards map off to his accomplice. Rather dirty trick, I'd say—leaving it to his mate to figure out what it meant. Well, it couldn't very well have been you," Wiggins said to Macenery. "Not if you had the necklace in the first place. Unless you'd given it back to him, but that's not likely in the circumstances."

Macenery's relief was palpable. "You're goddamned right it couldn't have been me."

Jury smiled. "I guess I run faster than I think, Wiggins."

Wiggins sat there beneath the hospital lamp, bathed in his own little glow, and unwound the tiny red strip from a fresh box of cough drops.

III

Only a slant of murky light showed through the partially open stable door where Emily was in Shandy's box, about to remove the pony's saddle. She had exercised him for twenty minutes, until the cream cakes seemed to start oozing around in her stomach, and then brought him back to the stable.

As she started to unbuckle the saddle, the stable door slowly shut, cutting off what light there was.

No place was darker than the stable at night when the door was shut. No windows, no chinks between boards, no knotholes were here that light might filter through. The structure was as sturdily built as a house. She hadn't bothered to switch on the electric light because she knew the stables like a blind man knows his own roomful of furniture.

Although she might have been afraid in her own room in the dark, she had never felt afraid in the stable; it had always been her sanctuary.

She was afraid now.

Anyone who had a legitimate reason for being out here would not have shut the door, would have flicked the switch inside, and, above all, would not have simply melted into the silence as though purposely becoming a part of it, the thick silence that fell after the first shuffling response of the horses to the sudden, sharp clatter of the door. The only sounds now were the usual rustling sounds of threshing hooves, soft whinnies and snorts.

Emily started to say, *Who's there?* and stopped. Instinct told her to hold her tongue. She stood there with the towel she had used to wipe the tack, hearing footsteps on the floor of the stable. If she could get out of Shandy's stall to the barrels ... Katie had always said they made her think of Ali Baba. But, no, whoever it was would look there ... for *her?* Who could be looking for *her?* The steps seemed to be moving very quickly straight down the line of boxes. Emily could hear the thrust of the outside bolts on each box door being shot — one, two, three — one after another.

Someone was locking each of the doors, locking the horses in. Someone was locking *her* in. There must have been an electric torch switched on down at the far end, because she saw the play of reflected light dimly on the boards and ceiling.

Why was she being locked in?

She heard the creaking of the door to the loose box at the far end, probably old Nellie's box, and then a high neigh. The horse was objecting to this invasion. The door rattled shut. And once again there was the sound of a bolt thrown.

She pulled her knees right up to her chest, scarcely breathing. Now there came the same set of noises: gate to box opening, rustling of hooves, gate closing, bolt thrown. All repeated in Jupiter's box.

There were seven boxes, three of them empty.

Now she knew what was happening: whoever it was was looking for her, and to make sure she didn't sneak out in the pitch-darkness, sneak through to the outside stable door — that person had locked them all and was now methodically inspecting each one of the loose boxes. Now the next box was being inspected and bolted.

There was no way she could see of getting out. She had her eyes tightly shut in an effort of thinking. What she wanted to do was just sit here, not moving a muscle, and hope that the thin light would pass over her and mistake her for another bag of feed.

The fourth box was being opened, scrutinized, locked.

Very slowly, Emily got up on her knees, then into a crouching position, and then moved quietly to Shandy's side. She gripped the mane for leverage and hoisted herself up on the pony's back. Shandy made snorting sounds, but that was all right, considering the racket the other horses were making at this intrusion.

There was nothing to do now but wait, lying flattened out on Shandy's back, her cheek against his neck. Whoever was there was now in the stall next to hers.

Shandy was whinnying and pawing the ground. He was not at all happy with this odd nocturnal performance. Emily locked her fingers round the reins and got her head as close to his ear as she could and waited.

She heard the bolt shoot back, saw the light from the torch stream across the horse's flank, just missing her, saw it searching the corners of the stall—

"Go," she whispered in the pony's ear.

Shandy exploded from the stall. When they got to the outside door, which was closed but not latched, she rammed it with her crop and the pony with his head and they shot through.

They left behind them someone, she thought happily, with the wind against her face, who must now be lying in the dirt.

Emily was across the cobbles and onto the drive in less than a minute. Another minute and she could have cut across the grass to the house—but obviously, she couldn't go *there* for help, because whoever it was in the stable could easily have come from *there*. To get to the High, she could ride through the gate at the end of the drive—

Too late she remembered the gate was shut; she'd been directed always to shut it behind her. Could she take the chance that the person (could it be anyone but nasty Derek with his wet mouth?) hadn't picked himself up off the ground and would grab her the moment she stopped long enough to unlock the gate? Any of the other horses in that stable she could have made jump it. But not Shandy. And Rookswood was bounded for a good quarter mile by a stone wall along the Hertfield Road.

There were only two choices — either follow the wall until it finally ended, which meant going through the Horndean wood, or cut back across the pasture, which would allow her to gallop to some point beyond Rookswood. . . .

It came down to one choice. The sound coming down the gravel behind her was not the sound of feet, but of horse's hooves.

So the Horndean wood it would have to be. Emily dug her heels into Shandy's side and slapped the reins. There was no way of doubling back now.

As she galloped along with the wall to her right, the wind was cold on her face and brought the smell of rain. She prayed it would rain. At least it would make some noise; it would cover the noise she herself made. The noise the hooves made behind her spewing up dirt and gravel thundered in her ears.

Just once before she entered the wood did she look back over her shoulder to see some dark outline coming at her. If the dark outline was Julia's horse, Jupiter, Emily knew she wouldn't have a prayer on the flat because Jupiter was simply faster than Shandy, even if Julia, who was a boring rider, was up on him.

When she reached the scattering of trees that began the Horndean wood, she picked out the line of an old bridle path and slowed Shandy to a trot. Somewhere off to her left, she heard the other horse gallop by.

Now she couldn't keep going ahead, toward the end of the wall and the relative safety of the Hertfield–Horndean Road — because the rider would be up there. And if he were already starting back toward Rookswood, then doubling back might be the worst of all.

She could stand on Shandy's back and scale the wall. But if Shandy were found riderless, the other one would know and be on the other side of the wall and looking for her. And he'd be on horseback and she'd be on foot. Probably he still had his torch, while she had nothing except her crop, and what good would that do?

He could leave false trails. The words of Superintendent Jury came back to her just as she heard the crackle of twig and brush, the sounds of the returning rider, now moving more slowly.

Leave false trails: it was as if Jimmy Poole, before he got so sick (and almost died, she was sure), were out here trying to tell her what to do.

Quickly and quietly she moved Shandy to a section of the wall, climbed up on his back, balanced herself carefully and clambered up on the wall. From her neck she took the towel which she'd used to wipe down the tack, let it fall on the wall, where it caught on a protruding vine. Good. It looked like it got caught there as she went over. She walked along the wall a few feet, caught hold of the lower branch of the tree, and swung herself up.

She didn't have to wait long.

There was a thrashing through the branches and bracken, and the thin beam of a torch pointing into space below her, searching the outlines of trees before it.

The torch had picked out Shandy's rump. The other horse stopped; someone got down from the saddle, squelched through the wet leaves, came to a stop just below her.

For the first time in her life, Emily Louise Perk's curiosity hadn't got the best of her. She was frozen to the tree, her face pressed against it, unbreathing.

In the few seconds when she knew this awful person was inspecting both horse and wall, she knew she should have looked down, but she couldn't. She was too much of a coward.

Emily Louise had cried three times in her life: once, when her father had gone; once, when her cat had died; once, when Katie O'Brien had gone into the hospital.

This was the fourth time, and she was crying because she knew Jimmy Poole wouldn't have been that much of a coward.

The rain stopped. The dark closed in, even thicker than before. The person had gone, getting back on the horse (she was sure it must be Jupiter) and trotting off. The rider would be looking for her somewhere else.

She climbed down from the tree onto Shandy's back and wished she had something to give him for a reward for waiting so still and patiently.

Emily made for the end of the wall and the Hertfield–Horndean Road. At the point where the wall ended, the road was bisected by another road, narrower, going to the hamlet of St. Lyons.

Shandy was tired and breathing heavily, shaking his head as if he'd like to shake free of the bit. She was on the St. Lyon's road now, and off to her right across the hedges and long pasture, she could make out the row of lights from the rear of cottages along Littlebourne High Street. That pink, milky light was cast by the lamp Mary O'Brien always lit in her bedroom. Far off and screened by trees, the lights winked on and off like stars. In just another quarter of a mile she would be at the turning where the little St. Lyons road went straight on and a rutted country lane branched off to the right and led back to connect up with the road that finally became Littlebourne's High Street.

Emily was so exhausted that she just lay her face down on Shandy's mane and let him walk on. In the distance, she heard a car.

It drove past her, a dark blur in the night. There was little traffic on the St. Lyons road.

Her mind went blank with fear when she saw it stop a distance behind her, reverse in the narrow road, trying to maneuver itself by backing halfway into the hedgerow.

And then she knew. She started Shandy at a canter and quickly changed from a canter to a gallop. Shandy was fast, at least with Emily riding, but no horse in the Bodenheims' stable was fast enough to outrun a car.

She'd better outrun it, if she wanted to live through the night.

The car was now some distance behind her, but it was clear from the position of its headlamps that it had managed to turn and was coming straight on.

The fork in the road was just ahead. The turn to the right would screen her for a few seconds from the car. She slowed Shandy to a walk, took off her tweed coat and stuck the arms, one each side through the loops of the bridle. It was a silly ruse, but she remembered all those time she'd fooled her mum by stuffing pillows under her bedclothes to make it look as if she were still there after she'd crawled out the window on some midnight adventure. Right now, she wished she'd listened a little more to her mum over the years, though she still wasn't sure what her mum had had to say.

She could hear the car gaining on the St. Lyons road and it was very near to the turn. With Shandy at a walk, Emily slid off, yelled, "Go!" and slapped his rump. Shandy broke into a gallop, the fluttering coat atop the saddle.

Just as the beam from the headlamps illuminated the legs of the pony, Emily fell back through the hedge, crying and hating herself.

What a traitorous thing to do to Shandy.

IV

Mr. William Francis Bevins Potts was clearly so proud of his position with the rolling stock engineer's department that he hadn't minded at all having his favorite television program interrupted to talk about London Transport. Whilst he offered up a smorgasbord of mind-numbing details about the history and adaptation of tube stock and rolling stock, Jury looked at the lathering of colorful Underground posters on the walls of Mr. Pott's flat in the Edgeware Road — marvelous Edwardians being helped by equally marvelous London bobbies in their outings on the Underground. Indeed, Mr. Potts's flat rather reminded Jury of a tube station, with its huge hoardings, but otherwise spartan furnishings.

Jury let him talk on for a few minutes, for he believed that people who were obsessed with a topic needed an outlet for that obsession and would come round much more quickly and fix much more clearly on the actual questions Jury wanted answered.

Occasionally through this morass of exquisitely boring detail would flash an intriguing fact like an exotic fish. He hadn't known, for instance, that the newer diesel hydraulic locomotives built in the late '60s had Rolls-Royce engines. Plant might be interested in that detail.

". . . surface stock is used on the District, Circle and Metropolitan Lines, you see, and the tube stock is used on Northern, Jubilee . . ."

Any mention of the Jubilee Line brought a spark to Mr. Potts's eye. His description of the building of that sounded pretty much as if he'd been around at the Creation.

None of this seemed to bore Sergeant Wiggins, however; Wiggins had a mind for minutiae equal to William F. B. Potts — it was one of the reasons Jury found him to be invaluable, especially in the note-taking arena. When Jury finally felt he had to interrupt this getting-onto-ten-minutes of monologue, Wiggins looked at him almost reproachfully.

"That's all very interesting, Mr. Potts. But what we're concerned with here really has more to do with the stations themselves than with the actual stock. We came to you because we were told you probably knew as much as anyone about the technical details of the building—"

Emphatically, Mr. Potts nodded; apparently having had his fix for the day with his own special interest, he was willing to move on to broader matters. He ran his hands back over his sparse gray hair, made a tent of his fingers, and riveted his attention on Jury.

"If you had to dispose of something, something relatively small, by way of putting it in a safe place where you could come back and collect it later — where would you leave it in an Underground station?"

Mr. Potts, who seemingly could not be taken aback by any question related to the Underground, simply asked, crisply, "How small and how long left?"

Jury made a circle with thumb and index finger. "Maybe the size of a half-crown. And how long is questionable. I'd say from a day to . . . indefinitely."

That, Mr. Potts's expression told Jury, was a facer. "You mean hide some article so that no one else would come on it, either by design or accident?" Jury nodded. Mr. Potts thought for some time, looking from one to the other of them, looking at the posters on the wall, started several times to answer, drew his answer back, as it were, from the brink, shook his head, and then said, finally, "Odd as it seems, there'd be hardly anywhere. Except, perhaps, one of the grates."

"Grates?"

Mr. Potts nodded. "You've seen them; everyone has. You just don't notice them. Ventilation grates. Of course, it depends what station you're talking about — there're different sorts. You could probably stick something in there and it wouldn't be found for a year. A lot of them are down at floor level. Just walk through the tunnel, you'll see them. People never look down at their feet, do they?"

Jury rose and Wiggins slapped his notebook shut. "Mr. Potts, we're extremely indebted to you. Sorry we can't tell you any more."

That did not seem to bother Mr. Potts at all, who could be, when it came to anything not connected with surface stock and tube stock, a master of economical language. "Pleasure," was all he said, as he showed them to the door.

There, Wiggins turned and asked, "I was wondering, sir. How do they clean them? The tunnels, I mean. Don't they have to clean them?"

William F. B. Potts's chest swelled up, not with pride nor vanity, but to get plenty of air in his lungs. "Certainly. It's the tunnel cleaning train that does that, Sergeant. It's equipped with floodlights outside each one of the motor cars and behind the driver's cab, that's where the cleaning operator is. There's the filter car and the nozzle car. Nozzle car draws the dust into the filter car. It operates at various speeds. Built at Acton Works, it was sometime in the '70s . . ."

"Thanks very much, Mr. Potts. We'll be in touch," said Jury, steering Wiggins toward the stairs.

The door closed behind them and Sergeant Wiggins said, "It's good to know that, isn't it, sir? I've always wondered."

V

The grate was almost directly across from the spot where Katie O'Brien had slumped. It was at floor level and beneath the *Evita* poster. With the help of two London Transport security police, Jury found it.

The necklace had been wrapped in a thin, dark handkerchief, fed through the opening in the grate — something which would have taken hardly more than a matter of seconds — where it had lain on a ledge collecting the soot of the whole last year. Had anyone actually looked, the small bundle would have been easy to see. But why would anyone bother to look into a ventilation grate in a tube station?

TWENTY-THREE

"KILL you?" exclaimed Melrose Plant to the bedraggled bit of child standing before him in the Bold Blue Boy. It was true that she did look as if she'd spent the night in hand-to-hand combat with thorny thickets and bogs and hedgerows. Her ordinarily unkempt hair was even more tangled than usual; her face was muddy, her jeans ripped.

She nodded, frowning at the floor.

Melrose had been looking for her everywhere for the past forty-five minutes. Peter Gere was not at the station. Polly Praed had seen Emily around eight, she had said. The Bodenheims denied any knowledge of her at all. Her mother was not at home.

It was ten o'clock when he had settled down to wait with a pint of bitter and a cigar and had been scared nearly witless by the sudden appearance of the small white face at the casement window and the demand to help her crawl through. No, she refused to come through the saloon bar or the public bar. So crawl in she had done, Plant dragging her by the armpits.

Melrose got up from the window seat to look out through the top of the glass pane where the lamp just outside the pub illuminated part of the road. He could see her pony tethered to the lamp. It seemed to be munching at a bit of grass. Why was her coat hooked to the bridle?

When he asked her, the look she returned him was one of withering scorn. "To make them think I was still on Shandy, of course. Then I was afraid maybe they'd run into *him*. But when I went across the pasture and finally got to the High he was just walking round Littlebourne Green. Shandy's very smart." The look clearly added: *More than some.* "I want to find Mr. Jury." The mouth downturned, prelude, he thought, to a fit of tears, although it was hard to imagine her crying.

"At the moment, he's in London. I expect he'll be back very soon. As a matter of fact, he wanted me to keep an eye on you."

The look now told him what a bang-up idea she thought *that* was.

"Come on." He dragged her over to the turnstile of crisps, went behind the little bar himself, and got out the lemon squash. If her mouth was full, she'd forget her misery. "Who knew where you were?"

Emily shrugged. "Lots of people. I always feed the horses Sunday nights. Here." The colored map, now damp, muddy and wrinkled, had been in her pocket all along. She showed it to Melrose.

He looked from the map to her. "When did you do *this?*"

She told him while rooting out the last crisp from her bag.

"Did you show it to anyone?"

"To Polly. We figured out what it was. It's the Underground. Why would anyone want to do a map like that of the Underground? London's ever so exciting, though. I hardly *ever* get to go to London." She sighed dramatically and glared at Melrose as if he were personally responsible for her countrified existence.

"Did you tell anyone else?"

Emily had made a ball of the empty crisp bag and was bouncing it in the air.

"Stop that and pay attention!"

She frowned mightily and slid down in her chair. "You needn't be nasty. I only told Mrs. Lark."

The Bodenheim cook. Wonderful. She, no doubt, immediately told all of the family.

He looked at Emily, wondering what to do. Young ladies in distress had never been Plant's métier. He expected mothers, nannies or old cooks to present themselves for such emergencies. Emily's mother seemed to be, as usual, unavailable. He hadn't seen Mary O'Brien. Polly Praed? He suggested it.

"No!" The single syllable was explosive. "I don't want to talk to anybody." She had gone round behind the bar to find her coloring book and crayons. Having secured them, she returned to her stool, all kitted out, seemingly oblivious to the awfulness of the previous hours.

"You're talking to me."

"That's different."

Either that meant he wasn't anybody, or that he had been admitted to that very select company thus far comprised of Superintendent Jury and whatever horses happened to be about. "I'm glad to know you–trust me."

Her look would have turned anyone more unused to her to stone. "Only because you're a stranger, and you don't ride horses, so it wasn't you."

Implying that in any other circumstances, he'd have all the makings of the born killer.

"You don't think it could have been *Polly?*" Emily didn't answer. "But that's—" He wanted to say *ridiculous,* but it stuck in his throat.

"It's why I didn't want to come in through the front. I don't know who's out there." From the other side of the wall came the warm if indistinguishable voices of the regulars, like something wrapped in cotton wool.

"Well, you can stay here the night. I'm sure Mary O'Brien can find you a nightie—"

"Nightie! I don't wear *those!* I sleep in my knickers." She finished up her green Bambi and slapped the page over.

Melrose got up. "I'm going to call the police."

"I'll only talk to that Scotland Yard man."

"He's in London. I'll call Hertfield. Maybe Peter's—"

She looked up from the blue squirrel she was coloring, with steel in her eyes. "Mr. Jury."

Part Three

MUSIC
and
MEMORY

TWENTY-FOUR

◆◆◆◆◆◆◆◆◆

M R. Jury was, shortly after this exchange, talking to six other policemen — Wiggins among them — who had been routed from their Sunday evening activities to assemble in the Wembley Knotts Underground station. Since three of them belonged to the Flying Squad, it probably wasn't the telly which Jury had interrupted when he made his call to Scotland Yard. The other two were security guards with London Transport.

"Nasty," said Detective Inspector Graham. "But what makes you think this villain will come back here tonight?"

"Tonight, or early tomorrow morning. Tonight is most likely because there won't be the Monday morning commuters. No matter how early, you always seem to run into someone who has to be at work spot on six, or something."

"Still," said Graham, "if this necklace has been lying in that grate"—he pointed below the *Evita* poster—"all this time, why now?"

"Because our friend knows that there's not much time, that's why. Ever since Katie O'Brien found that map, the whole thing must have been pretty nerve-wracking. Two women dead and another one in a coma. Don't tell me this person's going to wait around for *us* to find the bloody necklace."

"Then he's got exactly one hour and thirty-three minutes before this tube stop closes down." Detective Inspector Graham stopped at the sound of the echoing footsteps coming round the curve of the wall.

It was Cyril Macenery, carrying a violin case. He kept his eyes down, as if he were searching for something.

Jury introduced him to the assembled company. "Our itinerant musician," he said. "We've cleared the place out — not that it took much clearing — and the only ones here now are you" — he looked the group over — "and Cyril, Katie's teacher. I think it should be business as usual, and the thing that will make our friend least suspicious is if there's someone playing down here. As far as I'm concerned," Jury added, grimly, "it's only poetic justice." He looked at Cyril Macenery, who did not reply. He'd agreed to do this, to play his violin, but with some resistance, answering Jury in monosyllables when Jury had got hold of him at the hospital.

Temporary Detective Constable Tyrrwhitt, who was leaning against the wall, dressed in leather coat, Hawaiian shirt and jeans, said, "So there's two of us on the platform — not counting you two — one of us in the tunnel and one on the moving stairs. You're sure this creep knows where that necklace is?"

"I'm pretty sure," said Jury.

"Pretty sure," echoed Tyrrwhitt, stashing his gum behind the poster of Evita. She still dangled, dreadfully insecure, but sticking it.

Jury liked Tyrrwhitt. He was a T.D.C. now; he'd be in Graham's shoes, or shoes like them, inside a year, Jury bet. The sarcasm went, Jury thought, with the persona, half-developed through the clothes Tyrrwhitt wore for cover. He would have beat out the leather jackets Jury saw earlier any day.

"It's the best I can do," said Jury, handing round the photo he'd brought with him. "That's who you're looking for."

After they'd all had the picture, Graham passed it back. "Nasty, very nasty. I'd sooner suspect my old gran."

"Be glad it isn't your old gran. You might wake up with no fingers."

They were standing around the curve from the Evita poster, out of sight of the grate. Macenery had the violin — it was Katie's —

226

tucked beneath his chin. He plucked a string, stared at the wall, and said, "She's dead."

They had just been talking about what Macenery would play as a signal to the men on the platform if he saw the person they were looking for. Jury had turned to walk back down the corridor and thought he couldn't have heard him correctly. "What?"

"She's dead. Katie. She died just before you called."

Jury swallowed. "I don't believe it."

Macenery plucked a string of his violin. "Neither do I."

As he drowned himself in music, Jury stared for a moment, and then walked back down the corridor towards the platform.

They sat, Wiggins and Jury, in a murky corner at the end of the platform.

"You're kidding," said Wiggins, in as plaintive a voice as Jury had ever heard him use.

"I guess not. I wish I were." Jury took out his packet of cigarettes.

Wiggins was mournfully silent for a while and then he said, "But aren't you afraid Macenery will lose his head the minute he sees —?"

"No. If he could come here and do what he's doing, no, I don't. He's disciplined, see. I expect that's why he's so good."

The two passengers who got off the next train seemed to think he was good too. They stopped and listened before they started through the exit that led up to the little bridge and out the other side of the Wembley Knotts station.

And so it went for the next half-hour — Jury chain-smoking and studying the gray floor of the platform; Graham and Tyrrwhitt pacing; the others in the far corridor or the stair; Macenery playing the violin.

"What's he playing now, Wiggins?"

"I never heard it done except on a piano," said Wiggins gloomily. "It's called 'Pavanne for a Dead Princess'."

"Oh," was all Jury replied.

After another ten minutes, and thinking that he must be wrong, that nothing was going to happen that night, he heard the sound of the beeper. He pushed the button and over the speaker of his small radio he heard the quiet voice of the sergeant on the stair telling him the subject had just been spotted.

In a couple of minutes, they heard the first strains of the song Macenery had said he'd play — one of Katie's favorites — "Don't Cry for Me, Argentina."

Now they had to allow enough time for retrieval of the necklace. Jury gave it another three minutes and then signaled to Graham and the other detective sergeant. T.D.C. Tyrrwhitt was stationed in the corridor, ostensibly to listen to the violin and then to follow the suspect at a respectful distance.

The four of them — Graham, the D.S., Jury and Wiggins — went through the archway to the short flight of stairs and down.

Jury heard Tyrrwhitt commanding, "Hold it right there, mate."

The person frozen in a crouch by the grate was now looking from Tyrrwhitt behind him, gun leveled, to the others bearing down on him.

"Hello, Peter," said Jury.

Peter Gere had the handkerchief-wrapped necklace in his hands and said, "I should have bloody known. The minute I heard that goddamned song, I should have known. It was the same one *she* was playing, that afternoon."

Jury did not know where Cyril Macenery was. The music had stopped. But he was glad Macenery hadn't heard Gere say that.

In a voice so cold it could have frozen hell over, Detective Inspector Graham issued the usual warning to Gere. The provincial policeman — one of those whose incorruptibility was legendary. Apparently, Graham wanted to think they still existed.

Jury asked, "Why did you kill Katie O'Brien, Peter? Did you think she knew what that map meant?"

"I didn't kill her, did I? Just roughed her up a bit." Jury said nothing. "She found it when she was cleaning one day. Like a bloody idiot, I forgot to lock the desk drawer. Nosy little lass, that girl was. I overreacted. She gave me a funny look and went away. But then she came back: she got at it again by taking out the drawer on the other side. Well, I couldn't have her see me in Wembley Knotts station, could I?"

"And you wanted to take everyone's mind off Katie's accident, so you wrote those letters."

"It worked, didn't it? Anyway, I didn't kill her. She's in hospital."

"She's dead."

Gere went ashen. Jury knew, while the awful news was sinking in, that he had the advantage. "What about Cora Binns? Did you know she was Tree's lady friend? Or was she wearing some of Kennington's jewelry?"

Gere looked at Jury almost blindly. With Katie dead, it was a little late for denials. "I knew he *had* a girlfriend. Men like Trevor Tree always do, don't they?" he added. "What a fool he was to give her those rings. She'd got off the bus and was searching for Stonington. Said she had business with Lady Kennington. How the bloody hell was *I* to know what her 'business' was. I didn't know how much she knew or how much Tree had told her. And there she was with that jewelry that Kennington's widow was bound to recognize — I could hardly talk it off her fingers."

All of this was brought out in a rush, like a man fighting for oxygen, before he seemed to realize how much talking he himself was doing.

"What about Ramona Wey?"

Gere didn't answer.

Jury thought perhaps he could appeal to Gere's vanity. "You must have been damned shrewd, Peter, to get Trevor Tree to trust you."

"That's a laugh. Other way round, I'd say." He fell silent again.

"Get him the hell out of here," said Jury, turning away.

With false heartiness, Detective Inspector Graham said, "Well, Mr. Gere. We might just as well take the tube." Jury knew he was joking, and the joke didn't pay off.

As Graham was about to put cuffs on Peter Gere, the train stopped, disgorged a couple of passengers — a woebegone woman with hair to her waist and a gypsy skirt dragging a four- or five-year-old girl. Late for a kid to be up, thought Jury, his mind on Emily Louise. The mother seemed all unaware of this phalanx of men and commenced plowing straight through them.

Jury could not see how anyone could have been that quick, but

Peter Gere grabbed up the little girl and backed off with her. A look of surprise and then unspeakable horror crossed the woman's face.

Automatically, Tyrrwhitt went for his gun, realized that with the child as a shield, it was no good. He stood there, mutely staring. No one was close enough to Gere to get him before he was out of the exit door leading up to the bridge. Jury raced after him and reached the bridge as the doors of the train sucked shut and it began to move. He yelled to Peter Gere over the noise of the train and the sudden rush of wind to put the girl down, he hadn't a prayer, there were police at the other exit too. He made a grab for the little girl's skirt.

Gere looked desperately both ways — back at Jury, forward to that other exit — and thrust the child from him. Jury grabbed her back as Gere went crashing through the makeshift barrier across the broken wire mesh, hoping, apparently, to ride the top of the train.

Peter Gere's hands scrabbled wildly for purchase, but there was nothing there now to give it. He missed the last car by inches and hit the track.

Jury looked down, the little girl shoved against his shoulder, and was glad William F. B. Potts hadn't mentioned the voltage on the outside rail.

TWENTY-FIVE

◦◦◦◦◦◦◦◦

I

WHEN Jury found Melrose Plant at two o'clock in the morning, he was sitting with an overflowing ashtray, a bottle of Remy, and a book of French poetry.

"There's a message from Mainwaring. He wants to see you, no matter what time you get in."

Jury sat down heavily. "Let me have some of that, will you?"

Melrose shoved the bottle toward him. Then he told him about Emily Louise.

"Oh, my God," said Jury. He was silent for a moment. "And how's Mary O'Brien?"

"Dr. Riddley gave her some sort of sedative and I suppose it worked for a while, since he managed to get her upstairs and into bed. I was about to go to bed myself when she came down in her nightdress with a terrible blank sort of look on her face. Do you know, she was carrying an oil lamp. She made a slow circuit of the place; she held it up to all the windows, looking out; she might have been looking for some late traveler. . . . It was eerie." He lit a fresh cigar. "I think I know now what's meant about someone's being 'a ghost of his old self.' She was flesh and blood turned to vapor. Really, I thought I could put my hand through her." He was silent for a moment, and then added: "There's no such thing as being prepared for death. I'm glad I never saw her. . . ." He looked at Jury, as if half-afraid Jury might tell him about Katie O'Brien. Jury said nothing, and Melrose went on. "When Riddley told me about Peter Gere — I was baffled."

"How'd Dr. Riddley find out?"

"That music teacher of Katie's — what's his name?"

"Cyril Macenery."

"He called Riddley. Apparently, this chap had to have somebody to talk to who knew Katie. Very broken up."

Jury drew out the necklace, still wrapped in the handkerchief, and dropped it on the table. "The people who had to die for that little lot —" He shrugged unhappily. "Go ahead, you can touch it. It's not needed in evidence anymore."

Melrose gave a low whistle. "Beautiful, objectively speaking. Are you going to return it to Lady Kennington?" Jury nodded. Melrose turned the gem between his thumb and forefinger, ran his thumb over the carving. "So Peter Gere was Tree's accomplice?"

"It occurred to me after I thought about that search of the people there, the house, the grounds. How simple can you get? The person spot-on was Peter Gere, wasn't it? The village bobby gets called straightaway, and he calls Hertfield police. And he's the one who searches Trevor Tree; he said so himself. He could have either just left the necklace in Tree's dressing gown pocket, or palmed it himself and put it in his own and given it back to Tree later."

"Would Tree have trusted Gere with it?"

"Why not? It was only a matter of waiting until everyone had disbursed, finally. Police back to Hertfield, the Kenningtons back to bed. Gere couldn't have got very far with it, so a double-cross was very unlikely. All Tree wanted was to get the necklace out of the house and safely stashed somewhere else — we'll never know precisely what he had in mind — so he rises early, walks down the drive so as not to wake anyone, gets a ride to Hertfield, and does the smart thing: melts into the early-morning commuters to London. What went through his mind then, I don't know. But I'll guess. On the train he gets a bit worried that someone might not assume he's sleeping late, that someone might shop him, and there'll be a greeting on the other end. Police at his digs, at least. So he walks up that corridor and sees the grate. Bend down, tie your shoe, something like that, and slip this through." Jury held up the necklace. The stone winked in the light.

"Then there was Cora Binns. We talked about her 'running into someone.' But that's a bit coincidental, isn't it? She didn't run into her murderer by accident, she did what anyone might do — asked directions of the local bobby. Not only did he give her directions, he followed her into the Horndean wood. Peter Gere recognized the rings she was wearing and wondered what 'business' she'd got at Stonington. Carstairs's men found the rings in Gere's box room, in the bottom of a carton full of junk marked for the Jumble sale at the fête. Obviously, he never delivered it. Can't imagine why," added Jury wryly. "I guess he thought no one would bother looking there."

"What about Ramona Wey?"

Jury shook his head. "He stopped talking at that point. Ramona Wey must have known Cora Binns. Maybe she knew the death of Cora had some connection with the emerald. I may find out when I talk with Mainwaring."

Melrose thought for a moment. "I wonder what she said to Peter Gere at the gate when he was taking tickets. I was so interested in all the backs she seemed to be getting up — mainly the Bodenheims' — that I didn't give a thought to Peter Gere."

Jury drank some cognac neat. "Who would? He seemed such a pleasant, mild sort of chap. Over the edge, he was, and hid it wonderfully. He tried to direct out attention to everyone else. Those letters were just a blind, something to get people thinking about more intriguing things than Katie O'Brien. He must finally have figured out what that represented, and with all of that money at stake, he wasn't going to let mere human life stand in his way."

"But what would make him think of the *grate* as a hiding place?"

"Peter Gere once worked for London Transport. He mentioned it in relationship to the letter he'd got — written to himself, that is — 'skulduggery' when he worked for LT, he said. So he might think of it quicker than you or me." Jury poured himself another drink. "Where's Emily now?"

"With her mother. Oh, yes, she really does have one. Mrs. Perk came by and got her. Horrified at what had happened, but by that time Emily had had a kip and had washed her face, so she didn't look quite so fierce. Mrs. Perk said she'd told her to go home and to bed right after she'd finished at the stables. Mrs. Perk says Emily doesn't like sitters. Makes their life hell, so she finally gave up. Half the time when Emily is out, I believe her mummy think's she's in."

Jury rubbed his eyes. "Speaking of kips, I think I'll have one myself, as soon as I talk to Mainwaring. I'm going to Stonington tomorrow and then back to London. Finish up the paperwork. Wiggins'll do most of it, I hope."

Plant picked up the emerald again, held it up to the light, and adjusted his spectacles. "If I didn't know it was Peter Gere, I'd certainly have sworn it was Ernestine Craigie who was the guilty party."

"Oh? Why's that?"

The emerald necklace swung between them. "Surely, that bird carved there is a Great Speckled Crackle."

They sat there for another ten minutes, passing the bottle back and forth and talking about everything they could think of except Katie O'Brien.

II

"What did she tell you, Mr. Mainwaring?"

Freddie Mainwaring sat in robe and slippers, looking vulnerable, as men will who are routed out of bed in the middle of the night. "That she knew this Binns woman. I wasn't aware of it before, but Ramona worked for that agency. Funny, I can't think of her doing that. She always seemed too . . . worldly to be a typist."

"And?"

Mainwaring seemed to be speaking more to the silver-framed photograph of his wife than to Jury. Perhaps he was trying to explain his fall from grace. "Ramona told me she remembered this girl talking a lot about some 'Trev' — her boyfriend in London, though Ramona doubted Cora Binns would appeal much to any man for very long. Anyway, Ramona didn't make any connection between that and Kennington's secretary. I think she knew him better than she admitted, to tell the truth." Blood rushed into his face. He brushed his hair away from his forehead. "Until she saw the picture of the dead woman."

"Why didn't she tell us all of this?" Jury thought he knew why.

Mainwaring pulled a crumpled packet of cigarettes from his robe pocket. He seemed to have wilted in the last twenty-four hours, grown grayer, sadder. "Ramona seemed to think the Binns woman had blackmail on her mind."

"That's a strange conclusion to draw. After all, it was *you* who got her to come here."

"I know. But Ramona . . . To tell the truth, Ramona wasn't all that nice of a person. It's terrible to say, but—"

"You're relieved. That doesn't mean you'd run to murder to get that relief."

Mainwaring's look was grateful. Perhaps this late confidence, too late to do Ramona Wey any good, was intended to set the record straight. "I couldn't seem to shake that idea loose from her mind."

"Did she have any idea who it might be who was Tree's confederate—if that's what she did think? Obviously, she thought someone in Littlebourne was guilty."

"I don't think she knew at all. She laughed and said she'd take a shot in the dark. Or several shots."

"You mean random accusations? That's a very dangerous game to play."

They both looked at each other, knowing just how dangerous the game had been.

TWENTY-SIX

ထထထထထ

1

I T was shortly after ten the next morning. Jury had left for Stonington and Melrose decided to walk across Littlebourne Green in hopes of clearing his head of last night's brandy. There was a stile in the sub-post office and he could purchase one and write some vague nonsense to Agatha.

Inside, he found that Miles Bodenheim had come down off the mountain rather early to whip the devils out of the post office. The postmistress, leaning on the counter and resting her weight on her knuckles, seemed impervious to whatever onslaught the gods had seen fit to deliver to her door.

"I should think, Mrs. Pennystevens, that in the circumstances, and especially as you are a public servant, having kept your position pretty much by the sufferance of us humble citizens" (a brittle smile, here) "—you would not be so quick to imply niggardliness. The letter to the Chief Constable weighs exactly the same as the other; it must do, for I wrote just the same letter to both. To insist on another two p for the second letter merely proves your scales are malfunctioning—Ah, my dear chap!—"

His eye brightened at sight of Melrose. Fresh quarry. Melrose found himself pulled by the arm and being led between the tiers of MacVities' cakes, golden syrup, and water biscuits. "Of course you've *heard!* Peter Gere! We none of us could believe it. Sylvia is absolutely *prostrate,* and who can blame her—"

Melrose said mildly, "I hadn't realized she was so fond of him—"

"*Fond* of him?" Sir Miles careened slightly backwards, upsetting a few half-loaves. "Of course she wasn't *fond* of him. It's the idea we have all been placed at risk for all of these years, our very lives hanging in the balance—Sylvia's words exactly—'Our very *lives* hanging in the balance'—well, it's all in my letter to the Commissioner. I sat down straightaway and wrote to him and the chief constable, and I mean to point out the same things to Superintendent Jury when I see him, that we can't have psychopaths on our police force!"

"I don't believe," said Melrose, picking up a couple of packages of MacVities for Emily, "it's actually part of the requirement."

Miles looked at him with some suspicion, didn't quite get the gist of that, and steamrolled on. "It's the lack of *screening,* don't you see? They simply take anyone, obviously, and don't do a proper check into their backgrounds. Why, just look at that sickly type who goes round with the superintendent."

"Sergeant Wiggins is a very good policeman."

"A strong wind would blow him over. Got all sorts of things the matter—" He picked up the cream crackers, checked the price and replaced them. "—with him. I can't under—" Melrose was saved from further defense of Wiggins by Sir Miles's attention being diverted onto fresh paths. "There go the Craigies," he said, craning his neck to look out the window. "Please do excuse me, dear fellow, but I must have a word with them. I know they must be prostrate. . . ." And out the door he sailed. Melrose heard him trumpeting *Ernestine! Augusta!* all across the High.

Having posted his card (a view of Hertfield from the air) to Agatha, telling her that the village was a singularly unexciting place, he wondered what to do with himself. No one seemed to be about. It had started to rain and the sky was dull and the Green wind-whipped. Littlebourne reminded Melrose at the moment of one of those old movie sets, deserted and desolate.

As he was crossing the Green, heading toward the Magic Muffin, he heard the clip clop of a horse's hooves.

It was Julia Bodenheim, up on Jupiter, all kitted out for a nearby meet, boots polished, stock crisply white. He was awfully glad she did not stop. All she did was raise her crop to her cap and smile and sit a bit taller, giving him the advantage of her trim profile.

He watched her go. Three deaths in as many days and Julia Bodenheim was going out to chase a fox, demonstrating to Melrose the remarkable English propensity for silliness.

II

Most of Littlebourne seemed to have converged on the Magic Muffin, muffins and tea being considered, presumably, not quite so celebratory as ale and beer. The Bold Blue Boy was closed, at any rate, leaving the eleven o'clock tipplers without much choice.

Polly Praed was, fortunately, one of them. She was seated at a corner table with an elderly woman with gray hair who was just in the process of leaving, but who looked Melrose over carefully before giving up her seat.

"Everyone is simply . . . astounded. Did you guess it was Peter Gere?" She was leaning toward him, her glasses scooped up on top of her head, her eyes shining with a mixture of excitement and sadness.

Melrose decided not to lie. "No. I was wondering, Polly—"

She did not seem the least interested in whatever he was wondering. "And *Emily!* My God! Going after a poor little girl like that."

Melrose nodded, though he found it very difficult to think of Emily Louise as a "poor, little girl." "Yes, absolutely dreadful. I thought perhaps—"

What he thought was no more of the moment than what he was wondering. "I always liked Peter Gere. He seemed so . . . mild. Unassuming. The very picture of the village bobby."

"Polly—"

This time he was interrupted by Miss Pettigrew, who whisked over with a tray to clear up the used teacup and plate before Melrose. Her hair was flyaway, her cheeks pink. Whatever terrors had befallen the village, Miss Pettigrew was right there to offer succor in the form of tea and muffins.

"Nothing, thank you," said Melrose. She whisked the tray from the table.

"Well, I suppose you'll be leaving now it's all over."

Although he was delighted she had finally given him an opportunity to extend his invitation, he was less than delighted that her tone, when she said this, was hardly one of sadness, not even one of resignation.

"Yes. Tomorrow, after the funeral. I thought perhaps sometime, when you weren't in the throes of your latest attempt to kill off the Bodenheims, you might consider visiting me at Ardry End. It's quite a lovely old place; it's been in the family — the Earls of Caverness — for several centuries."

She broke off part of a muffin and buttered it. "I suppose you have heaps of money."

"Heaps."

"That's very nice of you, but I don't know. I never go anywhere, really. Travel is all in the mind, isn't it?"

He did not attempt to answer that conundrum. "We used to have a mystery writer in Long Piddleton. He's gone now," Melrose added, hinting that the vacancy was open.

But her mind was, apparently, still on the subject of money. "I wonder how much policemen make?" She studied her muffin.

Oh, hell, thought Melrose.

III

To Jury's eyes, the steps of Stonington were as wide as water and its gray facade even more impenetrable than before. The sky was like slate; the rain had stopped, but the trees rained on; rime edged the empty urns.

Not wanting to take her by surprise with the nature of his mission, Jury had asked Carstairs to ring up Jenny Kennington and tell her what had happened. Cowardice, that — his wanting to pretend he was only the messenger bearing news he had had little hand in bringing about.

She must have been watching from one of the windows, for she opened the door before he reached it. She was dressed as she had been yesterday, in a skirt and the same silver-gray sweater.

"Lady Kennington. I've come to—" Was he intending to hand over the necklace on the doorstep?

"I know why. Inspector Carstairs rang me. Come in. He rang up late last night . . ." She looked as if she hadn't slept very well afterward. She gave a vague little shrug, seemed about to say something, changed her mind, shook her head. "It's awful. I couldn't believe . . . I didn't know Peter Gere very well at all. But . . ." Once again, she led him through the door to the chilly-looking library and once again apologized for the cold. "It seems useless trying to heat these rooms, especially with the moving and everything."

The leather couch and chairs were under dust covers. "I'm leaving all of this. I've never liked it." There were packing cases by the bookshelves.

They walked through to the other, smaller room. Jury felt a twinge of regret when he saw the flowered, chintz-covered chair was gone. He had not realized until just then how it must have hung in his mind like a picture, that arrangement—the chair, the shawl, the teacup on the floor. "Where are you moving to?"

"I don't know. Once we lived in Stratford—outside Stratford, rather, in the Avon valley. A friend of mine wants to sell a cottage in the old part of town. Very tiny, two up and two down." She smiled slightly. "That's what I need."

"Do you?" Jury asked, not looking at her, but through the French window. Outside in the cloistered courtyard, where no trees were, leaves had gathered mysteriously below the figure in the dry fountain. Color had fled completely from the day, leaving behind only the monochromatic scene of white marble, gray stone, dark leaves.

Thinking his question perhaps rhetorical, she didn't answer, but led him through to the dining room. It was unchanged, of course, for there had been nothing here to change. "I thought we could go into the kitchen where there's a fire." Still, she lingered here, looking out the long windows. It was almost ritualistic, the way she stopped in each room, as if paying obeisance to some house-god to keep him from loosing his potent magic.

240

Certainly, she seemed in no hurry to collect her necklace, which Jury felt was burning in a small, green fire in his pocket.

In a moment she said, "Katie O'Brien's dead, too."

"Yes," said Jury, bringing out the necklace. "This is yours."

There was nothing for her to do now but hold out her hands, cupped like someone taking a drink from a stream. He dropped the emerald into it. She held it up, turning it in the light. "Four people died because of this."

"Don't be stupid about it," said Jury, brusquely. She looked at him, surprised. "I mean, it's yours, it belongs to you. If you don't want to wear it, then hand it over to Sotheby's or someone and let them auction it off. With that kind of money, you won't have to leave and move to Stratford-upon-Avon or anywhere else."

If she had paid any attention to this, she gave no sign. The next thing she said was, "You know, I always thought the burial rites of the Egyptians were somehow more hopeful than ours. Leaving food and wine and money and gems in the tomb, so that the person would have plenty in the afterlife."

"What are you suggesting now? That the necklace carries the Curse of the Pharaohs, or something?"

"No." Her cool eyes appraised him. "I get the feeling you think I'm not properly grateful. . . . Believe me, I am."

"I don't expect you to be grateful. I expect you to take proper care of yourself, though." He turned away to look out at the mournful statue, feeling irrationally angry.

"Oh," was all she said. Her hands fooled with the clasp of the necklace, which she then placed round her neck. "There, you see. I don't think it's cursed at all."

Jury was trying not to smile; he had no idea why he felt so cross. Indeed, she did look comical standing there in that droopy, gray sweater adorned with so much emerald elegance. "Okay," he said. "Just so long as you're sensible about it."

"I'm a very sensible person."

Jury wondered. He was moved to give her another brief lecture, but was saved from such foolishness by the door's creaking open at the other end of the room, and a reincarnated Tom entering. The black cat sat in the middle of the floor, slowly washing his face, as if its brush with death were a long-faded memory.

"The cat's back already?"

"Yes. It wasn't as bad as the vet thought after he looked at the X-rays. But it was still expensive."

Jury pointed to the necklace. "That'll pay a lot of vet's bills."

She fingered it, smiling. "It's rather pretty, isn't it? John told me that emeralds were valued for one reason because they're the color of vegetation. Regeneration, that sort of thing. . . . They were related to the flooding of the Nile and the restoration of life."

"Well, the cat certainly looks restored. Maybe that's a good sign."

She looked at the cat, who was squinting up at them as if it needed glasses. It yawned. "Ugly old thing, isn't it?"

"Yes. Too bad you don't like it." Jury smiled.

IV

Polly Praed was not the only one concerned with how much money policemen make.

Emily Louise Perk pondered precisely the same question as she was currying Shandy that Monday afternoon. Only she was more transparent than Polly Praed: Emily wanted to know how much a superintendent of police made.

"Why don't I just subpoena Superintendent Jury's bank account?" asked Melrose, from his seat on a bale of hay.

The sarcasm fell wide. Emily continued her discussion of the relative merits and cost of different kinds of horses. "A truly good horse can cost thousands of pounds. But, of course, I don't want race-horses or anything like that."

"That's lucky for the superintendent. Give him time to pay off his car." Melrose changed the subject. "I thought school was starting today." That should take the wind out of her sails, he thought, grumpily.

There was a retching noise from inside Shandy's box. "Tomorrow. But Mum said I'm not going because of the funeral. I hate school."

"Why?" Didn't everyone under twenty-five?

"Because it's stupid. You have to wear clothes, and everything." The velvet hat and a pair of eyes appeared over the edge of the gate to the box. "Are you going to Katie's funeral?"

"I am, yes. Are you?"

The furrow between her brows deepened. "Mum says I've got to."

"Don't you want to, then?"

"No. It's too sad. I don't want to see Katie put in the ground."

"None of us does." The eyes held his, clearly expecting an answer more profound. Melrose tried to get her mind off the funeral by saying, "I'll tell you what. Let's go for a ride!" This was said with an enthusiasm he certainly didn't feel.

"*You? Ride?*"

"You needn't take that tone." Melrose got up from his bale of hay and dusted his trousers. "I've been up on one or two horses in my life."

She came out of Shandy's box and stood looking him up and down like a tailor about to fit him for a new riding habit. "Well . . . I *suppose* the Bodenheims wouldn't mind if I put you up on old Nellie."

"Old *Nellie*. I daresay I could do with something sprightlier than that. . . ."

Fifteen minutes later saw Emily Louise Perk on Shandy and Melrose Plant on old Nellie riding off, if not into the sunset, at least into a September haze settling over the Horndean Road.

TWENTY-SEVEN

I

"So surprised I was to see you coming up the walk," said Mrs. Wasserman, her short legs trying to keep pace with Jury's long ones as they walked to the Angel. She occupied the basement flat in the house in Islington where Jury had also lived for years. "Did something happen? Where's your car? It didn't break down, I hope. You were going away on holiday, remember?"

Jury smiled. It was as if he'd misplaced his car, forgotten his holiday. "You know how it is, Mrs. Wasserman. Something interfered."

They were nearing the Angel. Mrs. Wasserman hated the Angel. She did not like its graffitied posters or its imprisoning lift or the foreigners who worked there. Sometimes she would go all the way to the Highbury-Islington station and take a bus back just to avoid the Angel.

She handed Jury a pound note to buy her ticket and continued her account of her most recent glimpse of the man she claimed had been following her. "He was there when I was walking from the Highbury station and down Islington High Street. There's a greengrocer's there I like to go to, you know. He followed me. And you remember the park there. We walked past it once and you said those trees, the two on the corner, how they looked like dancers, the way their branches were twined together." In her nervousness she was snapping her black purse open and shut. "He stood there, near those trees. He stood there all the while I was in the shop." The purse pressed tight against her bosom, she swayed slightly.

While Jury waited in the short line in front of the kiosk, he took out his notebook. "Describe him again, will you?" It was a ritual they went through often.

"So many times have I described him, Mr. Jury." This was said to a sad little headshake, a sad little smile. Jury was now cast in the role of neglectful nephew, whom she counted on, who had failed her, but who, perhaps, should be forgiven, he was so young and innocent and maybe even simple-minded. After all, he'd forgot his holiday and lost his car. "Well, he was small, and wearing a brown suit and coat. And a brown trilby. His eyes were not nice, not nice at all."

Jury wrote it down. There probably was such a man; there were many such men. But he knew the man wasn't following Mrs. Wasserman. Her obsession with her shadowy pursuer had grown over the years. Now for a few days she would avoid the greengrocer's and the little park and the trees that looked like dancers, before forgetting that that was where she had seen him last.

The new aluminum lift clattered to a stop and a bored Pakistani waited for his cargo to exit through the door which opened into a narrow alley.

Mrs. Wasserman looked at her ticket. "I have to change at King's Cross. I hate changing. Where are you going, Mr. Jury?"

"The East End. Wembley Knotts."

"Not a very nice place. You had better be careful. But I suppose that's silly, telling a policeman to be careful." She stepped on the lift. "It's just that, you know, the Underground's so awful anymore. Awful things happen."

"I know," said Jury to the closing doors of the lift.

II

Darkness was coming on quickly in Catchcoach Street. The windows of the Anodyne Necklace cast turbid half-moons of yellow light on the pavement.

When Jury walked in, he saw the women were still doing sentry-duty on the benches; their men were still propping up the bar. Shirl, in a sleeveless purple velvet so antique the nap was nearly worn away, stopped plying her trade long enough to smile and wave. Several of the others nodded to Jury, including Harry Biggins. He had become, apparently, a fixture, just another regular at the corner boozer.

Wizards — apparently the same game they'd been playing for months — was proceeding at the back table. They had all heard, by now, of the grisly affair at the Wembley Knotts tube station. To give them credit, they tried to maintain a proper air of solemnity. Glee kept breaking through.

"Come a cropper, dihn't 'e?" said Keith, with a wide smile. "Ruddy policeman, 'ow about that? Ruddy policeman. Always thought them country cops was so bloody 'onest."

"Apparently not," said Jury, matching the smile.

"They'd better be careful," said Dr. Chamberlen. "They'll be getting the same reputation as the Metropolitan police." He came close to giggling.

"I just dropped in to thank you for cooperating with us."

Their blank faces suggested they didn't know quite how to take this.

"Have you seen Cyril Macenery and Ash Cripps?"

"'Aven't set eyes on Cy all day. But there was a bleedin' copper come by not fifteen minutes ago lookin' for Ash. Guess 'e's been at it again." Laughter all round the table.

III

As Jury walked up the pavement towards number twenty-four, he saw a police constable leading Ash Cripps down the walk. From the way his hairy legs protruded from his buttoned-up overcoat, it would appear Ash was clad in nothing but the coat.

Standing in the doorway, hands on trousered hips, White Ellie delivered herself of an account of the proceedings, beginning as usual *in medias res:* ". . . Terrible it was, an 'er runnin' screamin' outta the ladies like all the devils in 'ell was after 'er. An 'im, there, stark, poppin' 'is ugly mug over the rail . . ."

"Shut yer bleedin' mouth, Elephant!"

As Jury said to the P.C., "What's the trouble, Officer?" White Ellie still lacerated the air with a few well-chosen obscenities.

The constable looked at Jury, frowning, until Jury pulled out his warrant card. "Oh, sorry, sir!" Then he took Jury aside, saying *sotto voce,* "You see, sir, I found him in the Ladies over to the little park off Drumm Street. Exposin' himself, he was. Name's Ashley Cripps. Ash the Flash they call him round here."

"It's okay, Constable — ?"

"Brenneman, sir."

"I need Mr. Cripps here for questioning. I'll take full responsibility if you'll release him into my custody."

Constable Brenneman looked as if there were nothing he'd like better, but he thought it only right to warn Jury: "Thing is, sir, it's not the first time I've had to take him in."

Jury also lowered his voice to say, "And I'm sure it won't be the last."

Constable Brenneman went whistling off down the walk and Ashley Cripps, trying to muster whatever dignity he could, squared his shoulders and preceded Jury into his parlor. "Gimme me strides, Elephant."

Without ceremony, she did so, then and there. Then she said to Jury, "Well, come on back, then; we was just 'avin' a fry-up. Missed our tea, we did, 'cause of 'im, and the kiddies was starved." The extent of the starvation was clear from the noise of cutlery, banging glasses and yelled demands for mash and rashers in the kitchen. As they passed through the parlor, Jury shoved some laundry back in the pram, away from the baby's head. Its rosebud mouth yawned. Alive.

White Ellie allocated what was left of the cooked rashers among the children. Sookey immediately tried to nick the girl's, but let go when she hit his ear with her fork. Friendly was slapping the catsup bottle and it came out in a rush.

" 'Eard all about it, we did. 'Orrible, 'orrible." White Ellie was peeling off some more rashers, dropping them into sizzling grease.

Having belted in his trousers and buttoned up a shirt, Ash said,

"Fell right on the bleedin' tracks, is what I 'eard. Well, there it is then. World's full of perverts." He shoved Sookey out of a chair. "Get outta 'ere, you kids. Give the Super 'ere a chair."

The kids mauled out of the kitchen, Friendly taking his bowl with him, and giving Jury a fierce look.

"Will you 'ave a bit of supper, then?" she said to Jury.

"Thanks, but no. I've got to get back to the Yard."

"Listen, thanks for what you did out there." Ash nodded toward the front, toward the scene of his latest debacle.

"Don't mention it. Actually, I came here to thank *you*. One good turn deserves another. Sorry I can't stay."

At the door they shook hands. "If you're ever this way again, look us up," said White Ellie.

Jury assured them he would, at the same time looking apprehensively at his car's windscreen. Clean.

As he was getting into it, he heard Ash Cripps telling the kids to wave. Small hands shot up over catsupped faces.

White Ellie yelled, "Your *'and*, Friendly! Your *'and!*"

TWENTY-EIGHT

◦◦◦◦◦◦◦◦◦

A BRIGHT pink balloon, relic of Sunday's church fête, had eluded the clean-up crew. It peeked incongruously above a listing headstone, its string apparently caught on some protuberance of gray rock. Now it rose a little more and a little more. As the service continued, Jury watched it being buffeted by breezes which mowed through the graveyard grasses, bounding and floating upwards and off into the Horndean wood.

He seldom thought of life in terms of what was or was not fair; today he did. It was not fair that the morning should glow like a pearl, the leaves shining, the very air like glitter, the sky milky with that bright pink oval pasted against it like a crayoned sun.

There had been more villagers in the Church of St. Pancras itself than were gathered here now. Jury was surprised to see Derek Bodenheim looking, for a change, strained rather than bored; the rest of the family had stayed at home; it was just as well. Mainwaring had come with a blonde woman who must have been his wife—rather pretty, unstylish, and with a face too expressionless for even simulated grief.

And Emily Louise, who had up to the last refused to come with her mother, was still there—back in the wood, camouflaged by branches and leaves, up on her pony. She would not come nearer, but she still participated. Her velvet cap was off, held in the circle of her arm like a Queen's guardsman might have held his tall hat.

Jury, Melrose Plant, and Wiggins stood bunched to one side as if unsure of their business there. And farther back, by herself, and perhaps even more unsure, stood Jenny Kennington. Her hands were stuffed in the pockets of a black coat; a lacy black scarf was wound around her hair.

Their heads were bowed as the vicar of St. Pancras commended the body of Katie O'Brien to the ground — earth to earth, ashes to ashes, dust to dust. When the coffin was lowered, a thickly veiled Mary O'Brien stepped forward and let fall from her hand a fistful of earth. The other mourners followed suit, circling the grave, each stopping to scoop up a handful of black earth, letting it trickle onto the lid of the coffin. It reminded Jury of some terribly sad version of a children's game.

He saw Emily turn her pony and disappear into the trees. He still stood there as the others dispersed, beginning their procession downhill. He stood there too as Wiggins and Melrose Plant made to leave. Melrose looked at him over his shoulder; Jury nodded to indicate he was stopping there for a moment.

He was watching Jenny Kennington. She had not left; she was still standing some distance off on the other side of the grave, as if waiting for everyone to leave. Jury stayed.

Finally, she walked to the graveside and gathered up a handful of earth and let it fall on the coffin. She raised her fingers to her forehead, and at first he thought she was about to cross herself. But she didn't. Instead, she smiled slightly and sketched a tiny salute in the air.

And then she walked away.